Sweet Surrender

Julia managed a faint smile, although she felt unnerved. "Do you always get what you want?"

"I've been lucky so far." Cyrus's free hand rose to touch her cheek, the long fingers softly caressing, and his expression tightened. "I want you," he said huskily, and it was not quite a question.

Julia felt her heart begin to beat unevenly, and all the impossible sensations she'd tried to deal with these past weeks surged inside her like a rising tide she hadn't a hope of mastering. Perhaps this was what she'd been waiting for, she realized dimly. To belong to him—if it was possible. He had taught her body to want him, and no matter what else she was uncertain of, she was sure of that much. She wanted him, and she had to take the chance. Whether it brought pain or pleasure, she had to offer herself to him.

She wondered briefly if he had put this price on her safety and Lissa's, but dismissed the idea before it could cause her any pain. It didn't seem to matter anyway.

"I—I want you too," she said unsteadily. . . .

The Matchmaker

♥

Kay Hooper

BANTAM BOOKS
NEW YORK · TORONTO · LONDON · SYDNEY · AUCKLAND

*This edition contains the complete text
of the original hardcover edition.*
NOT ONE WORD HAS BEEN OMITTED.

THE MATCHMAKER

A Bantam Fanfare Book / August 1991

PRINTING HISTORY
Doubleday edition published June 1991

FANFARE *and the portrayal of a boxed "ff" are trademarks
of Bantam Books, a division of Bantam Doubleday
Dell Publishing Group, Inc.*

*Bantam Books are published by Bantam Books, a division of
Bantam Doubleday Dell Publishing Group, Inc. Its trademark,
consisting of the words "Bantam Books" and the portrayal of a
rooster, is Registered in U.S. Patent and Trademark Office and
in other countries. Marca Registrada. Bantam Books, 666 Fifth
Avenue, New York, New York 10103.*

PRINTED IN THE UNITED STATES OF AMERICA

OPM   0 9 8 7 6 5 4 3 2 1

This is for Susie,
and the little one who surprised everybody.

Prologue

♥

It was early one chill November morning in 1870 when he was found in a basket on the doorstep of an elegant mansion in Richmond, Virginia, wrapped snugly in several spotlessly clean and seemingly new woolen blankets. A housemaid, coming out to sweep the step, nearly fell over him. He didn't seem the least bit concerned by his apparent abandonment, chortling happily at the young girl who, after a shriek that should have brought the neighbors bolt upright in their beds, seized the basket by its handle and dragged it into the house. (The baby boy, though obviously an infant, was not a small one. The housemaid, though an average-sized specimen, was totally unfamiliar with babies and had no idea if she could get this one out of his basket even if she could lift him. Which she doubted.)

Within minutes, a small group of servants surrounded the basket, all staring down at its occupant in varying degrees of bemusement or consternation. The infant blew a bubble at them with the greatest of goodwill and waved one pudgy—but surprisingly well-formed—little hand, in which was clutched a much-wrinkled and rather damp piece of paper.

The butler, no more familiar with babies than the housemaid but aware of his responsibilities neverthe-less, bent down and wrested the note from the child's hand. Actually, he didn't have to wrest very hard, because the boy gave it up willingly, almost as if it were his idea rather than the butler's.

The butler, whose name was, oddly enough, Stork, fastidiously smoothed the note, held it out, and read aloud in a tone of mounting astonishment: "This child is The Sun, born for great things. His father was a prince, his mother—"

"The son?" one of the footmen said. "That's a peculiar way to put it—"

"Not s-o-n. S-u-n," the butler corrected the footman. "Like in the sky. Now, where was I? Oh. Born for great things . . . His father was a prince, his mother a poor girl, but a good girl seduced"—Stork cleared his throat rather loudly, cast a quick glance at the young house-maid who was blushing furiously, then went on stolidly—"seduced by one immeasurably above her."

"Wonder if he really was a prince?" the same footman murmured, nudging contemplatively the basket with the toe of his boot.

Stork ground his teeth audibly. "—by one immeasur-ably above her. An old and wise Gypsy foretold—"

"Gypsies and princes?" the footman queried critically. "Doesn't sound right to me."

"Tom, if you say one more word!" Stork glared at the footman until he assumed the properly respectful ex-pression, then cleared his throat again and read the remainder of the note in the firm tones of a man who didn't mean to be interrupted.

"The Gypsy foretold a special destiny for the The Sun,

provided he was put into Fortune's hands. I so deliver him to Fortune, in good health."

The servants looked at one another, and it was the cook who said practically, "Well, of course the poor mother wanted her babe brought up in comfort, and Mr. Fortune's is the finest house in Richmond. I don't doubt the girl chose him because of that. And it's natural she'd make up a fine-sounding story, hoping to make the babe more acceptable."

Tom, venturing a comment since Mr. Stork was obviously finished reading, said with a heavy emphasis, "She picked right all the way around, didn't she?"

Stork was so much in agreement with the spirit of this remark that he could only sigh and look somewhat mournfully toward the stairs. "I suppose I'd better . . ."

The other servants vanished promptly, giving no more than one or two muffled grunts as elbows and feet collided in the doorway, leaving only the timid house-maid and the butler in the entrance hall. She twisted her apron between nervous fingers and said hesitantly, "Sir, shouldn't we get the baby out of that basket?"

Stork looked down his nose at the infant, who was sucking one fist as he stared gravely—and unblinkingly—back with very wide, very black eyes. "He looks comfortable enough to me," the butler decided. "Stay here with him, Mary, while I go inform Mr. Fortune."

He went up the stairs with a stately tread, returning some minutes later wearing a resigned expression. He stood eyeing the child for a moment, then bent and grasped the handles of the basket. A peculiar sound, a gasping grunt, escaped him when he straightened. The basket was a solidly made affair and with the large baby in it made a very heavy burden indeed.

Stork, aware of the housemaid's scrutiny, strove for an appearance of ease and staggered only a little as he carried it upstairs. He had to rest a moment on the landing, but it was all right as he realized that Mary couldn't see him. The child was perfectly quiet—and perfectly still whenever Stork lifted his basket, as if he were fully aware of his precarious balance.

The butler delivered the basket to the master bedroom, suffering the indignity of being greeted by a shout of laughter and the words: "Storks *do* bring babies, after all!"

He had expected it. He knew Mr. Tate Fortune rather well.

The entire neighborhood, in fact, knew Tate Fortune. So well did they know him that not a soul was surprised to discover he'd not only taken in the baby boy found in a basket, but also bestowed on the child his own surname—and the Christian name of Cyrus. The Sun might be the boy's given name, Tate explained when asked about the matter, but it was a cursed confusing one. And, besides, Cyrus meant sun.

No one had the nerve to ask if he'd considered the idea that "The Sun" might well have been only a misspelling and undue emphasis on the part of an overwrought mother.

In any case, young Cyrus thrived in his adopted home. He proved to be an amiable infant, sleeping a great deal in those first months and not at all fussy about what he ate. He ate a great deal. He was not a fat child; those who lifted him eventually discovered that his frame was constructed of large bones and very firm flesh that resembled muscle far more than it did fat.

He was, actually, a rather peculiar baby. When the first pangs of teething woke him from a sound sleep in the middle of the night, his bellow held more startled outrage than pain and roused the household from attic to cellars. Ears ringing, Tate gave the boy one of his best leather gloves, and young Cyrus seemed satisfied to chew on it. The first word out of the child's mouth was "Tate," spoken with perfect clarity. Tate had said several times in the boy's presence that he'd rather not be called Papa but, still . . .

Cyrus didn't crawl. One morning, sitting on a thick rug in Tate's study, he simply maneuvered himself upright and began walking. He never so much as staggered, and fell once only because Tate's big hunting dog accidentally knocked him over.

He was no more than three when he began reading, and his precocious curiosity seemed insatiable. Tate, highly entertained, spoke to the boy as he would an adult, answered his questions with total frankness, and generally encouraged him to think for himself, to ignore society's conventions whenever they didn't appear to make sense, and to carve his mark upon the world.

With Tate overseeing his upbringing, Cyrus was bound to become a hellion.

Which is exactly what happened.

A big child, he became a big man. A very big man. Both powerful and graceful physically, he moved with deceptive laziness and his deep voice held a slightly sardonic drawl. He was unusually dark and unusually handsome, and if he felt any stigma attached to his illegitimacy, it certainly wasn't apparent. In fact, he was somewhat arrogant.

In later years, even those who deplored Cyrus Fortune's outrageous ways and abrupt manners—if manners they could be called—rarely disliked the man himself. There might have been a devil in his peculiar black eyes, but it was a laughing devil, and if he presented a mortal danger to wives and daughters because of his sinful charm, he was also invariably honest in his business dealings and was a man any other could count on in a dangerous or difficult situation.

It was quite true and perfectly obvious that Cyrus liked women. He liked women so much that he probably would have been shot by a number of husbands if he hadn't been exceptionally fast for a big man and uncannily lucky. He was a bit more careful with daughters and confined himself to flirting with them, not so much because society frowned on the taking of innocence without sanction of marriage, but because he really did like women. And he didn't want any broken hearts on his conscience. . . . He *did* have a conscience. Still, he enjoyed flirting, and was gifted at the art whenever he set his mind to it. More than one sweet young thing had cried into her pillow at night because she couldn't manage to claim his wayward interest for more than an hour.

The people of Richmond didn't quite know what to make of Cyrus Fortune. Oh, his scandalous success with women was something his friends and neighbors could understand, even though they disapproved of it, but there was so much more.

Cyrus knew things. Things that logically he shouldn't have been able to know—in advance, at least. He didn't predict disasters or offer advice on business investments or any of that folderol. He merely possessed an extraordinary perception when it came to affairs, particularly amorous ones. He scarcely seemed aware of it, but others noticed. Young lovers, especially, seemed to flourish if they knew Cyrus. And it was also noted that whenever the love was obvious and true, Cyrus never made the slightest attempt even to flirt with the lady in question.

No one really understood him. And most were at least mildly relieved when, upon his adoptive father's death in 1898, Cyrus Fortune closed up the Richmond house and headed west.

In the years following, occasional word of him and his doings reached Richmond. Most of the rumors were so fantastic that few believed them, concerned as they were with social scandal and ruin on San Francisco's Nob Hill and deadly danger along the Barbary Coast—to say nothing of a *very* peculiar story involving Cyrus and a Turkish princess.

So, when the shutters came off the mansion in Richmond early in May 1902 and an army of workmen arrived to get the place in shape, curiosity was intense. Rumor had it Cyrus had notified his attorney in Richmond that he was coming home, but no one knew more.

It was midway through the first week in June when Cyrus returned to Richmond. It was a quiet homecoming, and for some time to come people wouldn't realize that this arrival, like the one nearly thirty-two years before, owed very little to chance.

Destiny, now, that was something else entirely.

What had she done?

She folded the newspaper carefully and stared down at the grainy picture while the words she'd read echoed in her mind. Her solution had seemed best at the time—

the only answer. Whatever the Old One foretold, she hadn't been able to destroy her own child. Flesh of her flesh . . . and flesh of his.

Now, haunted by a decision made nearly thirty-two years before, she looked at the picture, the face, and searched for some sign that she had not, after all, made a tragic error. As she looked, a coldness seeped into her. No resemblance there, not to her and not to him. And those eyes. It was obvious even in the newspaper photo that the eyes were strange and held an eerie flatness like the lifeless eyes of a doll. She didn't recognize the face, and the name was unfamiliar, but everything inside her screamed that she had given birth to this man more than three decades before.

It was wrong. *Wrong*. She unfolded the paper again and looked at another picture in another article on the same page. So much was wrong, she realized numbly.

She'd thought he would be protected and kept separate from the other one, thought she had been able to preserve them both. But destiny, it seemed, had other ideas. Destiny, the Old One had told her, could be altered only with finality. Anything less meant just a temporary detour away from what had to be. She had tried to break the pattern, and she had failed.

Had fate done that to her, filling an exhausted mind with doubt? Had it been the pattern trying to reweave itself?

"He has but two possible destinies. Death—or a life that will destroy others. What you carry in your womb is one true child—and the distorted, empty reflection of him."

"I can't kill my baby," she had whispered.

"You must."

"*No! There has to be another way.*"

"*Your lover was not an ordinary man; you know that?*"

"*I . . . suspected.*"

"*He had a gift, a gift which he has passed on to his son, one of the babes you carry. At all costs that gift must be nurtured. Your firstborn must survive; he is your true son. The other is the dark side of your lover's gift, the evil of it. It must be destroyed at birth. If you allow that other one to live, you risk the life of your true son, and all the good he will accomplish. The dark one will attempt to murder his womb-mate.*"

"*If they're separated? I can keep them apart—*"

"*Fate will bring them together no matter what you do.*"

She hadn't believed. What woman could have?

"*You must help me,*" she had begged. "*Tell me what to do, how to change the destinies of them both. There has to be a way.*"

With no more than a shrug of defeat, the Old One had told the young woman what she could do. In her voice was the weary acceptance of tragic mistakes, but her advice was minutely detailed. The two infants would be separated at birth, each taken to locations far apart and left in the care of carefully chosen strangers. Messages were dictated to provide each infant with the most positive start in life. The young woman was never to attempt to see her babies, for her mere presence could provide all that fate required to reconnect the two lifelines.

Now, staring down at the newspaper, the mother was very much afraid fate had worked to bring the twins together despite her absence from their lives. She rose, still holding the paper, and went upstairs, climbing all the way to the attic. She picked her way through the jumble of furniture and other items to a distant corner. Atop a sea chest sat a dusty oil lamp with matches nearby and a long, narrow box.

She lit the lamp and laid the newspaper aside, then opened the box. Inside was a cane made of polished wood and topped with an ornate gold handle. She touched it gently, gliding her fingers over the warm gold.

"They need you," she whispered.

One

♥

"Someone has his eye on you," Anne Butler murmured as she stepped closer to Julia Drummond.

Julia looked up from the refreshment table. Her long, graceful fingers quivered for an instant as they reached for another cup. Then she was ladling punch again with her usual composure. "Oh? Who?"

"Cyrus Fortune." Anne's gray eyes were bright with amusement and speculation. "I didn't realize you knew him."

Julia made certain no one was waiting for punch, then looked at Anne. She had been certain during the last half hour that someone had been staring at her, but she hadn't allowed herself so much as a glance around the room. "I don't know Mr. Fortune, though, of course, I've heard of him," she said. "I was still in the schoolroom when he left Richmond."

"He's been back more than a month," Anne remarked, still studying Julia intently. "Take it from me—a month is long enough."

Two things were clear, Julia decided: Anne was telling her she had recently enjoyed Cyrus Fortune's infamous

talents in the bedroom . . . and she was warning Julia.
Anne Butler was, in most ways, a nice enough woman,
but she was an incurable gossip; if she once got it into
her head that there was something between Julia and
Cyrus—or any other man, for that matter—it would be
all over Richmond within twenty-four hours.

Julia felt a faint chill of fear that she tried to repress.
Her acting abilities had improved over the past two
years, so she was able to smile with the rather haughty
scorn she'd perfected as her shield. The stuffy Brand
ancestors her father had often made reference to would
have been proud of her.

"Really, Anne, if you know nothing else about me, you
must at least know that I never stand in line. Not even at
the market, and certainly not for a man," she said
bluntly. "Aside from which, I consider it my duty to
avoid foolish entanglements, at least until I've presented
Adrian with an heir."

She relaxed almost imperceptibly when Anne chuckled.

"Yes, I suppose you should at that. Anyway, Adrian's
so charming and attentive that I suppose you've no cause
for complaint?"

The question was about as delicate as Anne's questions
usually were, but Julia was able to maintain her poise.

"No cause at all," she said with a slight smile.

Anne nodded, obviously detecting no irony, then
glanced fleetingly across the room. "Well, you'd better
scare up a chastity belt then, because Cyrus has that
look."

"What look?" Julia asked before she could stop herself.

"He's hunting fresh game—and he likes his bedmates
married." She obviously knew that much, since she
herself was married.

Coolly, Julia said, "As I hear it, he also likes his bedmates willing, which I certainly am not." She smiled across the table as several people stopped to get punch, then began filling more cups. She didn't look across the crowded room, even though she could still feel eyes on her. The sensation made her edgy.

Anne laughed again, but kept her voice low so that they wouldn't be overheard. "My dear, unless Adrian has you bewitched, Cyrus can make you willing. Trust me. Those black eyes of his are absolutely mesmerizing, and his voice is a quite expert caress. As I said, you'd better find a chastity belt." After giving Julia a very female wink, Anne moved away.

Julia continued to smile at the people who approached the table, and when they spoke she was able to answer casually, but her control was strained. If she hadn't promised weeks earlier to preside over the refreshment table at this charity dance, she would have avoided even coming here. But Julia had a reputation in Richmond for being as responsible and capable as she was elegant; having once made a promise, she kept her word if at all possible.

She knew most of the people at the dance, liked a number of them, and disliked some. If asked, many there would have said they knew her quite well. They would have been wrong; what they saw in Julia was only what she allowed them to see. The role she'd designed for herself was a convincing one. Barely twenty-one, she was often taken to be older because of her cool assurance. Other women seemed to trust her instinctively with their secrets, yet few had probed in an attempt to discover hers. Except, of course, for women like Anne, who wanted to know everyone's secrets.

Older women often told her with approval that she

was the perfect wife for a politician despite her youth. She ran her home with competence, did her husband credit in public with her style and grace, and lent her name and aid to charities without hesitation.

The perfect wife, Adrian had often said bitingly.

Julia shivered despite the heat of the ballroom, then pulled herself together. She lifted her chin, looking across the room unintentionally for the first time, and her strained gaze was immediately caught by the black eyes that had been watching her.

He was a big man; that was obvious even though he was lounging back against the wall. A powerful man, even though his stance held a lazy air. His shoulders were very wide, and there was a palpable sense of brute physical strength about him. His thick hair was as black as his eyes, his handsome face tanned dark gold, and a diamond signet ring flashed on the elegant hand holding his glass—not containing punch, Julia noted as he raised it in a slight salute.

To her. Julia knew she blushed as she quickly looked away. She was shaken. He had smiled at her, and even across the crowded room she had been conscious of a peculiar, almost sensual shock like nothing she'd ever felt before. *Dear God, if anyone had seen that look!* Those black eyes had met hers with the starkly intimate heat that belonged only in a bedroom.

She busied herself, resolutely avoiding any further glances across the room and trying not to think about anything, least of all Cyrus Fortune. It was surprisingly, unnervingly, difficult. She was almost feverish, suddenly uncomfortable in her clothing, as if it no longer fit, as if her body found the restriction of cloth unbearable. When Lissa joined her a few minutes later, the diversion was welcome at first.

"You've been doing this for more than an hour," Lissa said in her soft voice. "Why don't I take over awhile?"

Smiling at her younger sister, the thought in Julia's mind was the same one that had kept her going for the past two years. *It will be worth it. Whatever I have to do will be worth it if I can only see Lissa safely married. . . .*

Aloud, she said, "My part at this charity dance is to see to the refreshments; your part is to dance."

Lissa pouted, but her eyes twinkled merrily. "It's so hot. Honestly, Julia, why couldn't you send me to school in the North in summer, and bring me home to Richmond in winter? As it is, I'm getting the worst of things year round!"

Dryly, Julia said, "If I recall your letters correctly, you love the North in winter. Ice skating?"

Laughing, Lissa put an arm around her sister's trim waist and hugged her. She didn't notice Julia's flinch. "All right, ice skating is fun and so is dancing, even in the heat of July. But I really would like to rest for a little while, Julia, and I know a rest would be good for you. You look pale today."

"Lissa—"

"No one will notice if you leave. Just slip through that curtain over there, and you'll be in Mr. Tryon's study. It's nice and cool, and you can rest for a while."

Julia lifted a quizzical eyebrow at her sister. "How do you know it's cool?"

A mischievous imp laughed in Lissa's green eyes. "Because Mark Tryon thought it would be a good place to kiss me—and he was right."

"Lissa!"

"Oh, Julia, it was just a little kiss. I like Mark."

Looking at her sister narrowly, Julia said slowly, "He seems to be a nice young man."

"Quoth the graybeard," Lissa responded with tolerant mockery. "He's only a year older than you, in case you've forgotten."

The truth was that Julia had forgotten. Sometimes she felt very old. "Lissa, your reputation is so important—"

"My reputation is fine. Everyone knows I'm a good girl, including Mark Tryon. Now, why don't you go and rest for a few minutes, and I promise to stand here very decorously and ladle punch."

Knowing her sister, Julia was certain she'd be gently badgered and bullied until she gave in, for Lissa was not only sweet and loving, but also stubborn. Besides, Julia was tired, and knew that if she didn't take a few minutes to regain her customary calm, she would regret it later.

So she slipped away through the curtained doorway that was half hidden by a large potted fern. Though her host's study wasn't far from the ballroom, it was thick-walled. The muted sounds of music and conversation were as welcome as the room's coolness. It was a book-lined room that smelled of old leather-bound volumes and decades of pipe smoke, the carpet worn and the furniture comfortable. Only a small lamp on a table near one of the windows was lighted, and Julia went to sit in one of the wing chairs flanking it. The window was wide open to catch whatever breeze was forthcoming on the hot and muggy July night, but only the sounds of crickets in the garden found their way into the room.

Julia leaned back cautiously, wincing slightly as she did her best to relax in the chair. As uncomfortable as it was for her to be at the dance, she didn't look forward to going home. Home. The big, impressive house with its multitude of rooms and corridors and its quiet, efficient servants. It was a cold place even, impossibly, in summer. Or maybe, Julia thought tiredly, it just seemed so to her.

"Hello."

She stiffened, recognizing the voice even though she'd never heard it, because it matched the nakedly sensual warmth of black eyes. Slowly, she turned her head, recapturing her aloof mask with the ease of long and constant practice. She watched him stroll across the room, his size and lazy grace making her feel a panicky, threatened sensation. He sat down in the chair on the other side of the table and looked at her with that bold stare, and she felt suddenly exposed. Vulnerable.

With all the coldness she could muster, she said, "I don't believe we've been introduced."

His well-shaped mouth curved in a smile. "No, but then, we know who we are, don't we? I'm Cyrus Fortune, and you're Julia Drummond." The words were terse to the point of rudeness, his manner was definitely arrogant—but the voice was elegant black velvet.

Julia began to understand Anne's warning about the need for a chastity belt. She would have sworn she was the last woman in Richmond who could have felt any temptation to break her marriage vows, but that voice affected her like nothing ever had. In her mind was a strangely vivid little image of the way a cat arched its back when it was stroked, in an instinctive ripple of unthinking pleasure, and she wondered dimly if the sound of her racing heart was anything like a purr.

"I've been watching you tonight," he said. "But you know that. Do you know I've been watching you for days?"

That was a shock, but one she endured silently. She had to stop this before . . . before it was too late. Her own thoughts were scattered, panicked, and she didn't know why or how he could affect her like this. She drew a deep breath; it felt as if she hadn't breathed at all until then. "Mr. Fortune—"

"Cyrus." It was less a request than a command.

Julia ignored it. "Mr. Fortune, I'm a married woman—"

"Drummond must have robbed the cradle to get you," Fortune said abruptly, cutting her off without civility. "Somebody said you'd been married for two years, but you can't be a day over eighteen."

Oddly enough, Julia knew she couldn't accuse him of trying to flatter her; she had a strong conviction that Cyrus Fortune was too blunt a man to waste time with insincere compliments—even to get a woman into his bed. He wouldn't need to resort to such tricks, she admitted to herself silently, and was appalled at the realization.

Holding her voice even, she said, "I'm twenty-one, Mr. Fortune. And I am *very* married."

His mouth quirked again in that mocking little smile. "Not tempted to stray? Drummond can't be such a good lover; the man's heavy-handed with his horses."

The sheer effrontery of that remark made Julia gasp. Her own nature was toward frankness—or it had been, before her marriage—and she was hardly a prude, but for any man to speak to a woman in such a way went beyond the bounds of good taste *and* decency. But before she could gather her wits, he was going on, and if she'd thought he had gone as far as possible already, she was in for another shock.

"Drummond isn't making you happy, and we both know it, Julia. You're frozen inside; I can see it. You were never meant to be that way. Red hair is a badge of passion, and yours is like fire. I've never seen hair so red or eyes so wildly green. Or such an erotic mouth, like a lush flower. You have a magnificent body, a body made for pleasure. Even those dull colors and fabrics you wear can't hide your wonderful form. And you move with such grace, as if you hear music."

"Don't—" she got out in a strangled gasp, but he went on in his black velvet voice that made even the reprehensible words a sensual caress.

"Drummond wouldn't know what to do with a woman like you. I'm sure of it. He can't appreciate the fire in you. He probably takes you in the dark with your nightgown pulled up and thinks of nothing but his own pleasure. Does he apologize when he turns to you with his carnal appetites, Julia? Does he make it a hurried, shameful act instead of something joyful?" Fortune uttered a low laugh that was derisive. "Gentlemen like Drummond believe there are only two kinds of women: ladies and whores—and only whores enjoy bedding men. So the gentlemen marry ladies and fumble in the dark to breed. Is that all you want? To be a brood mare and never feel the hot pleasure of real passion?"

He laughed again, his eyes blacker than anything she'd ever seen, and filled with a heat that burned her. "I'm no gentleman, Julia. I don't want a lady or a whore in my bed—just a woman. A beautiful woman. I won't apologize for wanting her and I'll look at her naked in the light because God meant for a woman to be seen by a man. And touched by a man."

She wasn't conscious of moving until she was halfway across the room, her heart thudding, the smothering sensation of panic overwhelming her. She didn't go to the door that led back to the ballroom but another one, and she had no idea where it would take her. It didn't matter. Anywhere. Anywhere as long as she could escape him.

"Julia."

That voice. It tugged at her—and the realization she could scarcely resist terrified her. Her hand on the door handle, she half turned to stare at him. He had risen to his feet, but didn't move toward her. He was smiling almost gently.

"I want you. I want you in my bed."

"No." It didn't come from morals or consciousness of her marriage vows, or anything else of which society would have approved. It didn't come from a lack of attraction, shocking though that was to her; she felt the attraction, the strange, irresistible pulling at all her senses. The denial came from deep inside her, without thought, spurred by instinct.

"I can make you happy," he said.

"You can destroy me," she heard herself whisper. Then she wrenched the door open and fled, as if from a devil.

She found herself in a corridor, turning blindly, then again into a shorter hallway, ending up finally in a small sitting room. It was deserted. Julia closed the door behind her and locked it with shaking fingers. She didn't realize she was pacing until her wildly swinging skirt caught the leg of a delicate table, causing the vase on it to rock precariously.

Standing perfectly still now, her hands on the vase, she was conscious of her heart thudding and her breath coming in jerky gasps. She felt . . . shattered. Adrian had never been able to do that to her, no matter how he'd tried. She'd discovered a way to escape him, a way to preserve herself. In the first months with him, she had found a place inside herself that was quiet and safe, and when it became unbearable, she always went there. Where he couldn't reach her. Where she felt nothing.

She understood, if only vaguely, why that place was inaccessible to her now. Cyrus Fortune hadn't touched her, hadn't threatened her with harm; what he had said, though certainly incredibly indecent, had not been an attack. She knew she was afraid of him, and yet—it wasn't a simple fear, and escape wasn't possible.

Fortune would hardly force himself on her, Julia reassured herself, but her fear didn't ease. What he intended, she knew, had been plainly stated and was beyond question. Seduction. His own relentless, insidious, dreadfully effective brand of seduction. He had decided he wanted her, and she had the curious certainty he would stop at nothing to get what he wanted. He meant to add her name to his list of conquests.

What shocked her so deeply was that he could have any effect on her at all in an erotic sense. That any man could. But she had felt it. His frank sensuality, bold eyes, and disgracefully forthright words had penetrated her mask, settling in her body like glowing embers and evoking a heat she'd never felt before. It was something she didn't know how to fight.

Slowly, she turned toward the door. Her heartbeat had steadied, and her breathing. She was calm again. A few more weeks, she thought, and Lissa would return to school. Adrian was always more careful when Lissa was in the house. All Julia had to do was to avoid any chance of meeting Cyrus Fortune alone, and try her best to limit the possibilities of attending the same social functions. She had to stay out of his way, that was all.

She made her way back to the ballroom and slipped up beside Lissa at the refreshment table, where a number

of young men had congregated. That wasn't surprising;
Lissa was very pretty.

"There you are," she said cheerfully to Julia. "I was
beginning to worry that you—" She broke off to look
searchingly at her sister's face. "Julia, you're still pale.
Do you feel all right?"

"A little tired." She could feel his eyes on her again,
and had to fight not to look across the room. "I'll be fine,
don't worry. Some of the guests are beginning to leave;
we should be able to go in another hour or so. Why don't
you go and have a few dances."

"Are you sure? I can stay here and help."

"No, go ahead." Smiling, Julia kept her gaze on her
sister as Lissa chose a partner and whirled away in his
arms. Lissa would be eighteen soon; the upcoming year
was her last in school unless she chose to go on to
college. Adrian was encouraging her to do that; if she
didn't continue in school, she was likely to marry quickly
and leave the Drummond household for good.

Julia wanted her sister married. She believed that
Lissa wasn't ambitious enough to use a higher education
to her advantage—but even if she had been, Julia would
have encouraged her to marry instead. She had to be put
beyond Adrian's reach . . . and only a husband could
guarantee that.

A good husband, please God.

Across the room, Cyrus Fortune lounged against a wall
and watched her. He had seen her for the first time less
than a week before, walking through the park on her
husband's arm. Her lovely face had been shadowed by
the stylish hat she'd worn, but Cyrus had seen a more
somber shadow. Not a happy marriage, he'd thought,

vaguely disturbed by the darkness he'd fleetingly sensed.

The uneasiness had faded quickly, leaving a hot, intense desire behind. He had watched them walking together sedately, his attention wholly on Julia. She was a stunning woman, her body petite yet richly curved, her coloring vivid, and her face delicately beautiful. She carried herself with pride, and a grace that was unusually sensuous.

She intrigued him. And he'd immediately found out all he could about Julia Drummond. It was little enough. A younger sister in her charge, she had married Drummond two years before. No children yet, which made her less likely to take a lover if Cyrus knew women at all—and he did. Her reputation as the perfect wife was complemented by being well-liked. But she seemed to have no close friends.

Nothing of what he found out discouraged Cyrus in the least. He managed to see her from a distance several times during the next few days, and had attended the charity dance only because he had discovered that she would be there. Luckily, she had arrived without her husband's escort, and Cyrus had grasped the first opportunity offered to be alone with her. He could have kissed the pretty little sister who had obviously talked Julia into giving up her duties at the refreshment table temporarily.

Now, as he watched her, he frowned. After being closer to her and gazing into the vividly luminous depths of her green eyes, his desire was stronger than ever, but something was bothering him and he didn't know what it was. He felt oddly uneasy.

He'd been satisfied with her reaction to him and to what he'd said to her; she might have run from him, but

she hadn't been able to hide her own awareness of an
attraction. It was a good beginning. And though her final
words might have daunted another man, Cyrus more or
less ignored them simply because destruction wasn't
what he had in mind.

Still, there was something about her that he couldn't
bring into focus. He thought about it for a while,
watching her steadily, then pushed the question aside
impatiently. To hell with it. Perhaps he was sensing in
her a stronger than usual unhappiness. She was young,
after all, younger than any of his other women in recent
years; the young tended to feel things more deeply. Or
thought they did, at least.

Drummond had quite likely been as heavy-handed
with her as he was with his horses; on horseback he had
the necessary mechanics, but obviously no skill. It was
probably the same in the bedroom. No doubt he had
treated Julia like fragile china until the wedding night
and then shocked her with the coarse realities of panting, sweating male needs. She hadn't felt passion in her
husband's bed, Cyrus knew that. There was something
in her eyes that he'd seen only in the eyes of unawak-
ened young women, a kind of unaware innocence that
had nothing to do with physical virginity; it was another
barrier that some men were too inept or insensitive to
find their way past, and it was still intact in Julia.

Cyrus was confident about his own abilities. He'd be
patient for a while at least, let her protest to salve pride
or convention or whatever was her particular nemesis.
Give her a little time to get used to the idea. But she'd
come to him eventually, and she'd be willing. He would
make certain it was an enjoyable interlude, that he made
her happy.

In any case, Cyrus was prepared to do whatever it took to get Julia Drummond into his bed.

It was late by the time Julia said good night to Lissa at the top of the stairs. She was exhausted as she made her way past Adrian's study, a parlor, a few spare bedrooms, toward the master suite. Bedroom, bathroom, and dressing room, the suite was distant from Lissa's room and from the servants' quarters.

There was a light under the door, and Julia hesitated for an instant. She'd hoped her husband would be asleep. Her mouth was a little dry, but she opened the door quietly and went in, her mask firmly in place.

He turned immediately away from the window, where he'd apparently been watching the street outside, and looked at her with narrowed eyes. He was still fully dressed. A bad sign.

"Where the hell have you been?" he demanded softly.

Julia closed the door and leaned back against it, hardly noticing the protesting twinge of tender flesh over her shoulder blades. "I couldn't close down the refreshment table until after midnight," she said in a low, reasonable voice.

"I told you." His voice was harsh now. "I told you not to go to the party without me."

Julia would have protested that he'd told her at dinner he didn't want to accompany her, but she knew it wouldn't make any difference. Nothing would make any difference now. After two years, she was all too familiar with the irrational way his rage fed on itself. Something had made him angry since she and Lissa had gone to the dance, some small thing he probably didn't even remember now.

He came toward her slowly, like a predator, smiling. He had the strap. Julia stared at him, and as the cold dread formed in the pit of her stomach, what she saw became unfocused, then darkened slowly until she didn't see anything. Or hear anything. Or feel anything.

Until he was finished.

Two

♥

Cyrus Fortune wasn't one of the nine-member city council of Richmond and he wasn't particularly interested in politics, but he attended a meeting of the council a few days after the charity dance. He didn't contribute, just watched and listened with a slight smile, his black eyes flicking from one man to another unreadably.

"Cy, what are you doing here?" Noel Stanton slid into the seat beside Cyrus, his bushy brows lifted in an expression of exaggerated surprise.

Since another heated discussion was going on at the front of the room, Cyrus didn't bother to lower his voice. "Making certain the city isn't run by thieves and scoundrels, of course. Is it, by the way?"

"Well, of course it is," Stanton told him severely. "You don't think any honest man would want a councilman job, do you?"

Cyrus smiled briefly, but said, "I'm surprised they chose Drummond as mayor; he's a bit young for it."

"Your age." Stanton, who was eyeing forty as his next milestone and not happy about it, shrugged tolerantly.

27

"He sure as hell got the most votes in the election. Very smooth and charming."

Cyrus turned his head, studying the man he'd known for most of his life and one of the very few he trusted implicitly. "You don't like him."

"I don't like him. He's pleasant enough, I suppose. The ladies seem to think he walks on water. When he married Julia Brand, I expected to see black crepe on half the doors in town."

"And did you?"

"No." Stanton smiled in amusement, the mustache that was as bristly as his eyebrows twitching like something alive. "But you should have seen all the wistful faces at the first dance the Drummonds attended after their honeymoon."

Cyrus returned his gaze to the front of the room and singled out Drummond. Tall, athletic, handsome; a blond man with a boyish face the ladies would certainly find attractive, and muddy brown eyes set under unusually straight brows. He didn't like the eyes, Cyrus decided thoughtfully; there was a queer shine to them when Drummond turned his head a certain way. After a moment, he said, "Do you trust him, Noel?"

Stanton leaned back and crossed one leg over the other. "Depends. In business, yes, if he's risking as much as I am. Politics—maybe, but he's ambitious and I have a feeling he doesn't care who he steps on. I'd lend him money on his word, but I don't want him on any of my horses. An automobile is more suited to him, I'd say; he couldn't jab at its mouth if he was annoyed."

"Yes, I've seen him on a horse," Cyrus murmured.

Stanton looked at him inquiringly. "Why the sudden interest in Drummond, Cy?"

"Idle curiosity."

In a dry tone his friend said, "You're never idle despite your lazy air, and your curiosity always means something. Going into business with Drummond?"

"No."

"I see. She's very beautiful."

Cyrus looked at him. "She is," he agreed.

Stanton wasn't smiling. "And very young, Cy."

"If she isn't too young for Drummond, she certainly isn't too young for me."

"He married her."

"The only wife I want," Cyrus drawled softly, "is someone else's."

After a long moment Stanton said, "When you say something like that—and mean it, what's more—I could really dislike you."

With no change in his faintly sardonic expression, Cyrus said, "Do you mean you don't want to take my money tonight at the game?"

Stanton snorted and looked away half angrily. "No, dammit, I don't mean that. But I'll tell you honestly—if I didn't believe you drew the line at going after the wives of your friends, I wouldn't let you into my house."

"I would never bed a man's wife in his own house, Noel," Cyrus said gently. "Even my manners aren't completely hopeless."

"Cy, for God's sake—"

Chuckling, Cyrus said, "Relax. Felice is quite happy in your marriage—and I *do* draw the line there." He gave his friend a somewhat dry look, but offered no further remarks on the touchy subject.

Stanton wanted to remain angry. In all truth, he was often dismayed by his friend's unscrupulous pursuit of the women he wanted. It was a facet of Cyrus's personality that had always struck him as wrong somehow, not morally, though it was that, of course, but simply because it didn't quite seem to belong to the man he'd known for more than twenty years.

And he was so—peculiar about it. Almost philanthropic, in fact, though he'd never used such reasoning as an excuse. Cyrus didn't offer either explanations or excuses, and tended to become mocking or blandly uncommunicative if one of his friends pressed him for either. But Stanton had watched, and his friend puzzled him. On the face of it, most would say—and did—that Cyrus was a strongly sensual man who preferred a fleeting involvement with a succession of married women simply to avoid the entanglements of drawn-out affairs or the possibility of marriage for himself. There was more to it, though, Stanton thought—if that was even a part of it.

Cyrus became involved only with *unhappy* married women, and Stanton was almost positive he'd never been wrong in his assessment. Whether through instinct, perception, or just observation, he consistently chose women who seemed, afterward, to settle down in their marriages with perfect contentment.

It was strange, to say the least.

"You're frowning, Noel."

He looked at his friend and wished he could remain angry. But he couldn't. "Cy, one of these days God or the devil's going to teach you a lesson, and I hope I'm around to see it."

"A lesson?" Cyrus was smiling faintly.

"Yes. Either you'll pick the wrong lady, the wrong husband, or the wrong time, and find yourself up to your arrogant nose in trouble."

Cyrus laughed. "Consider me duly warned. Now, if you'll excuse me, I think I'll leave." He nodded toward the front of the room, where a discussion about property taxes was turning into a shouting match. "They're going to be at it for quite some time, and I have an appointment in the park."

"What's in the park?" Stanton asked blankly.

"Julia Drummond," Cyrus murmured, getting to his feet.

"Don't tell me you've persuaded her to meet you—and in such a public place—already?"

"Unhappily, no. I haven't seen her since the charity dance the other night. But she's in the park now, and I want to see her while Drummond is otherwise occupied."

"You know she's in the park? How?"

Cyrus looked down at him for a moment, then smiled mockingly. "How else? The devil whispered in my ear, Noel. See you tonight." He strolled out of the room as lazily as he'd entered, leaving his friend to sputter wordlessly.

Once outside the building, Cyrus quickened his pace, though it wasn't obvious since he merely took longer strides. He knew Julia was in the park, knew it without question, and if he did in fact owe his thanks for the knowledge to the devil, then so be it. It certainly wasn't the first time he'd known something with no rational way to explain it, and he'd gotten used to the odd sensation.

Today, at least, he was too eager to see Julia to care how he knew where she was. He'd made up his mind at the dance to be patient, but hadn't expected to not even see her in the days since. It had proved to be a novel frustration he didn't like at all. As far as he knew, she hadn't ventured outside the Drummond house. He had seen her sister the following evening at a large party, and

had overheard her telling an older woman Julia was a bit
under the weather.

The older woman, obviously an acquaintance, had
asked in a very discreet way if the "illness" was of the
nine-month variety, and Lissa had replied with refresh-
ing bluntness that, no, Julia wasn't pregnant.

Cyrus had been glad to hear it, though he was ruefully
aware even her pregnancy wouldn't have stopped him.
He felt a curious urgency when he thought of Julia, and
the sensation had been growing steadily. He'd become
aware of it the night of the dance, later when he was
home, an edgy feeling of restless disquiet that was
unfamiliar to him and not a little unnerving because he
didn't understand the cause of it. And if the disturbing
sensation wasn't enough, another puzzling thing had
begun that night. Even though he tended to sleep
soundly, that night he had awakened often from troubled
dreams he couldn't remember; each time, in the first
fleeting moments after waking, he'd felt a ghostly sense
of pain, terrible pain, that vanished when his eyes
opened.

For the next two nights the same thing had happened,
though the sensation of pain had gradually faded. He'd
always been prone to odd whims and notions, most of
which turned out to be accurate and positive no matter
how absurd they'd seemed at first, but this was something else, something new. It disturbed him. Once
again, however, he pushed the uneasy thoughts away as
he reached the park and saw Julia.

She was sitting on a bench just off the sidewalk,
smiling a little as she watched her sister and several
other young people attempt to get a kite airborne. Cyrus
slowed his pace as he approached her, taking the
opportunity to look at her without her awareness. Today,

she was dressed in the Gibson-girl style just coming into fashion: a dark, tailored skirt belted tightly at her tiny waist, a long-sleeved, high-necked white blouse with a scarf tied at the throat, and a small, neat hat.

Cyrus frowned slightly as he studied her very erect posture. He was no stranger to ladies' lingerie, and disliked the current version of the corset, which was very long with steel or whalebone strips and had to be, he thought, one of the worst instruments of torture fashion had ever imposed upon women. The style pushed the bosom forward and the hips backward in exaggerated curves, making walking, standing, or sitting hideously uncomfortable, and cinched at the waist so tightly that normal breathing was impossible. "Ladylike" swooning was a publicly accepted result of the unnatural constriction, but Cyrus agreed with the opinions of doctors who stated forcefully and with considerable heat that it was physically dangerous and ought to be banned.

It bothered him that Julia was obviously conforming to a ridiculous and dangerous fashion. She hadn't followed yet another practice and resorted to padding above and below the waist in order to make the S-curve look even more exaggerated, but since she had a naturally tiny waist and full breasts, the corset alone was quite enough to give her the stylish appearance. At the dance she'd worn a rather concealing gown with a great deal of lace. Of course he hadn't noticed any distortion of her slender figure. One of Cyrus's somewhat peculiar talents was the ability to gauge a woman's natural measurements accurately no matter what misleading fashion prevailed, and he'd known only that her figure was splendid.

He didn't like that corset, especially not on Julia.

He sat down on the bench a foot or so away from her, and smiled when her startled eyes met his. "Hello."

Immediately, she returned her gaze to the young people some distance away. Her smile was gone; she was expressionless now. But her delicate hands twined tightly together in her lap and he could feel her tension.

"Surely you can speak to me in public, can't you, Julia?"

"Not without being ruined," she said a bit grimly.

He couldn't help but laugh, pleased by her honesty, but said, "That's nonsense, and you know it. I often escort the wives of my friends, occasionally an unmarried young lady, and it does their reputations no harm."

"You are not a friend of my husband's." Then she paused and sent him a swift glance from guarded eyes. "Are you?"

Gently, he said, "One doesn't make a friend of a man and then seduce his wife. Not quite honorable, that. Friends are treated with more respect."

This time she turned her head and stared at him. "Of all the barefaced effrontery!" Her voice wasn't so much shocked as incredulous.

"I'm famous for it," he said, nodding. "But the real effrontery would be if I did seduce a friend's wife. In any case, if it's my plain speaking you object to, I'm afraid that's another trait I'm known for. It saves so much time, you see. I'm paying you the compliment of believing you'd prefer honesty to pretty speeches and bedroom lies. I want you, Julia. And no matter what you've been taught, real desire doesn't come dressed in silks and satins; it's naked."

She looked away again, a little pale except for the heated skin over her cheekbones. A blush suited her, he thought, and it was uncommon among redheads. She was really quite lovely. And young, Noel had been right about that. But she was two years married, and there was no doubt she was a woman—even though her green eyes seemed to hold even more innocence than he'd first thought.

"I'm married," she said in a soft, still voice.

"I hope you don't believe that's going to stop me," Cyrus said calmly. "If you were happily married, we wouldn't be having this conversation."

"Have you no sense of decency?"

He didn't fail to notice she let his remark about her marriage go unchallenged. "By society's definition? I suppose not. What does it matter?"

Julia drew a short breath and looked at him with glittering eyes. "Then we'll set decency aside, since that means nothing to you. And I'll be as blunt as you've been. I don't want you. I don't want an affair. Is that clear enough?"

"Let's walk," Cyrus said, rising to his feet and reaching for her hand.

"No—"

He grasped her hand before she could pull away, and gently but inexorably drew her up. "Don't fight me, Julia," he said, tucking her hand into the crook of his arm, "or you'll attract the kind of attention you'd rather avoid."

"Do you often resort to blackmail?" she demanded tightly, walking beside him as he began strolling toward one of the paths that wound among trees and neat shrubs.

"Only when necessary. Do admit you're more comfortable walking—if it's possible, that is, to feel anything but agony in that corset you're wearing."

It was one of the least shocking things he'd said to her, and since "agony" was a fair description of what her tightly laced stays caused, particularly today, Julia was a little bemused to hear her own defensive reply. "To be fashionable—"

"Fashion can go to hell. Forcing the human body to conform to an unnatural shape is foolish and dangerous, particularly in the name of fashion. And any man who'd choose to see his woman resemble a pouter pigeon ought to be forced to spend a few hours in one of those bloody contraptions."

She couldn't think of anything to say to that, and glanced up at him in faint surprise. It was unnerving to discover that the top of her head barely reached his shoulder, and even more unnerving to believe that his indelicate talk of corsets had been prompted by concern. He was a strange man; his black velvet voice made her feel things she didn't understand, his bluntness disturbed her and left her without the protection of conventional propriety, and though he'd been very calm and matter-of-fact about it, his determination to have her seemed unswerving.

Then he continued speaking in the same calm but forceful voice, and she wondered a bit numbly if there was anything, anything at all, that he considered improper to discuss with a woman. Somehow, she didn't think so.

"Besides that, you don't need any kind of artificial help to have a magnificent body. God gave you one. Seeing you naked has become my life's ambition."

Julia wanted to gasp or laugh hysterically, but her stays were too tight to allow her to do either without fainting at his feet. She almost told him so, certain he'd appreciate the remark. Instead, staring straight ahead and determined to keep her calm no matter what he said, she said coldly, "I'm terribly sorry to frustrate your ambition, but I must."

"Why?"

"I told you. I don't want an affair."

"I'll change your mind." He looked down at her as they walked along the winding path, wondering absently how long her hair was. It was difficult to judge, since the fiery mass was arranged in a pompadour. The hand he held firmly in the crook of his arm was very small and slender. Her left hand, he realized; neat gloves hid her wedding ring, but he knew it was there.

Too tight. The thought sprang into his mind, and he didn't know if it was literal or symbolic, if her ring fit too tightly, or her marriage vows did.

"I don't want my mind changed," she snapped. "I have no desire to be flung out in the streets and branded an adulteress."

"Drummond wouldn't do that even if he found out," Cyrus said coolly. "He's a politician. Infidelity means nothing compared to the damage a divorce would cause his career."

Until that moment Julia had believed she'd experienced all the pain a man could inflict on a woman, but this was a new hurt, an unexpectedly raw hurt. Another man, she thought bitterly, who discounted private torment as long as the world saw only a mask of contentment. Another man who would stop at nothing to satisfy his own needs. She wondered suddenly if even the scars of her private hell would evoke a shred of compunction in what passed for Cyrus Fortune's heart.

The concern she had thought she'd heard in his voice only moments before had obviously been no more than her imagination. Or perhaps his condemnation of corsets came purely from a man's desire to have the body he wanted undamaged by silly fashions.

"No," she said quietly, feeling empty.

"You don't love him, Julia."

Genuinely surprised, she looked up at him. "What does that matter?"

He stopped walking and half turned toward her, still holding one of her hands against his arm. The path they stood upon was shady and reasonably cool, with a few midsummer flowers perfuming the still air with sweetness. Now, in the middle of the day, only the young people and the two of them were in the park—and the others were so distant even their laughing voices couldn't be heard.

Cyrus looked down at her upturned face, and wondered why he'd even said what he had. She didn't love her husband, but, as she'd said, what did that matter? She wasn't refusing him because she loved another man, but because she was a married woman who wouldn't break her vows.

"I won't give up," he said.

Her green eyes were clouded with puzzlement and something else, something he couldn't read. "Why does it have to be me?" she asked.

"Because I want you."

She shook her head a little, her delicate features briefly holding a kind of bitter anguish. "Is what you want so much more important than what I want? Does it always have to be that way?"

For just an instant an unaccustomed hesitation took hold of Cyrus. This wasn't what he'd expected; she was different from the others. She was in pain, this was hurting her. He didn't want to hurt her, and honestly believed he wouldn't. All his instincts told him she needed him like the others had.

They had needed different things from him, those other women. Though no one who wasn't immediately concerned would have believed it, few of them had ended up in his bed. Some had needed a sympathetic ear or shoulder, some discreet help with problems they didn't dare take to their husbands, some a more nebulous assistance or comfort. Since he didn't particularly care about his reputation and since none of the ladies involved were harmed by their rumored affairs, he allowed people to think what they liked.

But with Julia . . . He acknowledged silently to himself that with her the instinct to help had tangled instantly and fiercely with a desire so powerful, his own needs *had* been more important to him.

Now her upturned face was filled with mute emotions that hurt him and made her even more beautiful to him in a strange, primitive way, and the intense desire for her swept over him like a tide. She needed him, he knew it. He *knew* it.

Julia was caught off guard by what she saw in his burning black eyes. She shouldn't have been, perhaps, because he'd certainly made both his desire and his intentions plain enough. But despite everything he had said, she really hadn't expected him to attempt a blatant physical seduction—and certainly not in broad daylight in a public park.

When his hands rose to her shoulders and his dark head bent toward her, she opened her mouth to utter some wild, wordless protest that never found a voice. His strong face blurred and she closed her eyes helplessly to try to shut out what had already gotten too close. His lips were hard, curiously hot, the demand in them so insistent she was aware of every suddenly throbbing nerve in her body. It was a shock greater than any he'd yet caused, stealing what little breath her stays allowed her and filling her mind with dizziness.

She was dimly aware of his long fingers tightening on her shoulders, of the whisper of pain as tender flesh protested even that slight pressure, but it didn't matter. He was drawing her down into some dark place that was velvet and fire, and she was lost there.

He muttered something against her mouth and then his slanted, deepening the kiss even more with stark possession. His tongue was sinuous as it stroked hers in a touch so intimate it sent a shudder of feverish pleasure rippling through her. Her body swayed toward his, and she felt the hardness of his chest press against her breasts.

Then his hands slid down her back to her waist, trailing new heat and the echoes of old pain, and the reminder was just enough to bring a chill of sanity to her mind and a moan of protest to her throat.

Whether or not he heard, Cyrus raised his head, staring down at her dazed face with eyes so fierce she almost flinched away from them. "You want the same thing I want, Julia," he said thickly. "That's what matters. It's all that matters."

She backed away from him slowly, and he let her go. She had a fatalistic certainty that next time he wouldn't . . . because next time she wouldn't be able to protest. It took more willpower than she thought she had to turn and walk away, but she did it. Her heart was pounding and she couldn't breathe except in shallow little gulps, but she walked with her head up and she didn't look back at him.

Some minutes later, as Cyrus continued on his way, frowning in thought, a man stepped onto the path behind him and stood gazing after him. He was a tall man, well-dressed and obviously prosperous. His lean face was without expression, but a shaft of sunlight fell across the powerful hands that clenched into fists by his sides repeatedly in a measured rhythm.

He turned his head and glanced back the way Julia had gone, then looked after Cyrus again. His hands continued to flex and clench steadily. A faint breeze stirred the trees, and a pattern of dappling sunlight shifted briefly over his face. His eyes reflected nothing in the light, like the windows of an empty house.

It was late that night when Cyrus returned home from the poker game at Noel Stanton's house, and he wasn't in the best of moods. He'd been on edge since Julia had left him in the park, and his luck with cards had been so abnormally bad that Noel had chided him on his lack of concentration—cheerfully, since he'd been winning every cent Cyrus lost.

Cyrus didn't care, except that it might have been another sign of his changing luck in other ways and it made him uneasy.

He let himself into the house and locked the door behind him, frowning when a soberly dressed man came silently into the hall. "I've told you not to wait up for me," Cyrus said.

"Yes, sir." The butler's face was impassive as usual. "A package came for you tonight, sir. On your desk."

"A package? From whom?"

"I couldn't say, sir. Someone rang the bell and left the box on the doorstep. Your name was written on the box, but nothing else."

Cyrus nodded. "All right. Go to bed, Stork."

"Yes, sir."

Cyrus crossed the hall to his study and went in. A lamp had been left burning for him, and in the light of it the wooden box on his desk gleamed darkly. He frowned as he stared down at it, surprised to see his name hadn't just been written on the box, it had been burned carefully into the wood.

There was no latch on the box; the well-fitted lid simply lifted off. Cyrus set it aside, surprised again to find a gold-handled cane inside. Real gold, he realized as he held it in his hands. This was old, he could feel it. The handle was ornate, but the design was subtle and exquisitely made, and the cane itself was heavy.

He saw the slip of paper a moment later, and laid the cane on his desk with unconscious care before reaching into the box for what he hoped would be a note explaining the curious gift. It wasn't exactly a note, however, merely a single sentence written in the same fine hand that had burned his name into the box.

Your father wanted you to have this.

Cyrus's first thought was that this had to be somebody's idea of a joke, because Tate Fortune had never used a cane in his life, even in his last years when age had taken its toll. . . .

His father?

Very slowly, Cyrus sat down in the chair behind the desk and stared at the slip of paper. Then he looked at the cane, and he was conscious of nothing except shock.

His *real* father?

Three

♥

Julia managed to remain very close to home during the next few days, even though she risked Adrian's suspicion by doing so. Despite his own busy schedule, he always seemed to know if she'd gone out and often where she had been. Any variation from her usual routine was a virtual guarantee he would spark an explosion of questions, accusations, and cruelty. Ironically, he was most suspicious when she *didn't* go out, apparently believing she was more likely to betray him in his own house.

Normally, she spent no more time in the house than necessary unless it was literally too painful to get dressed, keeping herself as busy as possible so she wouldn't have time to think, to dread. She tried to make certain she was either very much in the public eye or else indisputably in the company of other women, so Adrian had no grounds for suspicion.

The tactics made her feel the constant tug of an invisible leash, and they weren't always successful since he was sometimes completely irrational, but it was the best way she'd found to cope with an impossible situation.

After what had happened in the park, however, she didn't dare go out. She knew that hiding in the house was only a temporary postponement, but she needed the time to try to shore up her splintering emotional barriers. Luckily, Adrian had decided they would give a party—a large party—the following weekend, so Julia was able to claim preparation for it as an excuse to remain at the house.

In truth, there was a great deal for her to do, and since the visible evidence of her work greeted Adrian when he came home late each afternoon, he could hardly deny she'd been taking care of all the arrangements involved in hosting a large social event—especially since she made it a point to greet him with numerous questions regarding his preferences. It was another tactic she'd found to be generally effective; by focusing his attention on mundane details that he had absolutely no interest in, she could induce him at times to release the pressure inside him in small spurts of temper rather than devastating explosions.

"For God's sake, Julia, I don't care what you serve!"

She kept her voice brisk. "If you mean to discuss politics either during or after dinner, Adrian, then what we serve for the meal is quite important."

They were standing in the foyer, alone after a maid had bustled by with her arms full of linen, and Adrian glared down at Julia. His hat had been tossed aside the moment he came into the house; his blond hair was plastered to his scalp with perspiration, and a nerve beside his hard mouth pulsed visibly. He looked hot and frustrated; his duties as mayor were more difficult than he'd expected. The strains of office coupled with the intolerable heat wave gripping Richmond made his temper more ragged than Julia ever had seen it. At least for the moment it was just annoyance, not irrational rage.

"Why's it important?" he snapped, loosening his tie with a jerky movement.

"In this heat, serving something too rich will just put them to sleep or make them hideously uncomfortable. No one will feel like talking, especially about politics."

"Then serve something mild and chilled—use your head, Julia." He shrugged out of his coat, scowling. "Is my bath ready?"

"Yes."

She remained where she was, watching him ascend the stairs until he was out of sight. Only then did she swallow hard and slump a little as some of the tension left her. Perhaps this would be a good night. She wasn't sure yet, and wouldn't feel completely safe until he was asleep. He could still shout for her and demand she help him bathe, she knew. It was one of the little humiliations he enjoyed inflicting, forcing her to handle his naked body in the most intimate manner possible. The first time he'd made her touch him, she had been unable to hide her loathing and distaste, and she still carried the scars of his resulting fury. Since then she had learned to do as he wished without revealing any of her emotions, to detach the part of herself that felt ill and shamed and degraded.

Sometimes she wondered why she didn't go mad. Sometimes she thought it had already happened.

In the first weeks of their marriage, when Adrian's propensity toward violence had become all too dreadfully obvious, she'd been unable to hide her own shock and fear. Cowering in pain and terror from his blows, flinching from what he said to her and what he demanded of her, she had begged him to stop hurting her.

It made her nauseated now to remember, but she had. If anything, her pleading had only made him more violent.

When she had tried to fight his anger with her own and at least to make an attempt to defend herself, he'd nearly killed her, and when she had withdrawn into a frozen silence, it had been even worse. Gradually, locked into a ghastly cycle of abuse with no escape, she'd learned how to survive it. She had mastered all the little tactics designed to keep him calm, had sacrificed her independence, her pride, and her self-respect. She had learned that when there was no stopping him, the only thing to do was endure. The rest of the time she simply behaved as though nothing out of the ordinary had ever happened between them, as if their marriage was a normal one.

God help all women, she thought, if hers was a normal marriage.

He had only once struck her face, knocking her to the floor, and the resulting swollen bruise had made it impossible for her to be seen for nearly two weeks. After that he was more careful, even in his rages. Careful enough to mark her where only he would see. Whether he feared public censure or simply valued his favored position in the society in which they lived, she could not guess, but it was clear he intended to keep his bedroom brutality secret.

"Julia?"

She looked around with a start, then smiled when she saw her sister. "How was the picnic?"

"Hot," Lissa said, stripping off her gloves as she crossed the foyer. "Whatever possessed Mark to think today would be a good day to sit out in the sweltering heat, I'll never know. He and the other men could at least take off their coats and roll up their sleeves, but Susie, Helen, Monica, and I nearly smothered."

Julia frowned as she studied her sister's flushed face. "You should go up and get out of your stays, then take a nice, cool bath."

"That's what I intend to do. Is Adrian home?"

"Yes, he's bathing. We'll have something light and simple for supper and a quiet evening."

"I imagine Adrian will work in his study?" Lissa asked, starting up the stairs.

"He didn't say."

"In that case, I'll ask him at supper to give me another chess lesson tonight."

Julia kept her smile in place until Lissa was out of sight, then turned slowly and went toward the hallway that would take her to the kitchen. Lissa knew only one side of Adrian, had seen only the charming face he wore publicly. From the very first he had deliberately set out to make her adore him—and he'd succeeded.

She had gone away to school immediately after the wedding, and Adrian had been very careful to do nothing to upset Lissa's favorable image of him when she came home to visit for holidays and the summer break. When she was staying with them he was on his best, most charming behavior and, at least until this visit, had controlled himself and hadn't hurt Julia badly enough to force her to keep to her bed. Julia still didn't know what had set him off the night of the dance, and she hadn't dared ask. He certainly hadn't volunteered the information, and he'd long passed the point of apologizing for what he'd done to her, but it had been Adrian who had ordered her the next morning to remain in bed.

"I'll tell Lissa it's the heat," he had said, smearing ointment over the raw welts on her back. He always did that, and Julia thought it was because he enjoyed touching the marks he'd made on her flesh. "I'll tell her not to disturb you. And if she does come in here, tell her you're feeling exhausted and want to be left alone. Do you understand, Julia?"

"Yes." She understood only too well. And when her sister had visited her briefly, she'd been able to smile and say that it was only the heat, she'd be better in a day or so, and Lissa wasn't to worry. She had been careful to make certain Lissa saw nothing to betray the lie.

It would have been a dreadful shock if she had. Lissa thought Adrian was perfect. It was another of his deliberate little torments directed at Julia: weaving his charming spell so completely around innocent Lissa. Julia had considered telling Lissa the truth, but couldn't bring herself to do so. It was not to spare Adrian, but Lissa . . . and perhaps Julia herself.

Julia had had her own illusions shattered, and that wound had been the deepest of all; she didn't want to see the pain of it in her sister's eyes. See the dreadful knowledge of what a man could do to a woman. Teach Lissa what fear really was and teach her how terribly vulnerable she could be. And there was another reason she made certain Lissa suspected nothing—because of what Adrian had promised to do. There was no place Julia could go, no one she could turn to with even a faint hope of protecting her sister. Or herself. She had no money of her own, no friends who would take her and Lissa in if Julia dared to leave her husband.

And who would believe what she'd suffered at his hands? The scars on her body were faint, the result of her wedding night and those first few weeks when his rage had been totally out of control. Since then, he had used the strap or his hands and left no permanent marks on her. Not visible ones, at least.

She was his wife, she belonged to him. No one would question his right to punish her—and she doubted there were many who would even believe he did.

Trapped.

Julia went into the kitchen and spoke with the cook, automatically taking care of the details of supper tonight and the coming party. She'd become proficient at dividing her thoughts and attention, and one corner of her mind now worried at the awareness that she couldn't hope to avoid Cyrus Fortune much longer. There was a concert the following night Adrian had insisted they would attend, with a buffet dinner afterward, and Julia had a strangely certain feeling Cyrus would be there.

At the charity dance, his stare had been bold, and he hadn't hesitated to hold and kiss her in the park where anyone could have seen. How would he behave when she appeared on the arm of her husband?

The very thought terrified her. Adrian was always alert to how other men looked at her or spoke to her, though from his charming and attentive facade no one had guessed what demons of jealousy and possessiveness burned inside him. But she knew. She knew the price she would pay if Adrian caught even a glimmer of the naked desire in Cyrus Fortune's eyes.

She was also very much afraid her own feelings would betray her, even if Cyrus didn't. His kisses had affected her in a way she still couldn't quite believe, and being in his arms had felt so . . . right. Desire. He had, with the first touch, taught her body to feel desire. Her body, that had learned in agony to fear a man's strength, had swayed toward his in mute need and without fear. She found it incredible, and couldn't understand how it was possible.

But a moth seemed to feel no fear, she thought, as it was drawn to the flame that would destroy it.

Like all the women before her, she was bewitched, helplessly in thrall to a black velvet voice and heated black eyes, and what she felt about it was bitter resentment and pain. Another man who could control her with his force—even if his was a different kind of force. Another man who could make her do things she didn't want to do, feel things she didn't want to feel. Another man who wanted to use her to satisfy his own needs no matter what it cost her.

She managed to get through the evening, though watching Adrian smile at Lissa over the chessboard and tease her made Julia's stomach sicken and churn. For the first time, she wondered if she might be wrong in hiding the truth from her sister. Perhaps for Lissa's own protection she should teach her what men could hide beneath charming smiles. Perhaps innocence was something else that cost too much.

Julia was still undecided when they went to bed that night, but the morning brought the only decision possible. Whether Lissa did or did not deserve to know the truth, Julia decided that her sister's ignorance of what was going on was her safeguard. If she knew, she'd confront Adrian, and that was the one thing Julia had sworn to herself would never happen.

Adrian left for his office at the usual time, already looking wilted and irritable from the heat; Julia dreaded the mood he'd be in by the time he came home. Lissa helped around the house during the morning, then went out shopping with two of her friends. Julia tried to keep busy, but two days of steady work had accomplished everything necessary for the party, and by early afternoon she found herself at loose ends.

For the first time, the house felt hot to her, smothering almost, but she was still wary of venturing out in public for fear of encountering Cyrus. She considered and discarded an impulse to walk in the garden; there were no shady spots out there, and most of the midsummer flowers had been burned dry by the unrelenting sun, so it would hardly be a pleasant walk. Without really deciding to do so, she went to the stables in back of the house.

It was relatively cool inside the wide hall and very peaceful. Only the faint sounds of movement from the drowsy horses disturbed the silence. The men who cared for the horses were absent, so she was alone with them. Lissa had taken one of the carriages and a driver, giving in to Julia's suggestion because of the heat; Adrian had taken the other this morning, planning to send his groom and stableman to look over some horses due to be auctioned the following day.

For a few minutes she wandered from stall to stall, speaking softly to the horses and stroking satiny necks. Out of the house she felt more peaceful, though it was a tenuous peace easily disturbed. The shock of his voice shattered it.

"The horses are comfortable with you. I thought they would be."

She whirled around, staring in alarm. "Are you out of your mind?" she whispered.

Cyrus Fortune stepped out of the shadows, smiling faintly. "No one saw me come in," he said, knowing why she was so disturbed. "No one ever has to know I was here. The grooms will be gone for hours yet, and Drummond and your sister as well."

Julia took a step back as he came toward her, but there was no way for her to retreat farther without cornering herself in an empty stall. She felt emotionally cornered. "Leave me alone," she said shakily, control demolished along with peace.

Cyrus stopped immediately, a little more than an arm's length away, and his smile faded. In the dimness of the barn hall, his black eyes were liquid. "Are you afraid of me, Julia?" There was surprise and something else in his deep voice, something she could have sworn was anxiety.

Her laugh sounded a little wild to her own ears, and she wondered dimly if she had finally crossed the line into madness. "Afraid? Whatever I say, you won't stay away from me. Shouldn't I be afraid?"

"No. I won't force myself on you, if you've that in your mind. I want you willing." He still sounded surprised.

She closed her eyes, struggling to regain some control over her emotions. "I don't want an affair, can't you understand that? Please, just leave me alone. I won't . . . I won't break my marriage vows."

After a moment he said, "You're trembling." He reached his hand toward hers, and when she flinched he said sharply, "I'm not going to hurt you, Julia."

His tone caused tension to stiffen her body and her gaze to fall, but she didn't flinch again when he took her hand, and she didn't struggle or protest when he led her partway down the barn hall, where there was a rough wooden bench outside the tack room door.

"Sit down," he said.

It was only when she immediately obeyed that abrupt command that Julia realized what living with Adrian had done to her. Cyrus was angry. When she'd heard the emotion in his voice, she had felt an almost smothering panic and dread, an anxious need to find out what he wanted or what she'd done wrong so she could somehow satisfy him. It had become a compulsion to yield to an angry male voice, to submit instantly without question or even another word. To do anything in an attempt to avoid pain. Her recognition of the frightened, helpless response made sick shame writhe inside her, hot tears burn behind eyes taught never to shed them, and kept her silent as she sat on the bench with her head bent and her hands folded tightly in her lap.

He went down on one knee, careless of his trousers, and his big hand covered both of hers. She wasn't wearing gloves, and the heavy warmth of his hand made an odd little tremor go through her body. His was a gentle touch without force. His voice, no longer angry, was the familiar black velvet when he said softly, "Julia, look at me."

Instantly, she raised her gaze to meet his. His eyes narrowed briefly, and then he leaned over and kissed her.

She had been trying desperately to withdraw from him, to retreat into herself as she'd learned to do, but at the first touch of his warm, hard lips that escape was lost to her. His black eyes were burning, and she closed hers to shut out the awful temptation to lose herself in the fiery dark pools. This time she felt no shock except the shock of desire.

Everything but that faded out of her mind. The fear and anxiety, the sick shame at what she'd become, and all the memories of pain at the hands of a man were overwhelmed by the emotions and sensations this man made her feel.

He kept one hand on the back of the bench near her shoulder and the other gently holding both of hers, and made no attempt to draw her into his arms. His mouth was a potent seduction, moving slowly and sensuously on hers. His tongue glided between her lips in a caress that made a hot shiver ripple through her body, and she could no more resist him than she could resist her next breath. When her mouth opened to his touch in instinctive need, he accepted the mute invitation and explored deeply in a small possession so searingly intimate it seemed to brand her in a place Adrian had never been able to touch.

Responding was as natural as one beat of her heart following another. Julia wasn't aware that she was kissing him back, that her lips had softened and trembled in need, that her tongue touched his shyly and with hunger, and she never heard her own throaty little moan of pleasure.

His mouth hardened for an instant, but then he drew back to look at her, and murmured huskily, "Is that anything to fear?"

Julia opened her eyes slowly, feeling dazed and hot. Her lips were throbbing, her whole body was throbbing, and when she looked at him she knew only one thing: if she alone were at risk, she would give in to him without another word of protest. But it wasn't only she.

"Yes," she whispered, her throat aching.

His lean face tightened a little, but his voice remained soft and husky. "Do your vows mean so much to you?"

"Shouldn't they?" That reply was a mistake, and she knew it when he smiled slowly.

"When a woman answers a question with another question, then she's saying no. It isn't your vows stopping you. I know you've found no pleasure with Drummond, and I know you want me. I can be discreet, if that's what's worrying you. No one ever has to know we are lovers."

Julia swallowed hard, fighting to resist the lure of his beguiling voice. She barely managed to infuse her own voice with dry sarcasm. "Did you make such a promise to all the others? If so, I can certainly judge the worth of it."

His smile died. "That was different."

"No." She looked at him steadily. "No different. You were right about one thing; I prefer honesty to lies. Don't make an empty promise you have no intention of keeping."

"I don't make empty promises."

She heard a touch of his earlier anger sharpen his voice, and it made her nervous, but she forced herself to continue. "Shall I tell you the names of the women you've been with since you came back to Richmond? At least one of them told me quite bluntly herself."

"Anne Butler," he said flatly.

"Yes."

"She was the only one, Julia. The only one I slept with since I returned." *Slept with*, he thought, was an inaccurate term in addition to being euphemistic. He had never "slept" with any woman, and none had spent more than an hour or two in his bed.

Her steady gaze wavered slightly. "That isn't what I've heard. Gossip—"

"Gossip seldom has it right."

She shrugged and looked away. "Even so, you can't deny how quickly word of your affairs spreads. Perhaps the others didn't care about that, but I do."

"Stop saying *the others* as if the path behind me is littered with them," he said roughly, and tried to rein his temper when she darted him a quick, wary look. In a quieter voice he said, "I'm not a lecher, whatever you've heard."

Julia shrugged again. "I'm not an adulteress."

He was beginning to hate the sound of that word, and it had never bothered him before. He was also more baffled than he'd ever been in his life. Both frustration and worry were eating at him. She didn't love her husband—he was growing to hate, too, the word husband—she didn't care about her vows, and she wanted him. Was it really only a fear of public censure that made her refuse him? Whatever it was, he couldn't seem to find a way around it. He didn't want to hurt her, but surely finding pleasure in his arms wouldn't hurt her?

Despite his efforts, his voice had roughened again when he said, "If I kissed you again, would that matter? If I unbuttoned your blouse and opened it, touched you the way I ache to touch you, would you remember you're married? If I carried you to a pile of hay over there and pressed you back into it and lifted your skirts, would you be able to stop me?"

She looked at him, her green eyes appearing strangely blind, her lips quivering in a twisted smile when she whispered, "Probably not."

His hand tightened over hers. "It's what we both want, Julia, what we both need."

"I can't." She held her voice as steady as she could. "And if you—if you really do want me willing, then you have to believe I mean what I say. I won't betray my husband."

Cyrus rose to his feet with such an abrupt motion that she started and then looked at him nervously as he took a couple of steps away from her. His big, powerful body seemed unusually stiff, either through tension or pure anger—and it was the latter possibility that made her apprehensive. She couldn't see his face; he was standing in the center of the barn hall gazing toward the house. It wasn't until he spoke in a very low voice that some of her anxiety eased.

"Do you realize you've never said my name? Will you at least do that much, Julia?"

"Cyrus," she murmured.

He sighed. "If I wasn't so damned sure this was tearing you to pieces . . . but I am sure. I'm also sure if I did seduce you, you'd hate me for it."

She wondered if she would, but didn't voice the question.

Cyrus turned to look at her. He was smiling faintly, but his facial expression was a bit grim. "If I catch Drummond near the edge of a cliff, I'm going to push him over."

"There aren't any cliffs nearby," she said, trying for lightness because she was sure he didn't mean what he'd said.

"No, I suppose not. And I suppose it'll do me good to face the fact that I can't always have what I want. But I won't pretend I like it."

Julia didn't know how to answer, and so she said nothing.

"You don't have to worry about meeting me in public, and I won't try to see you privately. Whatever I feel, I'll keep to myself."

"Thank you."

He bowed from the waist, a gesture that was only partly mocking. "I know how to be a gentleman, even if I wasn't born one and never bothered to try to be one until now." He paused, then added in a voice more serious than any she'd heard from him, "Julia, if you ever need anything, any kind of help, then please come to me. I won't ask anything in return, I promise you. Just know you can trust me, and count on me if you're ever in need."

"Thank you," she repeated, shaken.

He gazed at her, an odd look of hesitation crossing his dark face, then shook his head as if to throw off a disturbing thought. "Will you attend the concert tonight?" he asked in his normal tone.

Julia was grateful the barn hall was dim, because she was afraid of what he might see in her eyes. "Yes. With Adrian and Lissa."

Cyrus nodded. "I had meant to go, but I believe I won't. And I'll send my regrets to your party as well, if you wish." When she started in surprise, he added, "Your husband invited me yesterday."

Unnerved, Julia couldn't help wondering if Adrian was merely interested in Cyrus because he was wealthy, or if he had some suspicion— No, ridiculous. Unless someone had seen her walking with Cyrus in the park? She didn't know, but the possibility was there.

"Julia?" Cyrus's voice was gentle. "Shall I send my regrets?"

Her thoughts whirled, then settled with a leaden feeling of dread. If Adrian did intend to cultivate an acquaintance with Cyrus for political reasons, he wouldn't let a social refusal stop him; if he was suspicious, he wouldn't rest until he could judge for himself if there was any reason to be. Either way, the party was a hurdle she had to get over.

She cleared her throat. "No, of course not. If Adrian invited you, he'll expect you."

"I don't give a damn what he expects," Cyrus said. "Will it ruin your pleasure if I come?"

It had been so long since Julia had thought of a party

with pleasure that for a moment she could only look at him blankly. Then she shook her head. "No."

He frowned slightly as he looked at her, that same hesitant expression returning for a brief moment. "All right," he said finally. "I'll see you on Friday, then."

Julia remained where she was long after he'd gone, sitting on the hard bench, staring at nothing. What a peculiar ending, she was thinking, to something that had barely begun. He had come to her today still bent on seduction, but different somehow. Today he'd been more aware of her emotions, and more responsive to them. She had no doubt at all he had decided to stop pressing her because he believed it was tearing her to pieces.

She should have been relieved. He wasn't a man to betray his feelings unless he chose to. Neither Adrian nor anyone else would see any hint of desire in his black eyes when they rested on her. She wouldn't have to worry about encountering him in public or in private and having her resolve tested. There would be no more improper or seductive remarks, no more heated kisses.

Her body would forget the astonishing pleasure it had known so briefly.

Julia rose slowly to her feet, feeling nothing but an empty ache now. It would pass, she thought wearily. Pain always did, given enough time.

She went into the house that seemed cool again, drawing the threads of her control around her tightly. She reminded herself that she must not betray knowledge of Adrian inviting Cyrus to the party—and concentrated on schooling her features into an emotionless mask so that she wouldn't betray herself when he did mention it. She didn't have to wait long, because Adrian

brought up the subject that evening as they were on
their way to the concert.

"Julia, I've invited Cyrus Fortune to the party," he
said, his tone easy because Lissa was sitting across from
them in the carriage. "And he'll be one of the dinner
guests."

The darkness aided her ability to hide her thoughts,
but it also denied her the chance to try to gauge his. She
replied in a tone to match his. "Oh? Where would you
like him seated at dinner?"

"On your right," Adrian said.

Lissa spoke up then, asking the question Julia wanted
answered. "Is he important to you, Adrian?"

"He could be, if I make a bid for governor one day."
Adrian laughed with a touch of dryness. "'Fortune' is an
apt name. He was rich before he went west, and has
more luck than a riverboat gambler. I just heard that in
'ninety-eight he bought up a few thousand acres of
supposedly worthless East Texas property—and where
do you suppose they struck oil last year?"

"East Texas?" Lissa guessed.

"Yes. Fortune won't be able to live long enough to
spend all the money he's making. I've heard he's never
had any political leanings, but it can't hurt to better my
acquaintance with him."

"I like him," Lissa announced in a definite tone.

Julia managed not to jump in surprise. "I didn't know
you'd met him," she murmured.

"I've seen him at parties, of course, but we were never
really introduced until— Well, I know you'll say it wasn't
proper, Julia, but there was really nothing I could have
done. It was the other day when I was coming out of the
library. My arms were full of books, and somehow I

tripped. I hadn't even seen him until then, but Mr. Fortune caught me. Wasn't that splendid of him?"

"It was lucky for you," Adrian said.

"I know, I might have broken my neck. He was very nice, and even carried my books to the carriage. I don't know why people say his manners are dreadful. They seemed perfectly all right to me. He was very polite and acted rather like an uncle. And even if his eyes *are* the blackest I've ever seen, they laugh in the nicest way."

"Don't lose your heart to him," Adrian warned in a light tone that deceived Lissa but not Julia. "Rumor has it that the last thing he wants is a wife—unless it's someone else's."

Lissa laughed. "I just think he's pleasant, Adrian, that's all."

They reached their destination then, for which Julia was grateful. All she could think of, unnervingly, was that she had never seen the laugh in Cyrus's eyes that so many people seemed to notice. It was a strangely painful realization. But she pushed it out of her mind, just as she had all the stray thoughts of him that had been tormenting her since the interlude at the stables. She pulled on her social mask and became the perfect wife.

"The other one isn't big enough?" Noel Stanton guessed, watching two dozen men busily working on the foundation of a huge house-to-be on lovely acreage that sloped gently back to the James River.

"Did you say something, Noel?" Cyrus asked, looking up from the blueprints spread out atop a corded stack of lumber.

"I was being nosy," Noel explained with an apologetic air. "Tate left you a perfectly good house closer in to the

city, and God knows it's big enough to hold an army;
why're you building out here?"

Cyrus, his coat off and sleeves rolled up, bent over the
plans again. "The city gets more congested with every
year, as you very well know. I want room to stretch."

"You'll have it," Noel said. He eyed a growing pile of
gray stone nearby as another wagonload was deposited,
and said thoughtfully, "That rock reminds me of the old
buildings they've pulled down recently."

"It should." Cyrus glanced up at him again. "I'm using
stone dating from colonial days. Since the city fathers
have been merrily destroying their heritage, I thought
I'd have a try at preserving a little of it."

Studying his friend, Noel pulled his hat off and began
fanning himself absently. They were standing beneath
the shade of a huge oak tree, but the heat wave hadn't
relented and there wasn't a hint of a breeze to disturb
the hot, still air. Cyrus, as usual, hadn't worn a hat, and
even though he'd removed his coat, the heat didn't seem
to bother him.

"Preservation, eh?" Noel's voice was mild. "Is that
why you've had most of the Fortune family paintings and
valuables removed from the house, crated, and stored?"

Cyrus looked up again, this time in surprise. "How did
you know about that?"

"Your groom told mine. You've got your servants in a
tizzy, Cy, they don't know what to make of all this."

After a brief frown, Cyrus shook his head slightly.
"There's no mystery. I wanted everything inventoried
and decided I might as well get the packing done at the
same time."

"It'll be months before this house is completed."

"I'm aware of that, Noel."

Bushy eyebrows rising, Noel said, "Are you also aware

of the fact that a bear with a toothache would be more amiable than you've been these last days?"

Cyrus stared at him for a long moment, but then a crooked smile tugged at his mouth. "Don't say I've been that bad."

"Worse. Your company manners never were much to brag about, but when even the ladies begin to notice you're in a temper as black as your eyes, the case has to be desperate."

"What ladies?"

"My wife, for one. Felice passed you on the street this morning, and swore that when she said hello, you growled in response."

"I'll offer my apologies the next time I see her," Cyrus stated.

"I'm less interested in apologies than explanations. Yes, I know you never explain, but this time you've really got me worried, Cy. What the hell's wrong with you?"

Four

♥

"Nothing," Cyrus said, frowning as he gazed toward the busy workmen.

"Maybe someone else would accept that," Noel retorted, "but I won't. I've known you for twenty years. When you left after Tate died, I thought you might come back changed, but you didn't. It's *since* you came back that you've changed. I thought at first it was because of Julia Drummond, but—" He broke off as Cyrus looked at him, then added quietly, "Maybe she does have something to do with it, after all."

Wanting to distract his friend from that possibility, partly because he didn't want to admit to himself how difficult he found it to accept her refusal, Cyrus said abruptly, "I received a package the other night. A gold-handled cane, very beautiful, in a wooden box. There was a note inside that said my father wanted me to have it."

"Your—?" Noel was effectively distracted because of sheer surprise. "Your real father?"

"Apparently. Did you ever know Tate to use a cane?"

"No. But who could have sent it to you?"

"I've been unable to find out. The package was left on the doorstep after dark. As far as I can determine, no one saw it delivered. I've taken the cane to half a dozen shops around town, including two jewelers, and all I've been told with any certainty is that it's very old. The craftsmanship of the gold is exquisite, but if the artist signed his work or left his mark, I haven't been able to find it."

"So that is what's troubling you?"

"Wouldn't it trouble you? Noel, Tate was always honest with me, and the fact that I'm a bastard never meant anything to him. It didn't mean anything to me. But now . . . 'Your father wanted you to have this' the note said. So who sent it to me? My mother? Is she still alive? Have I seen her across a street without knowing it? Why did she leave me on the doorstep of a stranger? Why didn't my father marry her?"

"You can't be sure he didn't," Noel objected quietly. "Perhaps he died before you were born, and your mother just couldn't raise you alone."

Cyrus shrugged a bit jerkily. "Perhaps. But I *can't* be sure, that's the hell of it. Always in the past I considered that my life began when Tate gave me his name. Whatever came before didn't matter. Then I got the package . . . and questions I've never asked myself have begun to haunt me. How common are black eyes, Noel?"

The question was abrupt, and Noel blinked. "Well, not very. To be honest, yours are the only ones I've seen."

"They're the only ones I've seen too. I've seen dark eyes, particularly out west—Indians, Mexicans, a few Gypsies—but not black ones, not like mine. Doesn't that strike you as odd, that in more than thirty years I've never seen eyes like mine in a single face?"

With a stab at humor, Noel said, "*You've* always struck me as odd, Cy."

His friend didn't smile in return. "I suppose I have."

"Hey, I was joking."

"No, you weren't." Cyrus did smile then, faintly.

A little uncomfortably, Noel shrugged. "All right, but what's that have to do with anything? We're all peculiar in our own ways."

"Yes, but most people can trace their peculiarities to a definite source. They can point to their ancestry as the reason they look and behave as they do; why they're tall or short, dark or fair, calm or bad-tempered. You yourself got those eyebrows from your grandfather."

"Family trait," Noel said automatically, then stopped when he realized his was a response Cyrus had never been able to make. "I'm sorry, Cy. I never thought."

"I never did either. Just as I never thought about the fact that the date I celebrate as my birthday is actually the anniversary of the day Tate took me in. I was a few weeks old then, apparently, so my actual birthday is sometime in October." He sighed. "The point is, none of that ever troubled me until the package came."

"I wish there was something I could say—"

Cyrus waved a hand in dismissal. "There isn't. And there's no one I can ask to find the answers I want, unless I somehow manage to find out who sent me the package. That's the only glimmer of a clue I have to any part of my heritage. Tate tried to find my mother in the weeks after I was left on his doorstep, and if he couldn't find her then, I'm not likely to have much luck almost thirty-two years later."

"You have to try, for your own peace of mind."

"Yes, I know. And I will. But even the basic answers I need aren't as important as . . . What disturbs me most of all is the cane itself."

Noel frowned. "What do you mean?"

Cyrus hesitated, but Noel was the closest friend he had in the world and he needed to tell someone, if only to check his grip on reality. "It's a feeling I've had since the package came," he said slowly. "A feeling I can't shake no matter how often I tell myself it's absurd."

"What feeling?"

"The feeling that there was a mistake made somewhere along the way, something wrong I should know about. I looked at the cane, and I realized there was something I should understand about it, some knowledge I'm supposed to have. I felt it. It's almost as if something inside me knows the cane was supposed to be the final piece of the puzzle. Only there are too many other pieces missing, and I can't even guess what to do with that one."

Noel's frown deepened. "Cy, what you're saying is definitely strange."

"Strange isn't the word for it." Not even to Noel was Cyrus willing to admit the cane seemed to have triggered other things as well, even stranger. His "whims and notions" were more frequent now and far more troubling. Some were literally compulsions, like this house he had to build.

He didn't know how or why, but he was certain beyond any doubt that the house in which he'd grown up would not be standing come winter. He *knew*. There was nothing he could do to save the house. Whatever was meant to happen to it was already . . . decided. Events had been set in motion, a pattern woven, and the destruction of the house was a part of it.

That was another thing, his peculiar recognition and understanding of patterns. He looked at places and felt the history of them, looked at people and sensed the ties that bound them and the emotions that drove them— sometimes even caught glimpses of what he believed were their futures. It seemed instinctive, yet he'd never been conscious of it before, not like this, not so strong and certain. He didn't like it.

He'd been changing since the first night he'd spoken to Julia, beginning with his strange dreams of pain; since he'd received the cane all the sensations and emotions had been growing stronger every day. Patterns. He was in the grip of one. He felt as if he were a pawn on a chessboard, all the moves planned out in advance, and it was a decidedly unsettling sensation for a man who had never believed anyone other than himself was the master of his fate.

"Cy?"

He looked questioningly at Noel.

"Going to the Drummonds' party tonight?"

The distraction, it seemed, had been only temporary. Cyrus had been trying not to think of Julia, but Noel was obviously too curious—and perhaps concerned—to let the subject drop.

"I was invited," Cyrus said briefly.

"That isn't an answer. Are you going?"

"Yes, Noel, I'm going."

"Is she a piece of the puzzle?" Noel asked softly.

The question surprised Cyrus, because Noel asked it and because the reply, spoken silently but emphatically in his head, was, *Yes, she is*. He went very still, consciously listening, but nothing else came to him. Julia was a piece of the puzzle, his puzzle, he was certain of it.

"Why did you put it that way?" he asked slowly.

Noel shook his head. "Because you're different. Because a few minutes ago, when I suggested you might be different because of her, I could see it in your face. You are. She matters to you, doesn't she?"

That was something Cyrus wasn't willing to think about, to question. There were so many damned questions already. Looking back down at the plans for his house, he said dryly, "Rejection matters to me. God or the devil must be trying to teach me a lesson after all. She doesn't want me."

"And you're accepting her refusal?"

Cyrus looked up quickly, his eyes fierce. "Dammit, Noel, does everyone believe I'm a lecher? That I'd seduce a woman no matter how unwilling she was, and not care how much it hurt her?"

Noel whistled softly under his breath. "You are certainly touchy these days. No one's called you a lecher as far as I'm aware, Cy. I certainly haven't, and I don't think it of you. It's simply that I've never seen you give up, much less this quickly."

"Let's drop the subject, shall we?" Cyrus's tone was testy.

Noel decided he'd better do as he was asked. It seemed as though Julia Drummond's refusal, combined with an enigmatic clue to Cyrus's beginnings, had pushed his friend well past the limits of his usual tolerance. Noel was more than a little worried about him. As odd as he sometimes was, during his entire life the one thing all of Cyrus's friends had been able to count on was the complete absence of a temper. No matter what was said to him or about him, Cyrus had always reacted with calm, sometimes with mockery, and often with amusement, but never anger.

And there was more to it, Noel thought. There was

something Cyrus hadn't chosen to tell him. He knew his friend too well to push, but it bothered him.

"Take a look at the plans and see what you think," Cyrus invited Noel now, his voice normal again.

Noel joined him in bending over the blueprints and made a couple of idle suggestions to improve the design, neither of which Cyrus agreed with. But the discussion helped to ease the remaining tension between the two men, and seemed to restore Cyrus to his usual calm temper. It wasn't until a few minutes later, when he was rolling up the plans, that Noel noticed something he'd forgotten about since long-ago childhood days of games and swimming in the river.

"I see you still have that birthmark. I'd forgotten it was so dark."

"Age changes everything, I suppose." Cyrus glanced down at the inside of his left forearm and felt an odd little chill feather up his spine. The mark he'd been born with was hardly bigger than a gold piece, a perfect crescent shape a shade darker than the surrounding flesh and hardly noticeable. Or at least, it had always been only a shade darker. Now it was deeper in color, almost bloodred, and it was very visible.

"We'd better start back if you don't want to be late for the Drummond party," Noel said casually, obviously not noticing anything unusual in his friend's expression.

Cyrus rolled his sleeves back down. He heard himself ask, "Are you going?" and his voice sounded normal to him.

"Felice says we are, so I suppose I will. It'll be stifling, too, with a house full of people. I swear if this heat doesn't end, I'm heading north until winter."

"You hate winter."

"I've learned to hate summer."

The conversation remained casual all the way back into town, and it wasn't until he was dressing later that Cyrus allowed himself to consider the question of his birthmark. He paused before putting his shirt on to study it, frowning. No soreness, no heat, no reason at all to suppose he'd done anything to injure that part of his arm and change the mark. But it was definitely different from last year, last week. Different from yesterday.

He went to his wardrobe and reached into the back to get the cane, then carried it to a chair near his bed and sat studying it. Though the carving of the gold looked merely ornate at first glance, a closer look revealed a number of symbols nearly hidden within meaningless decorative contours. Cyrus had found them the night the cane had been left for him, but they hadn't meant anything to him. Now he wondered if they should.

Stars, some connected with faint lines. Planets. The sun. And the moon. The quarter moon.

The crescent shape was carved into the gold on the top of the cane, where a hand would normally rest when it was in use, and it was more deeply carved than any of the other symbols. Cyrus looked at it for a long moment, then held the cane in one hand and pressed that golden quarter moon against the mark on his arm.

It was a perfect match in size and shape.

In the silence of his bedroom, Cyrus asked, "But what the hell does it mean?" And there was no answer.

The timing, he had decided, had to be perfect, and so he had been forced to curb impatience . . . and wait. He felt an odd fascination for the other, a strong curiosity. What interested him most of all was, the other had no awareness of him. A blind spot, perhaps. *He* had certainly recognized his womb-mate the first time he'd seen him.

It had been very difficult to contain his rage then, the first time. But it had gotten easier. Especially when he'd understood the other sensed no threat from him. Indeed, his womb-mate seemed not to know of his existence, of their connection. It was odd. He'd been given the knowledge, so why hadn't the other? He had finally come to the conclusion it was because *he* was the true son. He had, after all, meddled in the other's life with impunity, arranging several events so skillfully, his shaping touch had never been detected. It was clear evidence of his superiority.

He found it amusing to interfere with the destinies of people and course of events, to snip a thread here or there so the pattern became disturbed. He wanted to go on doing that, but a sense of urgency had come over him in recent days. Something new had entered the pattern. He didn't know what it was, but he felt it. The other was changing too quickly. Was it because of the woman? She annoyed him; he couldn't seem to affect her life entirely the way he'd meant to. He had known she was intended for his womb-mate, and he'd made certain she was out of reach, but she hadn't broken as he'd been sure she would.

Still, it might be amusing to watch the two of them struggle against fate. For a while, anyway. The only danger to his plans would be if they mated now—but she was too terrified to let that happen. He had made very sure she would be.

In the meantime, he had to consider carefully the best way to proceed. He had the gun primed and ready; all that remained was to decide when to point it and pull the trigger. He found it difficult to think of autumn in the

sweltering heat of summer—but it would come, then
winter, and it had to be over by then.

He thought he could afford a little more patience. A
few weeks, perhaps. But he'd have to keep a close
watch, and be alert to everything that was going on.
He'd have to try to discover if there really was something
other than the woman causing his womb-mate to change
and, if so, what it meant to his plans.

But he was confident.

"My compliments to the cook. This is excellent."

"I'll tell her. I'm sure she'll be pleased." Julia smiled
politely at Cyrus, conscious of the strong feeling of
unreality. At the opposite end of the long table, Adrian
was laughing at a joke someone had told him, and
between her and her husband a dozen guests talked as
they ate dinner.

Just a normal party, that was all. Except that from the
moment Adrian had formally introduced her to Cyrus,
Julia had felt the strange sensation of everything around
her being unreal and peculiarly deceptive. It wasn't only
her tension or her acute consciousness of Cyrus and what
had passed between them; it was almost like watching a
play, and knowing it wasn't real, knowing when the
curtain came down it would be over.

It unnerved her.

She couldn't fault Cyrus's behavior. He'd been the
perfect dinner guest, dividing his attention equally
between Julia and the lady on his right. His eyes
expressed nothing but mild enjoyment, his voice was
quiet and calm, and he hadn't betrayed by so much as
the slightest sign that he considered Julia anything other
than his hostess at a social event.

Julia hoped her mask was half as deceptive. Her emotional state was so odd, and between the heat, Adrian's ragged temper, and the tension of knowing she'd have to get through this party, she was so exhausted she just wanted to find a dark, cool place somewhere and sleep for a week. But she doubted anyone suspected her feelings. Social manners had been drummed into her all her life, and in the past two years she had perfected her public behavior.

So she was able to talk to both Cyrus and the man on her left calmly about casual subjects, performing her duties as hostess with the elegance and grace for which she was well known. No one, except perhaps Cyrus, could possibly have guessed her serene facade concealed a chaotic bundle of tense emotions.

It was a bit easier for her later, when the party guests arrived and the ballroom filled with the noise and movements of nearly a hundred people. Julia kept busy as hostesses always did, moving around the huge room speaking to people, finding dance partners for wallflowers, performing introductions, and overseeing the servants. She held on to her smile, acted by rote, and tried not to think at all.

"The Populist Party won't last much longer," Cyrus said, leaning back against the balustrade with his arms crossed over his chest.

"They sure as hell haven't been able to elect a president," Fred Daulton said with a laugh, taking a glass from a passing maid's tray and managing to "accidentally" bring his hand into contact with the breast of the servant.

It was fairly dark on the veranda, Cyrus thought, so

maybe it *had* been an accident. Then again, since the darkly handsome Daulton had a reputation among his male friends for preferring servant-girls or whores to ladies, perhaps not. Cyrus took a glass from the girl's tray with a nod of thanks, and returned his attention to the group of men who stood around him a few feet from the open French doors of the ballroom.

"They got a foot inside Congress," Adrian Drummond reminded the others.

"A small foot," Cyrus interjected. "But they have a few good ideas. The other parties may adopt some of them."

"Didn't know you followed politics, Cy," Noel commented a bit dryly.

"I read the newspapers."

"What's your party?" Drummond asked in a casual tone.

Cyrus lifted his glass in a faintly mocking salute. "I vote for the man, not the party."

Peter Reynolds slapped at a mosquito and said irritably, "There isn't a man worth voting for, not these days. Those fools in Washington are going to bring us all to ruin." He was a heavyset man of average height and excessive arrogance who had been known to knock another man down for expressing different views. He was also known for his unshakable belief that women's suffrage would destroy the country.

"If we give them the chance," Adam Prescott said. He was a tall man, blond like Drummond, and tended to be both cheerful and affable. Like the others in the group, he was personally wealthy and quite influential in Richmond. "We need to make changes, and soon."

"Perhaps it's time for fresh blood," Adrian Drummond suggested. "New ideas."

"Do you have any?" Noel asked him, and only Cyrus

realized that the question was more than a little ironic.

"I have a few." Drummond went on to explain where he stood on several subjects, expressing himself with such appealing candor and earnestness that it took even Cyrus a few moments to realize that the man's political ideas were old and stale rather than new, strongly favored the rich and influential, and contained more than a suggestion of about five different kinds of bigotry.

When the speech had ended, Cyrus said casually, "Interesting views. But there are other important issues. We all know where Reynolds stands on the subject of granting women the vote. What's your position?"

Drummond laughed. "I think any man would agree the ladies should tend to their homes. They aren't capable of logical thought, and certainly haven't the knowledge to form intelligent political opinions. Aside from which, can you imagine the lengths unscrupulous politicians would go to in order to secure female votes? We'd have population explosions of bastards born nine months after every election."

If he even knew that Cyrus himself was illegitimate, he seemed to have forgotten the fact. Cyrus didn't change expression, still smiling faintly when he said, "I see. Then you favor strong laws restricting women's rights—both in and out of marriage."

"Naturally. We know what's best for them."

"Not according to my wife," Noel put in.

Indulgently, Drummond said, "Oh, they may resent a few things, but the laws have to make sense. If we left it up to the women, they'd have us turn all our money over to them and be legally obliged to smile and give our names to other men's bastards."

Noel spoke up then with an innocent statement to the effect that he'd heard Congress was weakening on the subject of women's suffrage which, with Reynolds a part of the group, was tantamount to throwing the cat among the pigeons.

The attack on Washington instantly became a bit fiery as at least three voices hotly questioned the rationality and sense of the government. When Cyrus, who hadn't offered an opinion, slipped away to head toward the ballroom, Noel followed him as far as the French doors.

"Cy, are you out of your mind?" he demanded in a low voice. "I half expected you to ask point-blank if Drummond would mind his wife being unfaithful to him."

Calmly, Cyrus said, "I got the information I was looking for."

"Which is?"

"Have another drink, Noel. And enjoy the party." He strolled into the ballroom.

Julia had danced several times with guests, but it was still something of a shock when Cyrus approached her halfway through the evening and asked her to dance.

No one was near them, and Julia hesitated almost imperceptibly before she gave him her hand.

He looked at her very steadily, and said in a quiet voice, "I always dance with my hostess."

The musicians were playing a waltz, and as she went into his arms, very conscious of one big hand at her waist and the other holding hers in a light clasp, she fought a half-guilty, half-fearful impulse to look around for Adrian. Cyrus seemed to read her mind.

"He's out on the veranda discussing politics. Don't worry, Julia. I really *do* always dance with my hostess."

He danced beautifully, with astonishing grace for such a big man. She had to tilt her head back to look up at him, and only the fact that he seemed so calm enabled her to keep her own mask firmly in place. "Do you pick and choose social conventions according to what might amuse you to obey?" she asked lightly.

"I'm afraid so. The trick in life is to set your own standards. Now, I happen to believe showing appreciation to one's hostess is a sensible and polite thing to do. On the other hand, not speaking to a lady until I've been formally introduced seems quite ridiculous."

"Is that why you spoke to Lissa?"

"She told you about that, I see. Then you must know if I'd waited to be introduced before speaking to her or, God forbid, touching her, she would have broken her neck. Instead, I broke a rule. Sometimes we have to do that, Julia."

"You shouldn't—"

"I know, I shouldn't address you so familiarly. I won't, except when no one can hear."

His voice roughened on the words, and it made her heart skip a beat. Quite suddenly, she couldn't think of anything to say.

After a moment, his tone casual again, Cyrus said, "Lissa seems a very nice girl. I like her frankness."

"Oh, Lord, what did she say?" Julia asked involuntarily.

A gleam of amusement lit Cyrus's eyes. "Nothing scandalous. Just that I wasn't nearly as bad-mannered as people said."

Even as Julia was thinking, *He does have a laugh in his eyes,* she was saying, "I'm sorry, she shouldn't have said that."

"Why not? It's perfectly true. I'm bad-mannered only when I want to be. I hope you've noticed that tonight I'm on my best behavior."

Julia didn't quite know how to respond, so it was lucky
the dance ended then. He escorted her to an unoccupied
settee placed against the wall, collected two glasses from
a passing tray, and sat down beside her with the correct
foot of space between them.

Before she could say a word, he handed her a glass and
said, "I always spend a few minutes sitting with my
hostess."

She couldn't help but give him a wary look. "Do you?"

He smiled slightly. "I really do. I also spent over an
hour talking politics with your husband, and I'll make a
point of spending time with several other ladies before I
go. No one will notice anything out of the ordinary,
Julia."

Again he'd left her with nothing to say. She sipped the
chilled fruit juice in her glass, then unfurled her fan and
began using it. Though the French doors leading to the
veranda were standing open, the ballroom was uncomfortably hot, and with all the layers of clothing fashion
demanded—most especially the rigid corset—Julia felt
enervated. She hadn't been so conscious of it before, and
with all her attention focused on Cyrus she had even
enjoyed the dance, but now she could feel the effects of
heat and tension wearing away at her.

"Is it Adrian you're afraid of?" Cyrus asked abruptly.

Julia clung to her gracious and meaningless smile, but
she couldn't look away from those intent black eyes, and
was frightened that her own might be pleading. She kept
her voice low. "Please, you said you wouldn't—"

"I said I wouldn't show my feelings publicly and I
wouldn't keep pressing you. But I have to know the
truth, Julia. You didn't refuse me, you refused an affair.
The very idea seemed to terrify you. All evening I've felt
the tension in you, wound so tightly it could snap at any

minute. If it's because I'm here, then you're afraid of so much more than simply betraying what might have been between us." He drew a short breath, and the intensity in his voice didn't show at all on his face. "You act like the perfect wife, but it doesn't come from your heart. So where does it come from?"

"You have no right to ask me such a question," she said softly. "My marriage is my own concern." She wondered if her polite smile looked as unnatural as it felt.

"Julia—"

"Cyrus, please." She was at the end of her rope, and the strain quivered in her voice. She'd used his given name without thinking, realizing only when his eyes flickered.

"All right," he said immediately, gently. "All right, I won't say anything more about it. At least for now." Before she could reply, he began talking casually about a new exhibit at the museum, asking if she'd seen it. She replied almost at random, her mind worrying over his last promise—and it had been a promise. He wasn't giving up.

When another guest approached them a few minutes later and requested a dance with Julia, Cyrus gave way with perfect propriety and no apparent reluctance. She saw him numerous times afterward, dancing with several ladies, married and unmarried, and sitting with at least three others for a brief, socially correct interval. She saw him outside the French doors talking to a group of men that included Adrian. She saw him dance with Lissa, who seemed highly entertained by whatever he was discussing with her.

Remembering later, Julia was never sure how she managed to get through the remainder of the evening. No one looked at her oddly or commented, so she supposed her behavior was normal enough. By the time the last guest had departed, however, and Adrian had gone up to bed—cheerfully, for him—Julia was so drained she felt she couldn't put one foot in front of the other.

She told the servants they could clear the post-party clutter in the morning, then went slowly up the stairs. She met Lissa, already in her dressing gown, on the landing, and her sister's pretty face immediately tightened in concern.

"Julia, you look worn out!"

"It's the heat, I think," Julia responded with what ease she could muster. "I'll be all right once I peel away about three layers of fashion and have a cool bath."

"Didn't Adrian come up a little while ago? You can use my bath if you don't want to disturb him."

"No." Julia knew she'd answered too abruptly, and fought to keep her voice light. "My bath's filled and waiting for me."

Lissa shook her head slightly, a troubled frown on her face. "You have to stop pushing yourself so hard, especially in this heat."

"I wasn't the one who danced all evening," Julia returned.

"You certainly weren't a wallflower! And, anyway, I mostly danced with Mark, except for that waltz with Mr. Fortune. Do you like him, Julia? I saw you dancing with him. He's very pleasant and amusing, isn't he?"

Casually, Julia said, "Yes, very." Then she looked at her sister rather searchingly, wondering if Cyrus had made too strong an impression on Lissa. Other than Adrian, she'd never seemed to notice older men before. Slowly, she said, "It seems to be getting serious with Mark."

Lissa blushed faintly. "I think it is. He hasn't said anything, really, but—would you mind, Julia?"

Julia was relieved by the reply for a number of reasons, and this time her smile felt natural. "Why on earth would I mind? I believe he'd be good to you, and he can certainly take care of you properly."

"You don't think I'm too young? I know Adrian does."

"I think you should finish school before you marry, but I wouldn't object to an engagement," Julia said. "It might be best not to say anything to Adrian until—*if*—Mark proposes."

Smiling, Lissa said, "No, I won't. I just wanted to make sure you approved, even though I thought you would. Get some rest, all right? Good night, Julia."

I wanted to make sure you approved. Moving slowly down the hallway to the bedroom she shared with Adrian, Julia wished she could approve. She hoped her marriage was far from normal, but what guarantee did she have that Lissa would be luckier? Mark seemed a kind and decent man, but so had Adrian before she'd married him.

And girls went into marriage blind in so many ways. Blind and ignorant. Julia had been both. Blind to assume all her problems would be solved and her life made happy with a man to take care of her; ignorant of all the shocks and painful intimacies of the marriage bed. Fiercely, she made up her mind to have a talk with Lissa, whatever it cost her in embarrassment; no girl should go to her wedding night so abysmally ignorant, she didn't even know how a man's body differed from her own. In that way, at least, she could help prepare her sister.

As for the rest . . .

She went quietly into the bedroom, hoping desperately Adrian was still cheerful. At least then the little torments were almost playful and she could bear them. The lamp beside the bed was on, and he sat up as she closed the door. He'd kicked the covers to the foot of the bed because of the heat, and his nightshirt left his rather thin legs bare. He was frowning, but only with mild irritation.

"What the hell took so long? You should have known I'd want to talk to you." He gestured impatiently, beckoning her to the bed.

Julia went to the bed and sat down on the edge, turning her back to him. She bowed her head as she felt his fingers unfasten the row of tiny buttons that began at the high neckline of her gown and continued all the way down her back. "I sent the servants to bed and then talked to Lissa for a few moments," she said quietly.

Adrian grunted, but still with only mild irritation.

"What did you want to talk to me about?" she asked when she rose to her feet a couple of minutes later. She didn't go into the dressing room, but began getting out of her clothes in the bedroom because that was the way he always wanted her to undress. She left her gown and petticoat lying over a chair, and tried not to show the utter relief she felt when she'd unfastened her stockings, unlaced her stays, and dropped the corset on top of the gown.

"How would you like to be First Lady of Virginia?" Adrian asked, lying back on the bed and linking his fingers together behind his head as he watched her.

Julia had no real idea of what kind of politician he was, but everything inside her recoiled at the thought of him sitting in the governor's seat. She made certain that tangle of emotions didn't show on her face, however.

"Do you have the backing you'll need to run?" she asked calmly.

"I will have. It'll be a few years, naturally. But Fred Daulton's agreed to supporting me, and Peter Reynolds. Adam Prescott, of course. I'm not sure about Fortune yet. Leave the door open while you have your bath."

Five

♥

Since the command had followed immediately on the heels of Cyrus's name, she was, just barely, able to keep herself from reacting to it. She nodded, remaining in the bedroom as she removed her shoes and stockings, the chemise, bust bodice, and knickers. Then, naked, she got a clean nightgown and carried it into the bathroom, her expression tranquil. She knew it was tranquil because she saw her face when she walked past the dressing mirror in the corner.

Dear God, she hated this! Of all the torments he inflicted on her, she felt this one most deeply. Raised to be modest and naturally a bit shy, her personal privacy had always been important to her, but Adrian had lost no time in stripping her of it. She was his, he'd said, his to look at whenever and however he pleased—and he wanted to look at her naked as often as possible. To Julia, it was a ruthless invasion of her deepest self, and it hurt her so badly that she wanted to sob with the anguish of it.

It wasn't only that he looked at her naked in the light. It was the way he looked at her. Coldly greedy and lewd.

Almost gloating, as if he'd won some prize, even though
he made frequent disparaging comments about her body
whenever he was in one of his moods. She could feel his
eyes on her now as she stepped into the tepid bathwater,
and though her flesh didn't betray her, inside she
cringed.

"What did you think of Fortune?" he asked, watching
as she settled into the tub.

She couldn't relax with his gaze on her, but the cool
water at least made her feel she wasn't going to melt into
a puddle. "Polite," she answered. "Lissa was right about
that." For an instant she was conscious of a hysterical
urge to laugh. How she kept harping on the man's
manners! It was as if it were the only safe thing she could
think to say about him.

Perhaps it was.

"He's a cagey bastard," Adrian said with a slight touch
of resentment. "Couldn't pin him down. He kept saying
he wasn't inclined to politics, but he sure as hell knew
about everything that's going on, in Washington as well
as here. Hurry up, Julia, it's late."

She glanced through the open door to see him frowning, and quickly began washing. Were all men like
Adrian? She didn't know. His facade was so convincing;
perhaps every man possessed a public and private side
so dreadfully opposite. Her own father had been a stern
man, and Julia had no idea if her mother's frequent
"spells" during which she'd kept to her darkened bedroom had been the result of abuse. There was no other
married woman Julia felt close to, not close enough to
ask such terribly personal questions, so she had no way
of knowing if her situation was unusual.

Not that it really mattered, except that she was afraid
for Lissa.

She got out of the tub and dried herself, then pulled on the thin nightgown with a sense of relief. He usually allowed her to keep the nightgown on, and even if the thin cotton was a frail covering, at least she wasn't naked. She put out the light in the bathroom and went into the bedroom, sitting at her dressing table to take down her hair and brush it. He was silent while she smoothed the heavy, waist-length mass, but she could feel his eyes. She could always feel them. She began to braid her hair for the night, but Adrian spoke from the bed.

"No."

It wasn't an unusual command; he liked her hair to be loose in bed, and had forbidden her to wear a nightcap. But something she heard in his voice made nervous tension steal through her despite the normality of the order. She laid her brush aside and got up, going over to the bed, feeling chilled now. She crawled onto her side and lay back on the pillow without reaching for the sheet.

He extinguished the light, and in the darkness his voice was thoughtful. "Would you like to be First Lady, Julia?"

"I suppose any woman would," she answered neutrally, conscious of the heat of his body beside her.

"I want to go to the White House, you know that, don't you?"

"Yes."

"A man should leave his mark on the world. And he should leave a son behind to carry on his name."

She closed her eyes and swallowed hard, her stomach churning. God, no! He was in that state again, his mind filled with grandiose schemes and plans to "leave his mark" on the world, so strong and sure of his superiority.

He excited himself with those thoughts, aroused himself physically as a sense of power and promise filled him.

It had happened only a few times since their wedding night, but she dreaded it above all else.

"It's your fault I haven't been able to get a son on you, Julia. You know that, don't you?" His voice was growing thick, his breathing faster. The material of his nightshirt rustled as he pulled it up.

He hadn't touched her.

"Yes," she said from between dry, trembling lips, taking the blame because any other response from her made him furious. In the dark, it was always in the dark. Maybe because he couldn't bear to look at her then. Maybe because he couldn't bear for her to look at him. Or maybe it was because on some deep level of himself, he believed what Cyrus had so bluntly stated most gentlemen believed, that there were only two kinds of women—ladies and whores.

Adrian could—and did, she supposed—treat her like a whore, in private, most of the time. Like a possession he'd bought and paid for, his to use as he wished. But when he was like this, when he wanted a son, then she had to be a lady. They had to be a gentleman and a lady making a baby in their marital bed.

The problem was Adrian didn't really want a lady in his bed.

Julia felt him shift suddenly, heard the whisper of cloth as he tugged his nightshirt higher, and sickness rose in her throat so strongly she nearly choked. Not tonight, please God, she couldn't bear it tonight. She'd rather be beaten.

"Lift your nightgown," he said hoarsely, and rolled on top of her, his hands fumbling.

• • •

The stable smelled of sweet hay, leather, horses, and manure. It was hot and dusty, but she didn't notice either. She didn't care that hay made a poor cushion for her naked back and surging buttocks, or that the white blouse he'd taken off her would get dirty, or even that he'd torn her knickers instead of removing them. Her skirt and petticoats were rucked up around her waist, her stockinged legs wrapped about his hips, and the fingers of one hand were clenched in his thick hair while her other hand was pressed to her mouth to muffle the sounds she made.

He had pulled the top of her chemise down to bare her breasts, and the rough cloth of his vest rubbed her tight nipples rhythmically as he heaved on top of her. She hadn't worn her corset; the last time he'd taken her, the unnatural constriction of the garment, combined with his forceful passion, had caused her to faint dead away and left her feeling she'd been nearly broken in half.

Now, stifling her moans and whimpers, she moved with him the way he'd taught her, lifting and undulating her hips wildly as the unbearable pleasure carried her along on a rising wave. She squealed when the wave peaked, her body stiffening for a long moment and then going limp. Trembling and panting, she dazedly accepted his quickening thrusts until, silent as always, he went briefly rigid and then collapsed on her.

She wrapped her arms around as much of him as she could with a blissful feeling of satisfaction and delicious wickedness as he breathed heavily into her neck. He was so much larger. She scarcely could breathe under his weight, but she loved the sensation of being pinned in place by his body. She loved the way he made her feel.

It never occurred to her to think there was anything ugly or distasteful about being taken in a smelly stable with her clothing half off and her lover's trousers down around his knees. Months before, she wouldn't have been able to imagine such a thing without a shudder of horrified repugnance, but now it not only seemed perfectly natural, it seemed delightful.

He lifted his head and then raised himself on his elbows, smiling down at her. "Good?" he murmured.

"Ummm." She sighed happily, her flushed and sweating breasts glistening as they lifted and fell.

He put his hands on them, kneading slowly, and pressed his loins into hers in tiny, subtle movements. "I'll have you in a bed soon. You'll like that, won't you, honey?"

"Oh, yes," she said throatily, her eyes drifting half shut as her body responded to his skilled touch. She forced herself to think. "You said it wouldn't be long. You'll divorce your wife, and speak—speak to my parents."

"Soon," he said, lowering his head briefly to tease her stiff nipples with his tongue. "Then we'll be together all the time." His movements against her and inside her became more deliberate.

She moaned, tension filling her, and her thighs tightened around him convulsively. Rational thought scattered like leaves in the wind. "I love you," she whispered, arching to thrust her breasts harder into his pleasure-giving hands.

"I love you too," he murmured, his narrowed gaze intent on her face as he built her arousal slowly and expertly, until she was writhing beneath him and uttering desperate little pleas. Then he went still, holding himself deep inside her tense, quivering body. "I need you to do something for me. Something important. Will you, honey?"

"Yes," she gasped, her eyes glazed and wild. "Yes, anything . . . oh, please!"

"I'll tell you what I want you to do before you leave," he said in his soft, seductive voice. "And you'll do exactly what I say, without questions, and without telling anyone. Won't you, baby?"

"Yes! I will, I promise. Please . . ."

He broke the grip of her legs and withdrew from her, ignoring her whimper of protest. Before she knew what was happening, he had lifted and turned her, his immense strength handling her slight body easily.

"Oh! What are you—"

"You'll like this, honey," he promised softly, pushing her skirt and petticoat up over her back.

She might have protested again because this, at least, was deeply shocking to her young mind, but his hard flesh sank into her feverish body and his hands were on her aching breasts—and she did like it.

On her hands and knees with the hay caught in her tangled hair and clinging to her damp skin, she whimpered and rocked back to meet his hard thrusts, and never noticed the smell of corruption mingling with the scents of hay and sweat and horses and manure.

A few days after the party, Julia drove her buggy out of the city. As soon as she was clear of the more congested streets, she anxiously urged the horse to a trot. The message from Helen Bradshaw, a friend of Lissa's, had been waiting for Julia when she'd returned to the house at noon, and it had sounded urgent. Unfortunately, it had been delivered in the morning, hours before. Julia had been held up longer than she'd expected, first because of the crowded shops and later because of an accident in the streets that had snarled traffic for over an hour.

She kept the horse at a brisk pace, mentally apologizing to the poor animal for forcing him to exert himself in the building heat of the day. But most of her attention was fixed on recognizing landmarks as she left the city behind. She felt a touch of relief when she saw a tumbledown barn off to the right, and looked immediately to her left for the road turning between two giant oak trees.

No more than a hundred yards from the barn she slowed her horse and turned him onto the road. The ruts cut deeply into the dirt as if heavy wagons had frequently come this way. It was impossible to see much for a few yards, but then she saw a clearing ahead where a large house was under construction. The place seemed deserted, but she saw a buggy under one of the big trees, and guided her own horse toward it.

Now she felt puzzled as well as anxious. Lissa had left this morning with several of her friends, planning to spend the day with another friend who had recently given birth to her first child. But didn't she live on the other side of Richmond? Why would Lissa be far from the city where there was nothing but a newly begun house?

"Julia?"

She stopped her horse, her head jerking around in response to a voice she recognized instantly. He was coming toward her, moving with the ease of muscles under unthinking control, like a big cat, and it was more than surprise that kept her eyes fixed on him. He wasn't wearing a hat or coat, and his shirtsleeves were rolled up to reveal powerful forearms. His tie had been loosened and several buttons were unfastened at his throat; the first curls of the black hair on his chest were visible.

Julia's mouth went dry as he stopped beside the buggy, and she wished he weren't so tall, wished she didn't have the feeling they were very, very alone out here.

"What's wrong, Julia?" Cyrus asked, lifting one hand to rest on the back of her seat. As always, and even though his voice was the familiar black velvet, he spoke to her a little abruptly, direct and to the point.

She forced herself to think. "I—I received a message that Lissa was here and needed me."

He frowned slightly. "A written message?"

"No. It—my butler said a young lady delivered the message a few hours ago. A friend of Lissa's. She said that Lissa was ill, and was waiting for me here with another of her friends."

"I haven't seen her," Cyrus said, shaking his head. "And I've been here since early this morning."

Julia bit her lip and shifted the reins so that she could begin to turn her horse. "There must have been a mistake. I have to return to Richmond."

He reached out and grasped her hand. "Wait."

A flare of panic made her stiffen. "No. I have to—"

"Julia." His voice was quiet and steady. "Your horse needs to rest a bit before you start back to the city. So do you. This is the hottest part of the day; if you don't wait for at least an hour or two, you'll make yourself ill."

"I can't stay here," she said, the very idea sending a pang of dismay through her.

Cyrus took the reins away from her, knotted them

loosely, and then put his hands on her tiny waist and lifted her easily out of the buggy. "Yes, you can."

She was so startled by the abrupt action that for a moment she could only stare at him.

"No one will know," he said, wondering almost angrily how many times he'd said those words to her; every time he said them they seemed more and more wrong to him.

"But—"

"My workmen are gone for the day and I'm not expecting anyone else." He hesitated, then reluctantly dropped his hands from her waist. He wanted to pull her into his arms and kiss her with all the hunger that had surged wildly inside him at the first touch of her, but he couldn't. Not now, at least, not until he found some way to avoid hurting her.

For the first time in his life, he was wishing another man dead, and it was an effort to keep the grinding emotion out of his voice. "You don't have to worry about Drummond; he's halfway to Norfolk by now."

"Norfolk?" Julia watched him get the tether block from the buggy and tie her horse. She felt bewildered. "How do you know he's going there?"

"He and some friends of his stopped by here hours ago, and that's where they were headed. Didn't you know?"

She didn't. It was so like Adrian, she thought, to say nothing to her about a day-long trip; he preferred her to believe he was always near.

Cyrus took her arm and led her away from the buggies. He had been sitting among the clutter of lumber, brooding, when she'd driven up, and now guided her there. It was hardly cool even under the spreading oak, but at least the force of the sunlight was deflected and the lumber provided a place for her to sit. He folded his coat to make a cushion for her.

"I can't—"

"Sit down, Julia."

She sent him a glance and obeyed, saying only, "Your coat will be ruined."

"It isn't important." He reached into a bucket on another stack of lumber near Julia and pulled out a dark bottle. "Most of the ice has melted," he commented, "but this should still be fairly cool." He opened it and handed the bottle to her.

"Thank you," she murmured. It was fruit juice, and it was cool. She drank a little, feeling tense. They were too alone out here. And he was frowning, obviously not happy with his thoughts. Had she made him angry? Hesitantly, she said, "I'm sorry if I intruded."

He looked at her, and the frown faded as he smiled. "You could never do that." He was leaning back against the lumber no more than a couple of feet away from her, his arms crossed over his powerful chest, and his gaze was very intent on her.

She couldn't guess what he was thinking. Those eyes . . . they were so relentlessly black, they gave away very little of his emotions. Desire kindled a dark fire in them, amusement made them laugh, and anger made them fierce, but whatever else he felt remained enigmatic, hidden in the liquid ebony depths. At least with her.

Julia was even more conscious of the heat when he looked at her, more conscious of him, and she glanced away nervously. "I suppose Helen must have given the wrong directions, or my butler could have misremembered them. I really should try to find Lissa."

"She's with friends, you said. They'll take care of her."
His tone was reassuring.

"Yes, but, if she sent for me . . ."

Cyrus wondered if she had, but didn't question aloud.
He had a strong and strangely painful feeling Julia would
never be able to confirm that Lissa's friend had sent any
message at all. But he couldn't tell her so. Julia was
already disturbed; he didn't like to think of how she'd
react if he told her he thought she'd been deliberately
sent out here. If she had received the message when it
had been delivered, she would have arrived just about
the same time Drummond had stopped by—and even
the most indulgent of husbands might be forgiven a
twinge of suspicion when his wife turned up in this out
of the way place with an excuse that couldn't be proven.

Especially when the place was a lonely construction
site where a reputed scoundrel was building a house.

He wondered who could be suspecting she was unfaithful to Drummond or wanting it to look that way. It
had to be someone who would have known Drummond
meant to pass this way today, and when. Any number of
people might have been aware of the information, he
supposed. Except for Julia, who had been surprised at
the knowledge.

"Lissa will be fine, Julia," he said at last.

"You can't know that."

"Yes, I can," he said absently, occupied with his
thoughts. And he didn't like any of them. If someone had
gone to all the trouble to arrange this, the malicious
intent was obvious. Had that person meant to hurt Julia,
or simply to take the carelessly arrogant Drummond
down a peg or two by planting the idea his young wife
could betray him? He was certainly rabid on the subject

of unfaithful wives or, at least, children sired by lovers instead of husbands.

Julia felt peculiarly reassured, though she couldn't have said why. Searching for a casual subject to discuss, she said finally, "You're building a new house?"

"Yes." He pushed the thoughts out of his head because there was no way to find the answers now. And he didn't want to squander his time with Julia; very little would be granted to him, he thought. She belonged to another man, and whatever she felt for her husband, the marriage, at least, was one she was all too conscious of—and had made him conscious of as well. "The city's becoming too crowded for my taste."

"I always loved the country," she said with a fleeting smile so sweet and shyly unlike her social mask, it nearly stopped his heart. "We lived in the country when I was a child. But Papa needed to be closer to the city because of his business affairs."

"He and your mother were killed in an accident, weren't they?" Cyrus asked, needing to know more about her than the facts he'd uncovered. "A little over two years ago?"

Julia was surprised that he knew about her parents' deaths. "Yes, they were. It was—they were on a boat, on the river. No one knows why it went down."

"I'm sorry, I shouldn't have brought up a painful memory."

She managed another smile. "It's all right."

Cyrus hadn't intended to bring up any subject likely to trouble her, but heard himself say, "You married Drummond two years ago." He couldn't leave the subject alone, no matter how good his intentions were.

She looked away. "Yes."

"Why?"

"I told you I wouldn't discuss my marriage." She was staring off toward the house, expressionless. "I meant what I said."

"Julia, I have to understand." He sat down beside her on the stack of lumber, half turned so he could look at her. He knew he was pushing again, but he couldn't help it. He wanted to banish the look of fear that so often shadowed her lovely eyes, and he couldn't until he found out why she was so afraid.

There was another reason, he knew. A more selfish reason. He wanted her. She'd never been entirely out of his mind since the first time he'd seen her, and her refusal to accord him anything but social pleasantries was maddening. He hadn't felt even a glimmer of interest in another woman after he'd met her; it was Julia he wanted, Julia he needed in some way he couldn't even define, some way apart from the physical desire for her that ached in him.

She set the bottle of juice aside and laced her fingers tightly together in her lap, still not meeting his gaze. "There's nothing to understand."

"Don't lie to me." He didn't realize he'd spoken so harshly until she flinched, and that tiny indication of alarm went through him like a knife. He reached over quickly to cover her tense hands with one of his own, and made a conscious effort to hold his voice low and steady. "I'd never hurt you, Julia. It's just that I can't stand seeing you afraid, and I have to understand why you are. Is it Adrian? Does he threaten you? Has he hurt you?"

"I won't discuss my marriage." She turned her face completely away from him, her entire body rigid.

Cyrus was determined to get his answers this time. He looked at the fragile nape of her neck and told himself he had to find a way of winning her trust. He was concentrating on the problem so intensely that, for a moment, he didn't realize what he was seeing. She was wearing a high-necked blouse with a tie, so there was little flesh visible, but just below her hairline behind her left ear was a faint mark paler than the surrounding skin, like a—

He reached up and hooked a finger under the high neckline, pulling the material away from her neck slightly. She started and made a muted sound, but Cyrus barely heard it. The scar was nearly as wide as his finger and angled down the back of her neck to disappear beneath the white linen.

He was very still for a long moment, staring, something inside his chest tightening with a slow pressure so intense it felt as if the breath were being crushed out of him. Then he untied her tie and cast it aside. His hands were shaking as he grasped her shoulders and gently turned her so her back was to him.

"No! Don't!" She tried to pull away.

"Be still, Julia." His voice was very soft, hardly more than a whisper.

She wanted to run from him, to hide herself away where he'd never find her. She didn't want him to see, to know. Not him. Fear, shame, guilt, the remnants of her pride, all tangled together in a painful jumble inside her. But his voice held her more surely than his hands, and when he began unbuttoning the high neckline of her blouse she remained motionless, her head bent. She stared blindly at nothing, feeling every touch of his fingers as he unfastened the tiny buttons all the way down to her waist. Then she closed her eyes, her lips trembling, when he drew the edges of her blouse apart.

She heard an odd sound, a hoarse rumble like the

growl of some creature in the night, and his voice
sounded choked when he said, "Oh, my God."

Her frozen stillness shattered, she reached one hand
back over her shoulder in a pathetic attempt to cover
herself again, a shudder racking her body. But his arms
closed around her, drawing her back against the hardness of his chest, and his embrace was so gentle and
protective she wanted to weep.

Cyrus couldn't believe it. When he'd asked if Drummond had hurt her, he had thought her husband might
have slapped her or treated her roughly. That kind of
brutality would have been bad enough, but this— How
any man could hurt a woman as Julia had been hurt was
beyond Cyrus's comprehension, but what he had seen
when he'd opened her blouse was a sight so starkly
vicious he knew he would never forget it. Even when he
closed his eyes the image wouldn't leave him.

He hadn't seen it all; he felt the sickening certainty of
that. Above the lace-trimmed edging of her chemise,
very little of her back and shoulders had been bare to his
gaze. But it was enough. Thin, pale scars—God, so many
of them!—marked her creamy flesh with the pitiless
imprint of a horsewhip or some other kind of monstrous
lash, overlaid by more recent, half-healed welts that
were the wider marks of a belt or strap. And there were
tiny crescents, gouges in her skin that might have been
made by the heavy blows of a buckle—or a ring on a
driving fist.

Drummond wore a heavy gold signet ring, Cyrus
remembered, and a black fury stronger than anything
he'd ever felt in his life twisted inside him. He thought
of Julia, so young and frightened, her body small and
delicate, unable to defend herself against the strength of
a man. He thought of her in an agony that must have

been more than physical as the man who'd vowed before God to love and cherish her had brutally scarred her body and soul.

Burning in hell was too good for the bastard. Cyrus wanted him to suffer now.

Julia could feel tremors rippling through his big, powerful body as he held her silently, feel the hard tension in his jaw as it rubbed slowly against her temple, and she understood, with a wounded animal's bitterly learned awareness, that he was so deeply angry he literally couldn't speak. That anger made her apprehensive, but she was surprised by it as well, and a little bewildered. Until then, she hadn't thought that a man could feel both tenderness and rage in the same moment.

She couldn't believe it was possible. His kindness had to exist only in her imagination. "Please let me go," she whispered, rigid in his gentle embrace. She wanted to find some defense against him, and felt helpless. It was all she could do to hold her body stiff when it wanted to relax against his and accept a comfort her mind didn't trust. He knew the secret of her life, knew what no one outside her bedroom could ever have guessed, and she had a confused idea that this was a greater betrayal of her husband than infidelity could ever be.

"Julia . . ." His voice was a low rasp, as if it hurt his throat to speak at all. "You have to leave him. He's an animal, you can't stay with him."

She swallowed hard and repeated, "Please let me go."

His arms tightened a little, and then Cyrus slowly released her. She was painfully conscious of him behind her and of her unbuttoned blouse. She was shivering despite the heat, her emotions in turmoil.

"Julia—"

"My . . . my blouse. Could you—?" The sheer unseemliness of the entire scene struck her, and she clamped her teeth together to hold back a wild sound of despair. Unseemly? Dear God, what was the sense of worrying about propriety now?

He swore, so softly she barely heard him, then silently buttoned her blouse. She leaned down to pick up the tie he'd dropped to the ground and put it back in place, her fingers shaking. She couldn't look at him, didn't dare to meet his eyes.

"You can't stay with him," Cyrus said, a little roughly now.

She rose to her feet and then went still, because he'd gotten up as well and towered over her. "He's my husband," she murmured, refusing to meet those black eyes.

Cyrus grasped her shoulders. "Look at me, Julia."

"No," she whispered, more a plea than a refusal.

He surrounded her face with one big hand, gently pushing her chin up. "I said, look at me."

She flinched a little at the soft, fierce command and instantly obeyed. She thought his face was unnaturally pale and curiously hard, as if all the flesh had been stretched tightly over the bones beneath. And his eyes . . . so dark, for the first time nakedly expressive and filled with an incredible gentleness she didn't believe. She had the mad notion that there was safety in his eyes, and peace, and caring.

"Leave him. Come to me," he said.

"No." She didn't believe what she saw in him was real.

"Julia, I won't let him hurt you anymore."

He didn't know Adrian, she thought wearily, if he believed that. There were so many ways to be hurt. There was Lissa to fear for. Even if Cyrus could—and would—protect both her and Lissa, even if he wouldn't hurt her as Adrian had, and even if she could bear the public and private shame of leaving her husband for another man, what would she do when he tired of her? Men tired of mistresses, she'd heard.

"I won't leave my husband," she said quietly.

Cyrus swore under his breath again and pulled her into his arms, holding her so close that her breasts were pressed to his broad chest. Before she could do more than gasp, his mouth covered hers.

If he had been the slightest bit rough with her, she might have been able to fight the instant, bewildering response of her body to his desire. But the powerful arms holding her, though hard and curiously inescapable, were also gentle, and his warm lips moved on hers with a hunger tempered by tenderness. When he held her and touched her this way, her body had no memory of pain and her mind forgot even the last shred of reason.

She couldn't fight him. Or herself. Her mouth opened to him, her body molded itself against his, and her arms rose of their own volition to slide around his lean waist. A wave of heat that had nothing to do with the summer day washed over her, bringing all her senses so vibrantly alive, it was as if she had never felt before.

She was less aware of the differences between their bodies than she was of the rightness of how they fit together, as if all the contrasts had been designed specifically for this passionate contact. There was pleasure and excitement stirring to life inside her, a primitive and unfamiliar urgency she didn't understand, and a growing need to give herself to him that was almost a compulsion. She had the strangely certain feeling she already belonged to him, and if any man had the right to claim her, it was Cyrus.

"God, Julia," he muttered against her mouth. One big hand slid up her back and cupped her head as his other arm drew her even closer, and he deepened the kiss with a surge of desire so intense she actually jerked at the shock of it. Her breasts ached as they were pressed to his hard chest, and somewhere deep in her belly she was suddenly conscious of a throbbing emptiness. Fire inside her, molten in her veins and licking along her nerves until they felt seared and raw with a pleasure so acute it bordered on pain. A muted whimper caught in her throat and her hands clutched at his back almost desperately.

The strength of her own response was so stunning it brought her at least partway to her senses. She couldn't believe this was possible, couldn't believe it was any more real than the intense emotions she'd seen in his black eyes. Seduction . . . But that was it, wasn't it? He had a power over her she never would have thought any man could have, and with that influence he would compel her to do as he wanted.

His methods were different from Adrian's, but the result would be the same. One man controlled her mind through pain and fear; the other sought to seduce her mind by seducing her body. What she wanted counted for nothing.

"No, please," she whispered when his mouth left hers to feather over her upturned face.

"I want you so much, Julia," he said thickly. "And you want me. You can't deny that."

She was shaking with the desire he'd brought to life in her body and knew he felt it, knew she couldn't deny the painful truth. She couldn't force her arms to fall away from him, or struggle to free herself from his embrace.

So she clung to the only protest she could make, the only fact that was indisputably real. "I'm married!"

Cyrus lifted his head and stared down at her, his gaze fierce. "To a man who beats you! He might have married you in a church, but he broke his vows to you and God a long time ago. You owe him nothing. Julia, no one would blame you for leaving him."

"I can't."

"Come to me. I'll take care of you."

A chill trickled along her spine, and she finally found the will to put her hands against his chest and push herself back away from him. He let her withdraw only far enough to put an arm's length between them, his hands on her shoulders preventing her from completely escaping him.

"That's what Adrian said," she murmured.

For a moment Cyrus was so stunned by the comparison that his first emotion was sheer, incredulous rage. How could she liken him to the sadistic monster she'd married? Then he saw the blind look in her beautiful, wounded eyes, and for the first time he had some real understanding of how deep her scars went.

As far as Julia knew, he realized painfully, he was no better or worse than Drummond. She might even believe he was worse. His reputation as a rake certainly was. She lived with a man who appeared in public as the perfect husband, who had deceived everyone with his boyish charm, and no one had even come close to guessing her private torment. There was no gossip, no hint that Drummond was anything but what he seemed to be.

And the bastard had probably convinced her all men were like he was, that a wife's lot in life was agony and terrified silence. She was an innately proud woman and had no close friends. Who could tell her differently even if she could bring herself to ask? She hadn't confided in Lissa, Cyrus was sure. The younger girl's unshadowed adoration of her brother-in-law was proof enough of that.

"I must go," Julia murmured, looking toward the buggies with a slight frown.

For one of the very few times in his life Cyrus felt helpless. Trust had to be earned, and Julia's had been abused so dreadfully she might never be able to trust completely. Not trust a man, at any rate. He could make her feel desire, but the fear her husband had taught her was stronger.

His hands tightened gently on her shoulders, then released her. He didn't say another word, because he didn't trust himself to speak. He remained where he was, watching her walk away from him and, moments later, drive the buggy along the rutted track to the main road. As she disappeared from his sight, the resolve in his mind was cold, clear, and utterly implacable.

Julia was bound to Drummond legally and through fear. The only way to free her was to break those ties.

Six

♥

"Stupid bitch." He slapped her viciously, his normally handsome face twisted in a mask of rage. His voice was a chilling contrast to the enraged expression, because it was unnaturally calm, even conversational. "I told you what to do. I told you."

Helen Bradshaw cowered against the wall, her doe-soft eyes huge and frightened. A trickle of blood ran from the corner of her mouth. She was in shock. "I—I did what you said, I delivered the message to Julia." Her voice sounded high and thin to her own ears.

"Couldn't you have had sense enough to look for her if she wasn't at the house?" he asked in that eerie tone. "I told you to make sure she received the message at nine o'clock—not at noon. She was too late, goddamn you. And it gave them another chance to be alone together."

"I'm sorry—"

He slapped her again, with his left hand this time. It was a flat blow with the full strength of his arm behind it, and would have sent her to her knees if she hadn't been wedged into a corner of the stable.

Helen held a hand to her bleeding mouth and stared

at him in growing terror. What had happened to the lover who had brought her such pleasure last night—and all the nights before? It had been a delicious secret, her love affair with an older man. She hadn't told Lissa or any of her other friends, hugging to herself the knowledge of her own daring behavior.

It hadn't seemed wrong, even if she'd broken all the rules. He'd sworn he would marry her, after all. And it had been exciting, just as he'd promised, to slip away in order to meet him clandestinely. Barely eighteen, she'd been a virgin, but he had been so loving and gentle that first time, teaching her the ecstasy her body could feel. Teaching her so many exciting, pleasurable things.

It hadn't seemed wrong. But now she had a vivid mental image of herself lying in a smelly stable with her clothes half off while she moaned and panted beneath him and the taste of bile filled her mouth. Had she really done that? Had she let him— Dear God. Her flesh was crawling at the knowledge that he had done those intimate things to her, touched and—and used her that way.

It was as if she'd been blind until now. She suddenly had a dim, superstitious idea that he'd cast a spell over her. Now it was gone. Now she could see the grotesque darkness of what he really was.

"You ruined everything. Witless cow. I can't trust you anymore, you understand?"

His eyes were empty, she realized. Dead. Why hadn't she seen before? "You can," she gasped, trying to press herself harder into the corner. As if that would help, would protect her somehow. "You can trust me."

"You're a bad liar as well as stupid, Helen. That is your name, isn't it? Helen? You can't wait to rush out of here and tell someone about me, and we both know it. But I'm afraid I can't let you do it."

"Please," she whispered, the appeal born out of an instinctive certainty of what he meant to do.

"Oh, don't beg. It's so undignified. Besides, you should be thanking me. I was generous enough to let you enjoy yourself first. It's a pity that has to end, and I am sorry about it. You weren't bad at all, once you got the hang of it. There's just something about a sweet little virginal lady rolling around in the straw and bucking under me. Never met one yet who couldn't wait to hike her skirts and spread her legs, as ready for it as a cat in heat. You were no exception."

Helen nearly gagged, the taste of blood and revulsion thick in her tongue. "Don't—"

"Don't what? Don't shatter all your pretty, romantic illusions?" He shook his head in mild puzzlement. "We rutted in a barn, sweetheart. I dropped my pants, you lifted your skirt, and we used each other."

"I loved you," she whispered, tears beginning to trickle down her ashen cheeks. "I—I might even be—I might have a baby." It was the only thing she could think of that could possibly save her. But he shook his head again, amused this time.

"Nice try. Believe me, if my seed were any good, I'd know by now. It isn't. I'm one of a kind. Or will be, soon enough."

She didn't understand him, except to know he was finished with her. Sobs jerked her slight body, and her voice was terrified when she said, "Please . . . please don't hurt me."

He tilted his head to one side, an empty little smile quirking his lips. "Your mouth's bleeding."

"It—it doesn't matter. I won't say anything, I promise."

"Oh, you won't say anything." Still smiling, he stepped closer, his hands rising to her pale throat. "You won't say anything at all."

It was the longest, most severe heat wave anyone in Richmond could remember, and as July drew to a close it showed no sign of being broken. The sun burned the grass dry and brown, seared the midsummer flowers, and dulled the leaves that hung limp and motionless from the trees. Heat bounced from the pavement to shimmer in the air, so unbearable each afternoon, few stirred out of doors unless they absolutely had to.

All the energy seemed to drain from the city until every living thing moved slowly, and tempers were worn ragged by the heat. The sky was blindingly blue, day after day, with not a wisp of a cloud to hint at rain. Even the James River seemed to draw in on itself, receding from its banks and slowing to a muddy crawl.

The social activities in Richmond more or less ground to a halt. No one wanted to stand shoulder to shoulder in crowded rooms for any reason, and since the demand for ice had seriously depleted the supply, socializing had lost even the attraction of chilled drinks. Most preferred to remain in their relatively cool homes wearing the absolute minimum of clothing while they waited miserably for the weather to break.

Cyrus was one of the few who remained active in the heat. He allowed his work crew at the new house time off during the intolerable midday, but kept them busy in the early mornings and late afternoons. Surprising most of his friends, he bought office space in the city and began to handle his business affairs there rather than out of his house. Until he hired a couple of clerks who seemed to be frantically active, not even his friends had suspected he had so many business affairs.

"When did you buy a sugar cane plantation?" Noel demanded as he stood in Cyrus's office on a Wednesday afternoon in the first week of August. One of the clerks had just left to file paperwork that had raised the subject.

"Last year." Cyrus was sitting at a huge oak desk, his coat off and sleeves rolled up as he dealt with more paperwork. He didn't look at Noel as he asked dryly, "Did you stop by to stick your nose into my business?"

Unoffended, Noel said, "No, I stopped by because you have the coolest office in Richmond. I don't understand it, since both the windows in here face the southwest, but this is the most comfortable room I've found in the city, even in the afternoons. Why is that, Cy?"

"I have no idea." Cyrus leaned back in his chair and watched his friend move aimlessly around the room for a moment, then said, "I meant to ask you earlier—have they found the Bradshaw girl yet?"

"No. That's a hell of a thing, isn't it? A pretty girl from a good family steps out one afternoon to run a few errands, and no one sees her again. If there'd been an accident, she would have been found by now. The whole city's been searched. The police believe someone's got her."

"Or had her," Cyrus said quietly.

Noel looked at him. "You think she's dead?"

Cyrus nodded.

"Dammit, so do I. What do we have police for, I'd like to know, if not to prevent that kind of thing?"

"They do what they can. But sometimes evil doesn't wear a recognizable face."

Noel gave him a sharp look, then frowned as he drifted restlessly around the room.

After a couple of minutes, Cyrus said, "You didn't come here to talk about tragic news, my business affairs, or the temperature of my office. What's on your mind?"

Noel settled finally in the visitor's chair before the desk, and sighed. He sent his friend a curiously intent look. "I ran into Adam Prescott a little while ago. He wants to bring Drummond to the game tonight."

Cyrus didn't change expression. "So?"

"So, I thought you might want to know about it."

Lifting an eyebrow that was mildly questioning and nothing more, Cyrus waited.

Noel felt frustrated, and sounded it. "Dammit, Cy, I can't figure out what you're up to. Ever since their party, Drummond hasn't missed a chance to buttonhole you. He's even come here half a dozen times."

"He wants my political support," Cyrus said calmly.

"He wants your money," Noel snapped.

"That too."

"You have no intention of supporting him, and we both know it. You can't stand the man, no matter how well you pretend otherwise. So why are you stringing him along? From what I've seen, you hesitate and hedge just enough to keep his hopes up. In fact, I'd say you went out of your way to encourage him to believe you might back him politically, all the while being very careful not to commit yourself."

"It amuses me."

"No, it doesn't." Noel met those black eyes squarely. "What would amuse you would be to break the man's neck with your own hands."

After a moment Cyrus gave him a curiously chilling

smile. "That would be too easy. I'd much rather break every bone in his body. Inch by inch."

Noel barely felt his jaw drop, and had to try twice before he could ask, "What's he done to you?"

"Not a damned thing."

"For God's sake, Cy, you don't express a desire to murder a man—especially like that—unless he's crossed you in some way!"

"He breathes the same air I do. That's enough of an offense."

Noel stared at him, feeling very peculiar. Cyrus was still smiling, but his black eyes were deadly and Noel had never seen them like that. Without even thinking about it, he said, "It's because of Julia, isn't it?"

"Yes," Cyrus said flatly.

"Because you want her and she belongs to him?"

"She doesn't belong to him. She's tied to him—there's a difference."

Noel was conscious of another shock. If any other man had said those words in a voice so intense it shook, he would have believed . . . But, no. It couldn't have happened to Cyrus, surely, not so quickly. Managing a protest, Noel said, "Not in the eyes of God or the law."

"God turned His eyes away from that marriage a long time ago. And the law doesn't always recognize evil if it wears an appealing face."

"Evil? Cy, what—"

Cyrus immediately shook his head just once, a clear refusal to explain what he meant, and Noel didn't repeat the question. But he had another one, and he asked it.

"What is it you mean to do?"

"Strip away the charm. Expose the hideous face underneath."

Noel wanted to ask *And then?* but he didn't dare. He didn't want to hear the answer.

Julia was still puzzled and disturbed by the message that had sent her to Cyrus, and Helen Bradshaw's disappearance made the questions even more troubling. Until Lissa had returned home that evening in perfect health and spirits, it hadn't occurred to her the message might have been a deliberate ruse, and when she did consider it, she found the possibility chilling.

A casual question had provided the information that Helen hadn't gone with the others, and Julia's butler, Wilson, was positive it had been she who had left the message.

But why? If it had been a deliberate attempt to put Julia in a compromising position by causing her to arrive on Cyrus's property when Adrian was there, it seemed incredibly involved—particularly for an eighteen-year-old girl who, in any case, had no reason to plan it. There was no malice in Helen that Julia had ever seen, and like many young women, she didn't notice very much beyond her own self-centered interests. If she had suspected there might be something between Julia and Cyrus, she might have giggled and gossiped, but she wouldn't have done anything to either confirm or disprove her suspicions.

No, if Helen had indeed left the message, it was because someone else had persuaded her to, and the implication of such a possibility frightened Julia, especially now that Helen had vanished without a trace.

She didn't want to believe the two things were connected, but she had a sick feeling they were. Pawns were sacrificed; what if Helen had been a pawn? Who could be ruthless enough to use an innocent young girl and then discard her when she was no longer needed? Was she even alive?

If she wasn't alive, and if she'd been someone's puppet or pawn, then why? Why had someone used her in such a strange, involved way? Did someone suspect Julia had been unfaithful to her husband, or want it to appear that way? Adrian wouldn't have done it, she thought; he was too conscious of his public image to arrange such a thing when his friends would be witnesses to the result. But if not Adrian, then who?

It never occurred to Julia to suspect Cyrus, though she wouldn't realize that for a long time.

She didn't know what to think, but she was afraid. Adrian was so involved in his political aspirations he seemed to have little time or energy for her. He had more or less left her alone these past days. But sometimes when he looked at her, she had the eerie feeling he was just waiting. That he knew something. It unnerved her all the more because of her own feelings of guilt.

In Cyrus's arms she had convinced herself his seduction was simply another form of male domination, and the belief had enabled her to withdraw from him. But as the days passed, she slowly realized, to her bitter resentment and shame, that it didn't matter. He had brought something to life inside her, something she couldn't define except to call it desire—as astonishing as she found the very idea. His reasons for seducing her had no effect on the result; he had taught her to want him.

Now it tormented her. Her body, awakened by his touch, ached incessantly. Often it throbbed, as if the very center of her being had shifted from heart and mind to the primitive, overwhelming needs of her female flesh. Shockingly erotic dreams languid with heated pleasure disturbed her sleep almost every night, causing her to wake with silent gasps, and she would lay beside Adrian in feverish stillness, bewildered that her imagination could so vividly conjure physical sensations she had never experienced.

Sensations she didn't even believe were real.

It didn't seem to matter if she felt no trust for Cyrus, no certainty he was different from Adrian. Her body wanted his, and the force of the need was a compulsion that gained strength, day by day, until it was physically painful to her, until it seemed any risk would be worth taking if she could lie in Cyrus's arms just once. She didn't know if giving herself to him would bring pleasure or pain. All she knew was this terrible urgency, the confused but certain conviction that she had to belong to him. She had to.

Soon.

The days crept by, sluggish in the unbearable heat, and Julia struggled to hold on to her fraying self-command. In the face of so many tensions, it felt as if she would be torn apart by them. More and more her mask of calm was a tenuous thing, and when it finally shattered, she could never have guessed that her sister's loving hand would be responsible for the blow.

"Julia, what's wrong with Adrian?"

Looking up from her sewing, Julia studied her sister's troubled face for a moment before asking, "What do you mean?" They were sitting together in the parlor before lunch on the first Friday in August with the shutters closed against the heat of the day, and both had been silent for quite some time.

"He's so tense. He snapped at you twice last night at supper, and there was something in his face I've never seen before."

Julia hesitated. "The heat, I suppose. Everyone seems to be affected by it."

Lissa shook her head. "No, it was more than the heat. And you knew it too, because you were afraid of him. It was in your eyes. Don't tell me I imagined it."

Again Julia hesitated, but she couldn't bring herself to answer with the truth. Not all the truth, at any rate. Coolly, she said, "Like most men, Adrian has a temper. It seems to be the fate of a wife to bear the brunt of that, and I've learned to be wary."

"Julia—"

"Lissa, it wouldn't be fair to Adrian to discuss our marriage with you. Don't you agree?"

"Is that a polite way of telling me it's none of my business?" Lissa's voice was very quiet.

"I suppose." Julia managed a smile.

Her sister didn't return it. "I can't help being worried, Julia. I've noticed things lately. Since I've been home this summer."

Julia didn't want to encourage her sister to continue, but she couldn't help but wonder if Lissa's growing feelings for Mark had made her more aware of other people's relationships. Or was it that Adrian was slipping, showing more of his private nature outside the bedroom?

Lissa went on without being asked or urged. "He doesn't seem to notice how you feel at all, or care if you're tired or drained by the heat. You're so . . . so careful around him, as if you have to weigh every word. And even though he's very attentive in public, here in

the house he never touches you—I mean, when you're
around the servants or me."

"The realities of marriage," Julia said lightly.

"Mark's parents don't act like that, and they've been
married for twenty-five years. He teases her in the
sweetest way, and sometimes when you go into a room
where they've been alone, she's blushing and he has a
little smile on his face—and you know they've been
kissing and cuddling."

Julia felt a pang and hoped she didn't look as wistful as
she felt. "Every couple is different, Lissa," she murmured, wondering if it was true.

"Susie's parents hold hands when they walk, even if
it's just through the house. Monica's sister and her
husband smile when they catch each other's eye. Eliza-
beth and Parker laugh together all the time, and when
she was carrying the baby, he did everything he could to
make it easier for her. She told me. How he'd rub her
back, and help her get around when the baby got so big.
How he worried that something would go wrong, and
he'd lose her. Now that the baby's here, they're like
newlyweds again. He's so gentle and loving."

Lissa's green eyes were steady as they held Julia's. "I
always thought Adrian was wonderful, but,
Julia . . . you're so still when he's around, like you're
shut inside yourself. Your voice is—is so calm, it's as if all
the feeling has been squeezed out of it. I haven't heard
you laugh in two years. You never even smile as if you
mean it. I guess I always saw those things, but I didn't
really think about them until recently. You don't love
him. He doesn't love you. And I don't think—I don't
think he's kind to you."

Julia looked away, trying to gather her scattered
thoughts. "He's my husband, Lissa."

"Maybe he shouldn't be," Lissa said very softly.

Conscious of shock, Julia stared down at her sewing with blind eyes. "Do you realize what you're saying?"

"Oh, I know it's supposed to be wrong. Till death do us part, no matter what. It isn't easy for a woman to get a divorce, and when she does, people say she's fast. But you can't spend the rest of your life with a man who makes you unhappy, no matter what people say. If you made a mistake, you shouldn't have to go on paying for it."

"Lissa—"

"Why should you have to? Being in love is such a wonderful feeling. And to see love in a man's eyes makes anything seem possible. Every woman should know what love is like. You should. You deserve to be married to a man who loves you. Don't trap yourself in a bad marriage. Julia, if you stay with Adrian, and children come—it'll be too late. He'd never let you go then."

"He wouldn't let me go now," Julia heard herself say, and though she was appalled she'd said it, there was a certain relief in voicing that certainty aloud.

"Maybe if I talked to him—"

"No!" Julia felt cold with fear as she stared at her sister. It was too late now to pretend; all she could do was try to convince Lissa to remain silent. "If you say one word about any of this to Adrian, I'll never forgive you."

"Julia—"

"I mean it, Lissa. You don't know him. I do. He wouldn't give me a divorce no matter what anyone said to him, and bringing up the possibility would only make the situation worse for me. Promise me you'll say nothing to him."

Lissa stared at her for a long moment, a little pale and

very troubled, then nodded slowly. "All right. I promise."

Julia forced a smile, and knew it looked as strained as it felt. "I'll be fine, really."

"Will you? I have a feeling it's a lot worse than I thought. He hurts you, doesn't he? At least twice since I've been home this summer, you stayed in bed more than a day, and you were so white when I saw you."

"Lissa, please."

"I won't say anything to Adrian, but I can't help worrying. If he's hurting you, you have to get away from him. Even if he won't give you a divorce, can't you just leave him? He'd look awfully silly staying married to you when you didn't live with him."

This time Julia's smile held a touch of genuine amusement. To the young, most things were simple; Lissa was still very young even if she was maturing rapidly, and her uncomplicated solution seemed a reasonable enough one to her. "Honey, Adrian has a political career to think of, and scandals mean ruin. He wouldn't allow me to leave him."

"You could just—just leave. While he was gone during the day. He couldn't stop you."

"And go where?" Julia shook her head slightly. "I have no money of my own, and I couldn't ask any of our acquaintances for help, even if they were willing. Which they wouldn't be. Lissa, both society and the law consider a wife the property of her husband. How he chooses to treat her is his business, and no one has the right to interfere. There have even been cases where a man killed his wife, admitted it, and was found innocent of any crime because the jury believed he had just cause."

Lissa was clearly appalled. "You aren't serious?"

"Entirely." Julia had read of more than one such case in newspapers, and in a law book in Adrian's study—where she had gone to find out what her realistic chances for a divorce might be. What she had found had given her no hope at all.

"What did the jury consider just cause?" Lissa wanted to know.

"In the cases I read about, infidelity."

"Men have mistresses, and wives are expected to accept it. What's the difference?"

Julia had thought about it, and her reply was dry. "Men make the laws."

"Something should be done about that," Lissa exclaimed, outraged.

"A number of women are trying. A constitutional amendment granting the vote to women has been put before Congress during every session since 1878. Unless and until it passes into law, women have no voice in determining other laws."

"I should have paid more attention in school," Lissa said, then ruthlessly got the subject back on track. "But Julia, do you mean to say that if a woman was being hurt by her husband, neither the police nor any of her friends could help her?"

"Legally, they haven't the right. And there are social beliefs, first, that what goes on between husband and wife is a private matter and, second, that the woman is to blame."

"To blame? For being hurt?"

"For angering her husband." Julia shrugged a little tiredly. "Never mind that it isn't rational. Some realities of life aren't; you'd better accept it. The point is no one would dare to interfere."

"I know someone who would. Someone who doesn't

give a fig about the law or society. Someone you could go to for help." Lissa looked a bit startled and puzzled. "How strange I feel so sure of what I'm saying—but I do."

"Lissa—"

"Cyrus Fortune, Julia. He could—" She broke off abruptly, staring at her sister.

Julia knew she had reacted visibly to the name, and though she struggled desperately for control, she could feel her face burning. Between the past interludes with Cyrus, his insistence that she leave Adrian, and her own shameless thoughts and feelings of late, she was unable to hide the response. It was so ironic. Lissa had named the one man she believed could be trusted—and he was the very man who had tried every form of persuasion short of blackmail or physical force to induce Julia to have an affair with him.

"Julia . . ."

A bit disjointedly, Julia said, "You must have taken leave of your senses, Lissa. Mr. Fortune has the worst reputation with married women of any man in Richmond. And he has no use for runaway wives; he certainly wouldn't be pleased to find one on his hands. A man like him wouldn't want to be bothered with messy problems—"

"Julia, are you in love with him?"

A shaky laugh escaped Julia, and she thought with utter detachment that it had finally happened. She'd finally crossed the line into madness. Nothing else could feel this way. The unexpected conversation with Lissa had added to the tension inside her, until she wanted to cry out, or burst into tears or hysterical laughter—anything to relieve the awful pressure. She was out of control, dreadfully rudderless like the boat that had taken her parents' lives, and the sensation was terrifying. She didn't know how much more she could bear.

"Love?" She was unaware of the bitter cynicism in her voice. "No, I'm not in love with him. That wonderful feeling you've described is something I don't believe in. Not for me, not anymore." Trying to stop her naked flood of words, she clamped her teeth together so hard her jaw ached.

"I—I'm sorry, I just thought the way you looked for a moment . . ." Lissa didn't know what to say, and she was frightened. She had never seen her sister anything but calm. Now Julia's face was paper-white and there was a wild look of despair in her glittering green eyes that made Lissa want to cry. "We'll find a way for you to be free, Julia. There has to be a way."

After a long, still moment, Julia put her sewing aside and rose to her feet. In a flat voice, as if nothing unusual had been discussed between them, she said, "I don't feel like having lunch today. I think I'll take the buggy out and deliver the things for Mrs. King's thrift sale."

"I'll come with you."

"No. I need to be alone for a while." Julia walked out of the room. She put on her hat automatically and ordered a horse hitched to her buggy, the box of secondhand goods for the thrift sale loaded. She drove her buggy through the streets a few minutes later in the same numb state. No one seemed to notice anything peculiar about her, and her errand was completed within a half hour.

But Julia didn't return to the house. Instead, she drove out of the city. She wasn't aware of choosing a particular direction, and paid no attention to her surroundings.

Ever since the conversation with Lissa had begun, she

had known time was running out. Lissa was an honest girl not accustomed to hiding what she felt; with the best intentions to keep her promise, she still would be unable to hide her changed attitude from Adrian. He might not notice immediately since he was so preoccupied these days, but he would eventually.

Being Adrian, he would believe two things. He would believe Julia had confided in her sister about his treatment of her, and he would believe Lissa wouldn't remain quiet about it.

Julia didn't know what to do. Adrian had always held the threat of hurting Lissa over her head, and he was entirely capable of carrying out the threat. If he became enraged enough—and fearing his public mask had been destroyed or damaged beyond repair would certainly enrage him—then he'd stop at nothing.

She drove on through the early afternoon, barely aware of the scorching heat and blind to the dark gray clouds rolling heavily toward her.

It was after two when Lissa stood at the end of the walkway and looked anxiously up and down the street. The sun still beat mercilessly down on the pavement, but thunder rumbled in the grim storm clouds that were approaching steadily and the few people on the streets were hurrying to reach their destinations. Lissa was worried about Julia; she should have been home long ago, and with the storm coming . . .

When she saw Cyrus coming toward her, the relief she felt was almost staggering. She had trusted him from the first moment she had looked into his strange black eyes, and no matter what Julia said, Lissa knew instinctively that he could—he would—help her sister.

"Lissa? What's wrong? Where's Julia?"

Lissa found neither the familiarity nor the abrupt questions surprising, and it never occurred to her not to tell him. As soon as he was close enough, she reached out to him, catching his sleeve with unsteady fingers, and felt immediately reassured when his big hand covered them gently.

"Julia went out in the buggy; she should have been home ages ago. With the storm coming—and since Helen disappeared the way she did—I'm worried. Even if nothing has happened to her, Julia was so upset . . ."

"Why was she upset?" Cyrus asked quietly, his gaze intent on her upturned face.

"It was my fault. I was asking her about Adrian and their marriage. She didn't want to talk about it, but I kept pushing."

Cyrus's long fingers tightened over hers, and something as dangerous as a naked blade flashed in the dark sheen of his eyes. "Has he been hurting her again?"

Lissa blinked in surprise, but once more, she found nothing strange in the question or in his knowledge. "I—I don't think so. Not recently. She hasn't stayed in bed all day since before our party. And he's been so busy he's hardly been home at all. I told her she should leave him."

"And she refused," Cyrus said flatly.

"She's afraid." Lissa had been thinking of nothing else since Julia had left, and she felt cold now despite the burning heat of the sun. What she had seen in her sister's eyes had convinced her more completely than words ever could have that the man she had believed to be so wonderful was in fact a monster. "She told me about cases where a man had killed his wife, and nobody thought he'd done anything wrong. I didn't understand

at first, but I think she knows he'd . . . he'd kill her
before he let her leave him."

Cyrus looked at her for a moment, then said quietly,
"That is not going to happen. Lissa, I want you to go into
the house and pack a few things for yourself and Julia. As
soon as I bring her back, you're both coming with me."

To Lissa, his words brought only relief. She was
nodding with unquestioning acceptance even as she
said, "Adrian usually gets home around four."

"He won't today. I've sent him halfway across the state
to a political meeting. He shouldn't get back here before
midnight, if then."

"*You* sent him?"

"I'll explain later. Right now I have to find Julia before
this storm hits. Don't worry if we aren't back when it
does; we'll take shelter and wait it out. You just be ready
to leave the moment we return."

"All right. You won't let him hurt Julia?"

"No. I'll take care of you both."

"I'm going to marry Mark," she said, because it was
somehow important to her that he know that.

"Of course you are," Cyrus said calmly, patting her
hand. "After you finish school."

Lissa couldn't help smiling, but all she said was "The
storm's coming; you'd better hurry." Then she released
his sleeve and turned back toward the house, feeling an
absolute faith and trust in him so strong that for a very
long time she wouldn't even ask herself where her
certainty had come from.

Julia might not have noticed the approaching storm at all
if her horse hadn't shied nervously as a tangle of dry
brush blew across the road in front of him. She steadied

him, surprised to realize a strong, hot wind was blowing all around her, rustling through parched leaves and grasses. Becoming fully aware of her surroundings, she saw the angry dark clouds blot out the sun to produce an eerie twilight, and heard a low grumble of thunder.

She was a long way from the city.

The road wasn't particularly wide, but there was no side road she could see in which to turn around. She had no choice but to turn in the too-small space. Her skittish horse fought the reins, growing more nervous with every passing second. She was on the point of getting out of the buggy and leading him when the sense of someone approaching rather than the sounds made her look over her shoulder.

She felt absolutely no surprise at seeing Cyrus. He was riding a big Roman-nosed gray that looked powerful enough to carry even its large rider mile after mile, and both the man and horse seemed impervious to the approaching storm.

Cyrus rode directly to her horse's head and leaned down to grasp the reins, quieting the agitated animal seemingly by his touch alone rather than by force. Looking back at Julia and raising his voice to be heard over the wind, he said, "We have to take shelter. Hold on."

Julia wouldn't have been foolish enough to argue with him even if she hadn't felt a peculiar sense of destiny. As he led her horse along the road away from Richmond, she realized where—without being the least aware of her destination—she'd been headed.

Seven

♥

"Go inside," Cyrus told her minutes later, raising his voice again to be heard above the dry whine and crackle of the wind. "I'll see to the horses."

He held her horse steadily enough for her to get out of the buggy. She went up the temporary wooden steps at the side of his new house, where he had brought her. "Inside" was an arguably inaccurate term, since the house's exterior walls hadn't risen high enough to enclose even the first floor, but the building was in the dry, with flooring in place and a solid roof to hold off the coming rain.

Julia stood just inside, shivering a little even though the wind whipping her skirt was still hot. Thunder was booming almost continuously now, and lightning was forking through the leaden gray clouds, but the rain refused to fall.

She didn't want to go deeper into the house, not alone. It seemed a bit eerie, shadowed by the roof high above and the darkening afternoon. Bare studs marked the placement of walls, windows, and doorways like bones without flesh. A temporary interior stairway snaked

upward to disappear into the partially completed flooring
of the second story. The darkly hulking shapes of half-
completed fireplaces crouched here and there. Silvery
pipes protruding from the floor and walls glistened as the
vivid flashes of lightning touched them, and strands of
electrical wiring threaded their way among the studs and
beams of the wooden skeleton.

It was just a house, Julia told herself. It would be a
magnificent house, she thought, when it was completed.
And she didn't *feel* an eeriness from it, she simply had a
sense of strangeness inside herself that the unfinished
building seemed to echo. Like her, the house was
incomplete, the bare bones of something that needed
flesh before it could become real.

Cyrus had disappeared with the horses; she had no
idea where he'd gone. She waited, the peculiar ideas still
filtering through her mind. Waiting? Yes. She'd been
waiting for a long time. It had been hard, but she'd held
on. She hadn't been defeated, even though the battle
had left her too weary to feel very much except pain and
fear.

As she saw Cyrus come toward her, her feelings
changed to fascination and longing that was almost
painful. She saw him look up at her as he reached the
steps, and wondered why he stopped so suddenly. He
looked shocked, she thought.

Cyrus had been brooding as he'd hurried back to the
house, trying to decide how to convince Julia to come to
him. He didn't want to force her, but at the same time he
was absolutely determined she wouldn't spend another
night under Drummond's roof. The man wasn't only
vicious, he was unstable; Cyrus had kept a close eye on
him for weeks now, and he was convinced that whatever

madness or sickness twisted inside Drummond's mind was worsening rapidly.

He was beginning to betray himself, to voice political statements and opinions so grandiose and blatantly lacking in reason even his staunchest supporters had begun eyeing him uncertainly. Cyrus had subtlely pushed and prodded, gauging the response with care because he was wary of having his efforts to expose Drummond backfire into anything hurtful to Julia. The consuming fire inside Adrian, he'd determined quickly, was the burning of ambition, and Cyrus had worked to focus Drummond's full attention as well as his full energy on the political aspirations that fed that ambition.

But during the past few days Cyrus had grown more and more uneasy. He couldn't put a name to what he was feeling except to know it concerned Julia. And time. Time was running out, he realized. He couldn't afford to wait until he goaded Drummond to expose himself publicly; he had to get Julia away from her husband, and quickly. So he had maneuvered to get Drummond out of Richmond, and he'd gone to talk to Julia.

He was grateful, now, that the storm gave him the opportunity to be alone with her, but he still didn't know how to convince her to leave her husband. He was grappling with that problem when he took the first step into the house, looked up, and saw her.

The incomplete exterior walls of the house didn't block the wind very well; fitful gusts were tugging at her dark skirt and white blouse so that she seemed in motion even though she stood still. She had lost her hat sometime during the drive to the house, and the wind made wisps of her fiery hair flutter around her pale face. Her wide eyes were dark and colorless except when lightning flashed, but then they came vividly alive with green fire.

When the truth hit him, it was like being paralyzed for an eternal moment, as if everything inside him stopped. Then his heart began to pound heavily in his chest and he felt dizzy.

He hadn't questioned his own feelings very deeply because there'd been so many other puzzling and disturbing questions in his life since he'd returned to Richmond. He'd known he wanted her; the desire that had grown more intense with every passing day ached inside him now almost unbearably. He had known he wanted to help her, to ease her pain and take away her fear. He had even known she was important to him beyond those things, that she was somehow a piece of the "puzzle" his life had become.

He hadn't known he loved her.

Now, in a moment so intense it was almost blinding, he knew. It was akin to knowing his heart was beating, a certainty that didn't have to be examined because it was so irrefutable. She was part of him, and he'd never be whole, never be complete until she knew that, and believed it, as surely as he did.

Cyrus realized he'd stopped as though he'd run into a wall. Perhaps he had. The woman he loved was so physically and emotionally wounded, she might never be able to return his feelings even if she wanted to. Getting her away from Drummond would be only the first step; he would have to take many more slow and careful steps before Julia healed.

Cyrus drew a breath and continued up the steps, vaguely aware of the storm building all around them with an electric tension he could actually feel. If it didn't rain soon and drain some of the storm's fury, he thought, the lightning would grow more dangerous, and begin to touch off fires that would be deadly.

He reached Julia and took her hand gently in his. "We should remain near the center of the house," he told her. "It will be safer."

She allowed him to lead her deeper among the maze of fleshless walls and gaping doorways. She wasn't so aware of the strange thoughts with her hand lost in his, but she was still aware of tensely waiting . . . for something. She didn't know what it was, but she wanted it, needed it, and she didn't know how much longer she could wait for it.

It was darker near the center of the house, and she felt the wind more than heard it. Only an occasional draft of hot air disturbed the stillness. Cyrus led her into what would probably be a parlor, with a rock fireplace half completed blocking most of the light from the front of the house.

"Wait just a minute," he said, squeezing her hand gently before releasing it. "I think there's a lamp on the mantel block." He stepped away from her and moved between several looming shapes toward the fireplace. There was a brief silence, then the scrape of a match, a blue-white flare, the smell of sulphur and then the light of a kerosene lamp sent out a yellow circle.

Julia looked around. The looming shapes had become a wheelbarrow piled high with stones to continue building the fireplace, two corded stacks of lumber, and an open crate containing plumbing fixtures. There was also a smaller, empty crate, upended to form a table on which sat a second kerosene lamp, and a pallet of thick quilts.

Following her gaze, Cyrus said, "I've hired a watchman to keep an eye on the place at night; it looks like he's been doing more sleeping than watching."

"Were you worried about theft?" she asked, wondering why her voice sounded so hollow. Then she realized. The house, of course. Voices always sounded strange in a half-completed or empty building. Except for his voice. His voice was always curiously distinct no matter what tone he used.

"Lumber is valuable," he said with a slight shrug. He decided not to explain yet another of his "whims," especially since he hardly understood it himself, and since the last thing he wanted to do was add to Julia's fears. He wasn't worried about lumber being stolen. All he knew was that he felt the need to guard this house as strongly as he'd felt the need to build it.

Julia started nervously as a crash of thunder shook the entire house. She had the sensation they were more alone then ever before, cut off from the rest of the world by the angry but oddly protective force of nature itself. She tensed when Cyrus took a step toward her.

"You don't have to be afraid of me, Julia," he said quietly. As he had done on her previous visit, he shrugged out of his coat and folded it, then placed it on the smaller of the two stacks of lumber. "Come over here and sit down, please. We're going to be here awhile; we might as well be comfortable."

She obeyed the request, but her tension was heightened when he joined her with no more than a few inches between them. Searching for something to say, she finally asked, "Were you going somewhere? I mean, with the storm already so rough . . ."

"I was searching for you," he replied.

Julia turned her head quickly to stare at him. "For me?"

He nodded, watching her intently. "I'd gone to the

house to talk to you, and found Lissa very upset and worried about you."

"You went to the house?" She was shocked, and a chill of fear feathered up her spine. "But, Adrian—"

"He's attending a political meeting halfway across the state, and shouldn't return before midnight," Cyrus reassured her. "I made sure of that before I took the chance."

"Even so," she said unsteadily, "the neighbors . . . people will wonder."

"They'll think I went to see him, if they think anything at all. At least until—" He hesitated, then said, "I asked Lissa to pack a few things for the two of you, and to be ready to leave when we returned."

"I can't leave," she said automatically, wondering why her mind felt so sluggish. Why couldn't she think?

"Sweetheart, you can't stay," he said softly but with an intensity in his voice she'd never heard before. "It would be bad enough if Drummond were just a brutal bastard, but he's more than that. He's twisted. He could cross the line into insanity at any moment—if he hasn't already. Even his closest friends are beginning to wonder about him, and he's never betrayed himself to them before. The next time he gets violent, he could kill you. Or Lissa. Do you understand?"

Julia couldn't look away from Cyrus, even though she felt terribly vulnerable. Words welled up and escaped without her volition. "He'd said he'd hurt Lissa if I left him," she whispered. "That she'd never be safe from him. I thought if I could just hold on until Lissa was married, then maybe I could find a way out."

Cyrus reached over to touch her hand. "You can't wait that long. Julia, I know you can't be sure I'm different from Drummond. I know you don't trust me, can't trust

me right now, but I swear I would never do anything to
hurt you. I'll take care of you and Lissa, and I'll make
certain Drummond never touches her or hurts you
again."

"You don't know him. He—"

"Sweetheart, I'll keep him away from you if it takes a
bullet to do it."

Julia felt a shock, but a peculiar one. She didn't doubt
Cyrus was capable of killing another man if the reason
were strong enough; what surprised her was his apparent determination to do whatever was necessary to
protect her and Lissa. Just because he desired her?
Could passion drive a man to such lengths? The endear-
ment he'd used surprised her as well, and puzzled her a
little. Did he believe she'd expect pretty words and
phrases if she did go to him and become his mistress?

It seemed strangely out of character. From the very
first he'd been blunt with her, often shockingly so. He
had even once told her he wouldn't offer pretty speeches
or bedroom lies, and she had decided he wouldn't find it
necessary to resort to such tactics in order to get what he
wanted. Yet he had twice called her sweetheart, his
black velvet voice sober and gentle—and she had the
odd feeling he wasn't aware he'd done it.

"Julia?" In the lamplight his lean, handsome face held
an expression of unusual anxiety. "I swear I won't make
you do anything against your will. I won't force you in
any way. But you have to let me take care of you. Please.
Give me a chance to prove you can trust me."

She swallowed hard, unable to summon even a flash of
resentment this time at how easily he was swaying her.
She wanted to give in to him, wanted to take the risk, no
matter what it cost her. And it would cost her, even if he
didn't deliberately hurt her. Fleetingly, she thought of

how shameful it would be, and how people would condemn her for living with a man as his mistress with her younger sister under the same roof, but then she wondered vaguely if he meant to set her up in an establishment of her own. Wasn't that how it was done? She'd never heard of a man moving his mistress into his family home.

Not that it mattered where he meant to keep her. He was right about one thing at least—she had to leave Adrian immediately, before he could do something dreadful to Lissa. As for going to Cyrus, what choice did she have? There was no place else she could go. Besides, her body insisted she was his, and she was too tired to fight him anymore.

With a little difficulty she asked, "What did—did Lissa say when you told her?"

He smiled. "She just nodded. She trusts me, it seems." His smile vanished. "But then, she trusted him too, didn't she?"

Julia nodded jerkily. "He made sure she did. This summer though, she started to notice things. If I'd handled her questions differently, perhaps she wouldn't have realized the truth, but I—I couldn't pretend anymore."

"She needed to know, sweetheart." He hesitated, then said in a soft voice, "I wish you could believe you'll be safe with me. I'll do everything I can to make you happy, Julia, I swear it. Please, let me try."

Looking back later, Julia often thought how odd it was that the storm broke at the same moment as her resistance. Even as she was nodding, she heard the heavy drumming of rain on the roof and felt a cool, damp breeze touch her cheek.

"All right," she murmured, and the relief of simply

making any kind of decision was almost numbing. "All right, I—I'll leave Adrian. I'll come to you."

Cyrus lifted one of her hands and kissed it, smiling. His eyes were liquid, shining, and there was a note of fierce satisfaction as well as tenderness in his voice when he said, "You won't regret it." Then his gaze dropped to the hand he was holding, her left, and his smile faded slowly.

Julia had seen it too. A flash of lightning had reflected brightly off her wedding band. Very softly, she said, "A few days after our wedding, Adrian took the ring he'd put on me in church and replaced it with this one. He had it made too small. I can't take it off."

Cyrus studied her hand in silence for a moment, his face very still. The ring was tight on her slender finger, biting into the skin. The lamplight was barely strong enough to show him tiny scars on either side of her knuckle where flesh had been torn when the ring had been forced over it. It made Cyrus feel sick. How insane would a man have to be to do such a thing to his own wife?

"God damn him," he said quietly.

To Julia, his words sounded less like a curse than an invocation, and one very deeply felt. She had the sudden, surprising notion that Cyrus possessed a rare, inborn conviction he wasn't even aware of. He would seldom set foot in a church, she thought with a flash of intuition, yet he innately felt and understood the value of faith in a way few overtly religious men could come close to matching.

It seemed a strange trait for a man of his reputation, yet she felt certain she was right about it. For the first time, Julia began to wonder if she had any real under-standing of the man he truly was. She stared at him as his dark head bent slightly over her hand, then tensed a little, her thoughts scattering when she felt him take hold of the ring with a light touch.

"It's all right, sweetheart," he said in a low voice. His fingers turned the ring slowly, then eased it painlessly over her knuckle and off.

"How did you do that?" she asked in surprise, knowing only too well how tightly the ring had fit her. She hadn't been able to get it off no matter how hard she'd tried, yet he had slipped it from her finger as easily as though it had suddenly grown two sizes larger.

Cyrus held the ring for a moment, then slipped it into the pocket of his vest, saying, "I'll get rid of it on the way back to Richmond; I don't want it near this house."

"You didn't answer me." She watched his face as he gently rubbed the mark the ring had left on her finger.

After a moment he lifted his gaze to meet hers. There was something a bit hesitant in his black eyes and, finally, he shrugged. "It didn't belong on your finger. I didn't want it there," he said simply.

She managed a faint smile, although she felt unnerved by what he'd done. "And you always get what you want?"

"I've been lucky so far." His free hand rose to touch her cheek, the long fingers softly caressing, and his expression tightened. "I want you," he said huskily, and it was not quite a question.

Julia felt her heart begin to beat unevenly, and all the impossible sensations she'd tried to deal with these past weeks surged inside her like a rising tide she hadn't a hope of mastering. Perhaps this was what she'd been waiting for, she realized dimly. To belong to him—if it was possible. He had taught her body to want him, and no matter what else she was uncertain of, she was sure of that much. She wanted him, and she had to take the chance. Whether it brought pain or pleasure, she had to offer herself to him.

She wondered briefly if he had put this price on her safety and Lissa's, but dismissed the idea before it could cause her any pain. It didn't seem to matter anyway.

"I—I want you too," she said unsteadily, still shocked she could say those words to any man.

Cyrus made an odd, rough sound and leaned toward her. His mouth touched hers, very gentle at first but quickly hardening with desire. Julia felt herself being gathered into his strong arms, and for the first time she permitted herself to respond to him and to the hunger he had created inside her.

Her arms went up around his neck as her upper body molded itself to the hard contours of his, and her mouth opened eagerly to permit the kiss to deepen. She felt a burst of heat somewhere near the center of her being, and the force of it made her tremble. How could she feel this way? How could he make her feel this way? Her body seemed alive only when he held it, and she didn't understand how it could be possible.

It was so strange, like her dreams, a restless, burning pleasure that was a growing ache inside her. An empty ache. The intimate touch of his tongue against hers soothed the ache and yet made it worse, and she wanted—needed—to be closer to him. The hunger he had brought to life in her body had some instinctive knowledge of its own, a certainty of ultimate satisfaction, and it demanded she reach for that.

She made a faint sound of protest when he lifted his mouth from hers and opened her eyes to stare up at him dazedly.

"Julia," he said, kissing one corner of her mouth and then the other as his hand cradled the back of her head.

The tanned skin of his face was taut and his eyes were burning, and his black velvet voice was low, a little rough. "I had a better place in mind for our first time together, sweet. But I don't think I can wait for you any longer."

The clean smells of new wood and rain, the shadowy, lamplit room, unfinished though it was, and the pallet on the floor all seemed perfect to Julia. There was so much newness in this place, such a feeling of vigorous beginnings. She no longer saw it as eerie. She wanted to lie with Cyrus where there were no bedroom memories of pain and humiliation.

Even to the storm outside replenishing the parched earth it was an ideal place for her to start afresh.

"I don't want to wait," she whispered.

He kissed her again, then murmured against her mouth, "You deserve better."

She hesitated, then slid her hands down over his broad shoulders and reached for his tie. There was a part of her still capable of being shocked by the brazen action, but the compelling hunger she felt was too powerful to fight or deny, and she met his eyes steadily as she unknotted the cloth. "I don't want to wait," she repeated, beginning to unbutton his vest.

He was still for a moment, but when his vest hung open and she had reached the third button of his shirt he groaned softly and bent his head to kiss her again. He removed her dark tie by touch alone, then just as blindly worked to release the tiny buttons down the back of her blouse.

He drew her to her feet, shrugging out of his vest and shirt, allowing them to drop carelessly to the floor. Julia unfastened her skirt and let it fall, then fumbled at the tight cuffs of her blouse. Oddly enough, she didn't feel at all the way she did while undressing in front of Adrian, a fact she hardly noticed at the time. All she was aware of was the need to rid them of the barriers of clothing. She had to be closer to him.

Still, a pang of nervousness shot through her when she saw his imposing torso. He was so big, so obviously strong. His strength had been noticeable under layers of clothing; without those civilized veils he was so starkly powerful it took her breath away.

And he was so undeniably male. Golden skin taut over hard muscles. A mat of thick black hair, almost like a pelt, covering the broad expanse of his chest, narrowing over his flat stomach. She wanted to touch him, and yet at the same time nagging little fears were pricking at her.

He could hurt her with such dreadful ease. . . . And even though his desire seemed to her both strong and genuine, what if Adrian had been right about her? What if there were something in her that would destroy any man's desire before it could be fulfilled? Would Cyrus turn from her, horrified and sickened, his skin clammy with disgust, when she caused his passion to wither? Would he find that ironically, fate had cursed him to want a woman he could never possess even though she offered herself to him?

Please, God, don't let it happen. Not with him. I couldn't bear it to happen with him.

For a brief instant Julia wanted to run to avoid discovering what could be an agonizing truth. But then he kissed her again, his fingers taking over the job of unbuttoning her cuffs, and the heat of her own response held the stinging fears and desperate anxiety at bay. She felt the blouse slip free of her, then her petticoat, and a slight tug as he unfastened her stockings and began working to release her corset.

"Damn these things," he said, lifting his head reluctantly so that he could see what he was doing.

She helped him, more adept through sheer daily experience, and drew a breath in relief when the constrictive garment fell to the floor. "Fashion," she murmured huskily, then gasped when he pulled her closer and her aching breasts were pressed to the hardness of his chest.

His lips were trailing over her throat, and she felt the vibration of his words when he muttered, "Fashion can go to hell." He wrapped his arms around her and pulled her tighter against him.

Julia slid her arms around his lean waist, her fingers probing the smooth, rippling muscles of his back. She felt him removing pins from her hair until it tumbled freely below her waist, and then his hands slid down to guide her hips firmly to his loins. Her head fell back to bare more of her throat to his caressing mouth, a hot shiver going through her when she felt the shockingly intimate sensation of his hard manhood nestle against her softness.

That evidence of his passion reassured her, if only for the moment. He wanted her. He did. Nothing about her would change that. She tried to push Adrian and his bitter condemnation out of her mind, frantic to convince herself he'd been wrong. This was passion, not his frenzied, desperate fumblings in the dark. This was so incredibly pleasurable, fate couldn't be cruel enough to take it away from her. . . .

A little moan of stunned desire escaped her trembling lips, and she couldn't breathe properly. The sensations were so acute, and she felt so vibrantly alive . . . so overwhelmed by something she couldn't begin to control. Frightening. Yet wildly exciting. She was dizzy and

felt drugged, feverish. Her breasts were throbbing, and
the worst of the heat had settled deep in her belly,
where it burned almost beyond bearing until she wanted
to cry out some desperate, wordless plea.

It was difficult to think, but there was something she
had to tell him, something he needed to know before he
made her his. With her mind dazed and her body in the
grip of these strange, maddening sensations, it wasn't
until he lifted her in his arms and carried her to the
pallet that she tried to get the words out.

"Cyrus . . ." She caught her breath as his big hands
glided down her legs, removing her stockings and shoes,
and the warm touch affected her peculiarly. Her heart
was pounding so rapidly she thought it might burst, and
her entire body was quivering. Lying back on the quilts
that were surprisingly comfortable, she forced her eyes
open, not realizing until then that they'd been closed.

"What is it, sweet?" He was raised on an elbow beside
her, looking down at her with eyes that were tender
despite their burning. One of his hands brushed a strand
of her hair away from her face, while his other hand lay,
warmly heavy, over her stomach.

The last thing she wanted to do, especially now, was to
bring up the subject of her husband, but she had little
choice. She had a superstitious urge not to tempt fate by
confessing the truth, terrified her own words would
cause Cyrus to see whatever it was Adrian saw in her and
make him draw away from her in aversion. Even the
possibility sent a chill through her aching body.

She was glad she was still wearing her chemise and
knickers; partially clothed she felt a trifle less vulnerable.
But she was nervous, apprehensive, painfully embarrassed—and though her body still throbbed feverishly,
she was so aware of the suspension of his caresses and

her own terrible fears, she felt almost sick with dread. Her gaze skittered from his, and she said diffidently, "There's something I—I have to tell you."

Cyrus had kept a tight rein on the clamorings of his body, fiercely determined to make certain she would have nothing to regret in giving herself to him. But at her words an entirely new kind of tension clenched in him. The way she looked away from him, and sounded so anxious. God, she couldn't be pregnant! He didn't know if he could bear even the idea of Drummond's child growing inside her body.

But as he looked down at her, so delicate and lovely, her beautiful face framed by bright hair tumbled loosely over the quilt, he knew he would bear it if he had to. He loved her. He leaned down to kiss her, then drew back. "Then tell me. You can tell me anything, sweet."

She bit her lip, her eyes meeting his again, then took a breath and said softly, rapidly, "I—I've never—my marriage was never—consummated."

It was the last thing Cyrus had expected, and for a moment all he felt was shock. "Drummond didn't . . ."

Heat burned in her face, and Julia looked nervously away again. "He—he couldn't," she said in a stifled voice. "He tried, because he wanted a son. But he said it was my fault, that I made him ill."

Cyrus gathered her into his arms and held her against him, still so shaken he could hardly think, but hearing in her voice the damage Drummond had done to her confidence as a woman. "Shhh. It wasn't your fault, my darling."

Her voice was muffled against his neck as she clung to him, but he heard the words all too clearly. "It did make him ill to touch me . . . it was horrible when he tried. I felt so ugly and ashamed. I didn't want him to—to do

that to me, but he was my husband, and I knew he had
the right to, but he couldn't. He couldn't. And he said
things to me that hurt worse than the strap. . . ."

Cyrus held her tighter, his emotions chaotic. He hated
Drummond for what he'd done to Julia, for her pain and
for the healing that might take years. But he also felt an
almost numbing surge of primitive pride and crushing
responsibility. He, he alone would initiate this woman
who was his heart's desire into the mysteries and beau-
ties of making love.

"It's all right, sweetheart," he murmured huskily,
easing her back down onto the pallet.

"He said I was repulsive," she whispered. Her face
was white now, her eyes anguished.

Cyrus kissed her trembling lips very gently. "No sane
man could say that to you." He touched her cheek with
tender fingers, and his soft words were fervent. "You're
so beautiful, Julia, so amazingly lovely. The first time I
saw you, I couldn't take my eyes off you. And I couldn't
stay away from you. You've haunted me, awake and
asleep, every moment since."

Almost against her will, she believed at least that he
found her attractive and desirable. He had certainly
pursued her with a single-minded intensity. Still, she
had to force the difficult words out. "But passion can
change, can't it? It can . . . wither."

Cyrus was certain she had never talked of this to
anyone, and even though just the thought of Drummond
in bed with Julia sickened him, he was determined her
marriage not become a kind of Bluebeard's chamber
between them. Trust began with honesty; Julia had to
believe there was nothing she couldn't say to him, no
subject she couldn't discuss with him, no matter how
painful it was to either of them.

He made his voice gentle but matter-of-fact. "My sweet, there are a number of reasons a man might be physically unable to make love to a woman even if he feels desire for her." He hesitated, then said, "His sexual organ has to be erect to enter a woman's body. You understand that?"

Julia half nodded, her face burning again with embarrassment. Since she'd grown up in the country, with animals about, she had at least a basic knowledge of the mechanics of reproduction, but Adrian had confused her about sexual relations between men and women in addition to everything else. Since he'd always attempted to take her in the dark, she hadn't been certain what had gone wrong at first. Then she had realized he became aroused when he hurt her, but not when he tried to possess her. He hadn't been able to enter her, no matter how frantically he'd pushed and prodded. Even when he seemingly aroused himself—she judged that by his changing voice and movements beside her—before touching her, his arousal had vanished as soon as he did touch her.

"I—I understand," she murmured, unable to meet his eyes except fleetingly. "But you said—he might not be able to even if he wants to?"

Cyrus nodded. "Reasons like exhaustion or illness. If he's upset about something that has nothing to do with her, and yet affects his own body. Or if he's emotionally disturbed—like Drummond. His problems have nothing to do with you. Any man would find you desirable."

Part of Julia's mind was shocked by the conversation, but her painful confusion drove her to try to understand, and Cyrus didn't appear to mind. "But when Adrian . . . when he tried, he seemed to . . . arouse himself without even looking at me, or touching me. In the dark. And when he did touch me, his passion just . . . died. How could it not be my fault?"

Cyrus hesitated, praying he could find the right words. He'd never been so conscious of how young she was, how terribly young to have such wretched questions. "His passion was empty. Hollow. It wasn't the desire of a man for a woman; if it had been, touching you would have made it grow stronger. He isn't normal, Julia. What he taught you of men is distorted, unnatural. You have to believe that, because it's the truth."

"Men don't . . . beat women?"

"Normal men don't," he said flatly, his heart filled with pain because she should never have even imagined that question.

Julia hesitated, then said, "Sometimes he—Adrian makes me touch him. But not because the touch pleases him, or even arouses him. It's to hurt *me*, to—to shame me. That's why he does it. Do all men—"

"No." Cyrus leaned down and kissed her gently. "Sweetheart, touching between men and women should be nothing but pleasure. I want to touch you because it's a need inside me, because you're so beautiful and I want to be as close to you as I can. I want to please you, more than anything, to show you how wonderful lovemaking can be."

Almost without thinking she lifted a hand and touched his cheek with unsteady fingers. A little shy now, still uncertain, she said, "Before you touched me, I didn't know I could feel desire. Or pleasure. I'm sorry to be so stupid about it, but there was no one I could ask—"

"God, don't be sorry." He kissed the inside of her wrist softly. "You can ask me anything, my sweet." His smile was warm and gentle. "And you aren't stupid, don't think that. Just young, and even though you've seen more cruelty than anyone should, you're innocent as well."

Her fingers were stroking his cheek of their own volition, almost compulsively, and she loved the way his skin felt under her touch. "My mother never talked to me of such things," she murmured. "I promised myself I'd talk to Lissa."

"I hope you'll be able to tell her a man can bring her pleasure with his passion," Cyrus said quietly. "I hope you'll be able to say to her that she never has to be afraid of a man who loves her."

Julia was puzzled. Love?

Cyrus took her free hand and carried it to his chest, where she could feel the strong beat of his heart. Even as she felt the steady thuds, the tempo of them quickened, and his voice grew taut with intensity. "To make love to you isn't just a desire in me, it's a need. Do you understand, sweetheart? Not just passion. Love. I love you."

Eight

♥

That shocked her more than anything he'd said or done, and pushed all thoughts of Adrian out of her mind. She searched his face with bewildered eyes, seeing the tenderness stamped in his hard, handsome features, seeing a glow in his black eyes she'd never seen before, as if they were lit from within.

It was beautiful, what she saw. It even moved her in a way that was almost instinctive, as if the ancient core of her female being recognized and valued the primitive conquest of a male heart. But she couldn't feel anything except surprise and disbelief.

Love? He loved her? It wasn't possible. She'd heard tales of him while she was still in the schoolroom, and even allowing for the exaggeration of gossip, one fact had stood out: His attachment to any one woman, if there even was an attachment other than passion, had never been more than fleeting. A single woman, she thought, could never hold him, not for long.

Then again, perhaps his definition of love existed only in the moment. Perhaps he loved all his mistresses.

In any case, Julia wasn't foolish enough to assume

anything from the declaration. She was a married woman on the point of leaving her husband; Cyrus was a man who wanted an affair with her. If it pleased him to say he loved her, then so be it.

Finally, hesitantly, she said, "You don't have to say you love me. I didn't expect you to."

His expression didn't change, except for the curve of his mouth, which turned a little wry. "I said it because it's true. I'll never lie to you, Julia. Never. I do love you. I know you don't believe it, but you will one day."

She didn't know how to reply, so she said nothing.

He leaned down and covered her mouth with his, the first gentle touch deepening with hunger. Her arms went around his neck, and she was suddenly aware that the interruption had only held desire at bay, not destroyed it. Her body was throbbing again, feverish, and her response to his intense kisses was as fervent as it had been before. She heard herself murmur a protest when his lips left hers, and her own unexpected wantonness was no more than a tiny shock this time.

"I need you so much," he said huskily, his eyes burning down at her again.

Her heart was thudding, her breathing quickened, and the yearning inside her was so strong she was only dimly aware that the storm had intensified in its fury. She didn't hear the booming thunder or wailing wind, or the heavy drumming of rain on the roof; all she heard was his voice. His wonderful, black velvet voice.

"Yes," she whispered, because she had a peculiar feeling he had asked her a question, even though she'd thought it had already been answered.

He hesitated, then said, "Sweetheart, the first time for a woman . . . there's pain. I promised I wouldn't hurt you."

Julia had known too much pain not to be wary of more, but common sense told her women could hardly have been blessed with desire and cursed in the same breath with an agonizing consummation of it; God wasn't that cruel, surely. Still, she couldn't help but ask, "Only the first time?"

He nodded and touched her cheek gently. "Only the first time, and only for a moment."

She wouldn't realize it for a long time, but the first grain of trust for him formed inside her then. She wanted to believe him, so she trusted he was telling her the truth, trusted he wouldn't hurt her more than he could help.

Her arms tightened around his neck, and there was no hesitation in her voice when she said, "I want you, Cyrus."

He made a soft, rough sound, kissing her again and again. He could feel the banked desire inside him flare up hotly, his entire body burning and throbbing with need for her, and forced himself to concentrate fiercely on the even greater need to teach Julia the pleasure that was possible between a man and woman.

Love gave him patience; he doubted anything else could have.

Julia felt one of his hands touching her side, then her stomach, and realized he was unbuttoning her chemise. She was glad he was doing that, because even the thin barrier of sheer cotton was suddenly a torment to her. The primitive desire to lie naked in his arms, such an unfamiliar urge, was so strong in her she didn't try to examine it. She simply obeyed the demands of this incredible need she felt, and stopped thinking at all.

She shifted on the pallet to help him when he removed her chemise and knickers, gazing at his face as

he looked at her, because what she saw in his burning
eyes, an expression almost of wonder, was beautiful in a
new way and caused the heat inside her to run wild.
Instead of cringing inwardly and feeling rawly degraded,
she was aware only of a curious sense of uninhibited
delight in the clear evidence that he found nothing at all
ugly or revolting about her body.

"Julia . . . you're so lovely. . . ." His mouth
brushed hers very lightly, then trailed down her throat
slowly, and one big hand slid up over her rib cage to
warmly surround her breast.

She gasped, almost jerking at the shock that was both
physical and emotional. She had never felt a man's hand
touch her naked breast. But if it was unfamiliar to her
mind, her body responded so instantly to the caress, she
could only tremble as a hot wave of pleasure swept over
her. His long fingers stroked her flesh, and her breast
grew tight and hard as it swelled, throbbing under his
touch. Then his thumb brushed her nipple and she did
jerk, the burst of sensation so acute she didn't know if it
was pleasure or pain.

But whichever it was, her body wanted more of it. She
couldn't believe what he was making her feel. His mouth
moved against her throat, the hot darts of his tongue
sending shiver after shiver rippling through her. His
hands caressing her breast, fingers kneading gently and
thumb circling her taut nipple rhythmically until it was
a sweet, aching torment, until she gritted her teeth to
hold back the frantic sounds she could feel rising up
inside her.

His mouth touched the base of her throat, then moved
to her breastbone and slowly, so slowly she was almost
rigid with a breathless suspension, slid up the slope of
her swollen breast. She literally couldn't breathe; all her

consciousness was focused on what he was doing, a wordless, instinctive plea in her mind. When his mouth finally closed over her aching nipple, she gasped and moaned raggedly.

Her fingers tangled in his thick, silky hair, her eyes tightly closed as she helplessly endured the blazing shock of exquisite sensation. The wet heat of his mouth on her nipple, the burning, tingling pressure of suction, and the swirling caress of his tongue, was a pleasure beyond anything she had ever imagined.

She hadn't been able to control the wild feelings his touch evoked, but now her entire body seemed a thing apart from her mind, a thing of passion and relentless need with a life and instincts all its own. It arched against him, pleading mutely for more, quivering and burning as his hand and mouth pleasured and tormented her, and husky little sounds welled up in her throat to escape her trembling lips.

Her body wouldn't be still, and the fleeting idea that her feverish response was somehow shameful had no power to command muscle or flesh. She felt his hand touch her stomach, sliding warmly downward and then curving along her hip to slowly stroke her tense thigh. She had a vague impression her legs had been moving restlessly, but they were taut now, pressing together, and a new kind of urgency was gripping her body. The heat inside her was spreading, intensifying, and his touch seemed to guide it to burn hotter in the pulsing ache of her loins. His strong fingers were at the inside of her thighs now, gently insistent as they eased between them, and she felt her tight muscles suddenly give way as her legs parted for him.

He made a hoarse sound, his mouth fiercely hungry on her breast, almost frantic, as if the taste of her were something he couldn't get enough of. If her mind had been in control of her body, she would have tried to push him away, because she was burning alive and didn't know how much more she could bear, but she had no choice. Her body wanted more. Then he touched her, his fingers brushing the soft curls covering her mound, and her eyes flew open as alarm jolted through her.

For a single instant, even her body remembered bewilderment and sick humiliation, but then he was stroking her damp flesh very gently and a shock of pure pleasure burned the memories away. The whimper that left her seemed to come from deep inside her, an unfamiliar sound, hoarse and ragged. Her hips were rising mindlessly to his touch, sharp tension winding tighter and tighter in her body until she couldn't breathe except in gasping pants.

Her wide eyes fixed on his face when he lifted his mouth from her breast, and her nails dug into his shoulders as her body arched helplessly. "Stop," she whispered, the maddening tension tormenting her. "Please . . . I can't . . ."

He covered her lips with his, and his mouth was so hot and hard it should have burned her or bruised her, but it didn't. She needed that touch too, her mouth opening to his eagerly to accept the deep thrust of his tongue. She wanted him to stop, yet she didn't—and he seemed to know what her desperately striving body needed most. His intimate caress was insistent, driving her higher and higher until she was writhing, moaning wordlessly into his mouth.

Just when she knew it was possible to die from pleasure because she couldn't bear another instant of it and death had to be the end, the awful tension finally shattered. Her entire body convulsed, rising against him

with a shudder, and she cried out wildly as an unbelievable ecstasy swept through her. Her body remained
rigid for a long moment, gripped by the pulsing rapture,
and then she went limp, almost sobbing.

Cyrus held her for a few moments, kissing her trembling lips and flushed cheeks, then drew away from her.
She opened her eyes, so dazed she could hardly think,
watching him as he removed what was left of his
clothing. Was that how it was supposed to be, she
wondered dimly, that incredible pleasure? If so, pain
would be a small price to pay for it.

She knew it wasn't over. Cyrus had made her feel
things she had never imagined; now it was his turn to
find satisfaction in her body. She looked at him, her
mouth going dry, and tried to squelch her rising fear.

He was starkly masculine. In the yellow lamplight
brightened by frequent flashes of lightning, his body
looked even bigger than before, stronger. Muscles rippled when he moved, and her gaze clung to his body
with a mixture of fascination and alarm. He was beautiful
the way a blooded stallion was beautiful: powerful,
dominant, graceful, blatantly male, and unmistakably
dangerous. His manhood was swollen erect, huge, and
terror roiled through her as she looked at him.

He'd said there would be pain for her only the first
time, and even though she'd trusted he was telling the
truth, she couldn't help but doubt him now. She had
seen Adrian fully aroused when he used the strap on her,
but Cyrus was a much bigger man—and she just didn't
see how it would be possible for her to take him into her
body.

But when he came back to her on the pallet, she didn't
flinch away from him. Nor did she reach out to him.
Adrian had wanted her perfectly still when he lay on her,

and she wasn't sure if she was supposed to do anything at this point. To her surprise, however, Cyrus didn't immediately roll on top of her. Instead, he kissed her, and his warm, hard hand surrounded her breast.

Cyrus was holding on to the last threads of his control with all his will. He'd wanted her for so long, desire was a throbbing torment now. He had never in his life felt such an urgent, desperate need. He'd been able to ignore his own hunger for a while, intent on loving Julia until she understood the difference between lovemaking and the cruel perversions to which her husband had subjected her.

But now, as he kissed her and touched her, he felt the faint stiffness of her body. And when he raised his head to look down at her, he saw fear shadowing her beautiful green eyes. It went through him like a knife.

"Don't be afraid, sweetheart," he murmured, kissing her with all the gentleness he could command. "I just want to love you again, please you. Will you let me do that?"

Confusion flitted across her tense features. "Again?" Her soft voice was hesitant. "I thought—I thought you wanted to take me now."

"When you're ready," Cyrus said huskily. "When you want me to take you, my love."

Julia didn't understand what he meant. She was ready now, resigned to the promised pain, braced against it. But before she could ask him to tell her more, he bent his head, his mouth closing over her nipple, and the banked heat inside her flared to new life.

As badly as his body needed the release it would find in joining with hers, Cyrus's pleasure in merely touching her was so strong, it was a kind of satisfaction in and of itself. All his senses delighted in the textures of her body, the rising heat of her desire, the sweet taste of her, and the soft sounds she made as he caressed her. Her response was astonishing, and he was both relieved and intensely exhilarated to know that with all she'd suffered, she was able to desire him.

He'd been worried about that, but now he was sure Julia could heal from what had been done to her heart and mind. Once she experienced the full range of a woman's pleasure and no longer feared a man's desire, the worst would be over, he thought.

So he concentrated fiercely on arousing her now, ignoring the pounding urgency of his own body. The stiffness of fear left her, replaced by the sensual tension of rising passion as she responded to his touch. Her breasts swelled, round and flushed in his hands, the delicate pink nipples tight and almost pulsing in his mouth. Her hands rose to his neck, restlessly probing, and her breathing quickened.

Her belly was soft and firm under his touch, muscles contracting in little spasms of pleasure as he stroked her skin. The triangle of silky hair at the base of her belly, burnished copper over her creamy flesh, enticed him almost to the point of madness, and when his fingers explored gently, her damp heat drove his feverish desire impossibly higher.

Cyrus didn't know how much more he could take. Every muscle in his body was so rigid it was quivering with strain, and the fire inside him felt as if it were burning him alive. He caressed her insistently, until she was moving to his touch, her body totally caught up in the primitive drive toward release.

When he finally lifted his head from her breasts, she was whimpering, and looked at him with wide eyes filled with instinctive feminine panic.

"Please," she whispered, trying to pull him back down to her. "Make it stop, please . . ."

Groaning, he gently widened her legs and slipped between them, rising above her. Fighting all the urgent demands of his body that he bury himself in her, he moved very carefully, guiding his aching flesh to probe her wet heat gently.

Julia was so gripped by her body's need that she was barely aware of what he was doing until she felt the blunt hardness of his manhood seeking entrance. Her mind was shocked by the starkly intimate touch, but her body welcomed it and her physical need was far stronger than thought could ever be. Her awareness shifted, centering on the slow, burning invasion. She could feel her body stretching, admitting him, and the sensation was both strange and wildly arousing. There was something ancient and primitive about the insistent male demand, and everything in her that was female was compelled to surrender to it. She had never felt so vulnerable, or so aware of the most basic functions of her body.

Staring up at his taut face, she flinched slightly at the twinge of pain when something in her body suddenly resisted his possession. She felt a tremendous pressure, catching at her breath and sending hot shivers rippling through her. Part of her wanted to push him away, to resist the intrusion, yet another part of her welcomed it with desperate longing.

"Easy, love," he murmured in a voice thick with strain. He was braced on his elbows, liquid black eyes holding hers as his body slowly bore down.

It wasn't what she had expected. There was pain, but the burning pressure was worse, and she felt smothered. At the same time, she was acutely aware of the aching emptiness deep inside her, waiting just beyond her body's stubborn barrier. She whimpered as the pressure increased, then cried out when a sharp pain jolted through her.

Astonishingly, the pain was brief, and when the moment of shock passed, she could feel his hard, throbbing flesh sinking into her body. The pressure was still there, but different, all internal now as her narrow passage struggled to accommodate him. She felt more of his weight settle onto her, her aching nipples nestling into the thick hair on his chest, and then he was fully inside her, his loins cradled by hers.

She hadn't realized she was crying until he kissed the tears away and groaned her name softly.

"It's all right," he whispered, kissing her with fierce tenderness as his arms went under her shoulders to hold her even closer. His fingers were tangled in her hair, moving caressingly, and he held himself still inside her. "No more pain, sweetheart, I promise. I'll never hurt you again."

She wondered vaguely why she didn't feel crushed, but somehow her body seemed designed to bear his weight with no discomfort at all. The pressure inside her eased; she could feel her flesh adjust to the foreign presence as it gripped him snugly. The sensation was so intimate it shocked her mind, but her body was heating again, trembling, and her hips rose a little in an instinct older than the caves.

Cyrus groaned, her tiny movement nearly snapping the last thread of his control. She was so tight around him, it was almost painful, her silky heat caressing his flesh in soft pulsations like nothing he'd ever felt before. It was something beyond pleasure, a sweet torment he could hardly bear. He thought the strain of holding himself back for so long would tear him apart, and his body demanded an end to the torture.

He moved as slowly and carefully as his screaming instincts would allow, and the restraint provided a whole new world of sensation for him. It was as if her passage closed up when he withdrew so that every lingering inward thrust felt like the first. The pleasure was so intense he wanted it to last forever, but the quickening inside him refused him the luxury of time.

Julia hadn't believed he could make her feel even more than he had already, but this was so powerful it was almost frightening. She was being carried wildly on a rising wave of pure excitement, her body striving frantically for a release from the spiraling tension. Her legs rose to wrap around him, and she was moving with him instinctively, matching his hastening rhythm.

She didn't know if the thunder she heard was from the storm outside or the one raging in herself. That inner storm was surging and churning, buffeting her senses until she was writhing and whimpering, until she thought it would shatter her into a million pieces. Then, finally, she was hurled over the brink, and nearly screamed as overwhelming pleasure jolted through her. It seemed to go on forever, wave after throbbing wave of it, until she went limp, dazed, and almost boneless. She barely heard Cyrus's hoarse groan, and held him with what strength was left to her as his powerful body shuddered in completion.

Julia didn't know how much time passed before she became aware of her surroundings again. It could have been hours for all she knew. Or cared. A wonderfully cool, rain-damp breeze brushed her skin, and she could hear grumblings of thunder, but the storm seemed to be dying. Cyrus held her securely, his forearms underneath her shoulders and his cheek pressed to hers, his body still covering hers heavily.

The only emotion she was aware of was utter astonishment. If anyone *had* tried to tell her that such things were possible between a man and woman, she wouldn't have believed it. She wasn't entirely certain she believed it even now. And he'd been right in saying she would want him to take her; there had come a point when she had been more than ready for him, when her body had needed his so desperately she hadn't thought of pain or anything else except satisfying her overwhelming desire.

Cyrus lifted his head and kissed her lingeringly, then smiled down at her. "I'm sorry I hurt you, sweetheart," he told her softly.

She touched his face with wondering fingers, and felt her own lips curve in a smile. "It wasn't bad," she murmured. "The pain. And after . . . I didn't know I could feel that way."

"No regrets?" he asked.

Julia shook her head without hesitation. She didn't regret this, couldn't regret it. Something inside her, perhaps all that was left of her pride, quailed at the prospect of becoming his mistress in the condemning eyes of society, but she didn't regret her decision. She thought he would be kind, even though her mind told her not to set her hopes too high; he seemed certain he could protect her from Adrian; and the pleasure she'd found in his arms was something she didn't want to lose.

Shyly, she asked, "Is that—the way it's supposed to be? Every time?"

"Except for the pain. I'll always try to please you, love." He saw a momentary uncertainty cloud her eyes, and asked, "What is it?" very gently.

Julia hesitated, then said with some difficulty, "Adrian

only tried . . . a few times." She looked up at him helplessly, not sure how to phrase the question and dreadfully embarrassed by her shameless hunger to experience more of these astonishing feelings he'd shown her.

Cyrus understood, and was delighted. He brushed a strand of hair away from her face, his fingers stroking her soft skin. "How often will I want you? I have a strong feeling it'll be often, love. Very often." Still smiling, he moved his lower body slightly.

Her eyes widened. She could feel him inside her, feel the slow, swelling renewal of desire, and her body responded with an instant surge of heat. "Oh," she murmured, hoping she didn't look as brazenly pleased about that as she felt.

He chuckled and kissed her. "I seem to want you again now, in fact." Then, his black eyes growing intent, he said, "I'll stop if you're too sore, sweetheart."

Julia was aware of a number of sensations, but none was painful. She moved tentatively beneath him, lifting her hips, and caught her breath as the heat intensified wildly. "I don't feel any pain," she whispered.

"Do you want me to stop?" he asked huskily.

"No." She raised her lips eagerly to meet his, and thought dissolved in a fierce, heated surge of pleasure.

"The storm's over," she said a long time later as she reached for her corset. He was dressing as well, and though she didn't feel uncomfortable or self-conscious with him, she'd been careful not to turn her back to him. He hadn't seen her naked back, and she didn't want him to. Not yet, at least. She didn't want the peaceful, curiously sweet mood between them to be damaged.

But now he eyed her corset with a frown as he was buttoning his shirt, and she went still, waiting.

"We're going to have to talk about that thing," he said matter-of-factly.

Julia didn't move, and her voice was soft. "All my clothes are designed for it, and they don't fit without it. Adrian insisted."

Cyrus looked at her for a long moment, then stepped closer and turned her face up gently as he bent to kiss her. Smiling a little, he said quietly, "If you're determined to be fashionable, I won't protest too much—but aside from the fact you don't need any artificial device to look beautiful, that style of corset is too rigid and too tight to be anything but dangerous. There are less drastic designs available, and I hope you'll agree to choose one of them. Your clothes can be altered."

She drew a short breath, a flicker of relief showing in her eyes. "I—I hate this thing," she said. "I hate the fashion, too, when it's taken to extremes."

"Good, then we agree. Don't tighten your stays any more than necessary for now, and we'll see about making a few changes first thing tomorrow. All right?"

Julia nodded, realizing only then that she'd been unnerved because he had frowned. It had been an automatic reaction, and even though she despised her own timidity, she knew it would take time—as well as a better understanding of Cyrus and trust in his rationality—before she could stop fearing punishment for the slightest mistake or problem. He seemed to realize that too.

"Julia my sweet, never feel you have to do anything just to please me." His low voice was very gentle. "You have an intelligent mind and will of your own, as much a part of you as those beautiful green eyes. If you don't like what I say, tell me so; if you don't agree with anything I ask of you, tell me. Don't be afraid to be honest with me. No matter what you said or did, I could never hurt you."

She almost believed him. Nodding again, she began fastening her stays, eyeing him uncertainly as he stepped away and continued dressing. It would have been very easy for her to believe what he said, but she didn't dare. Not yet. Shattered illusions hurt too much to be risked.

"What time is it?" she asked as he opened his pocket watch and studied it.

"After six. We'd better start back."

Julia was both surprised it was so late and surprised so much had happened in a few short hours. The rain had stopped only minutes before, and since there was no break in the clouds to the west, the sun hadn't made an appearance; it was still like twilight outside, and could have been any hour before nightfall.

Cyrus waited until she put on her blouse so he could fasten the buttons for her, then went to get the horses. While he was gone, she got into her skirt and collected as many hairpins as she could find on the floor. It was a struggle to get her hair into some kind of order without a brush or comb, but she managed to wrestle the heavy mass into a reasonably neat knot and secure it with the pins.

There were, she thought with an unexpected spurt of amusement, definite drawbacks to taking a lover in a partially completed house with few amenities. Not that she minded.

Cyrus had left his coat. She picked it up, cast a last look around at what had been a haven from more than a sudden storm, then blew out the lamp and made her way through the house. Oddly enough, she wasn't worried about the turmoil ahead when Adrian discovered she'd left him. Whatever happened, she had burned her bridges and there was no going back.

Physically, she felt better than she had in a long time. She was relaxed, yet she'd never been so alive, as if all her senses had been heightened by the joining with Cyrus. There was a faint soreness in her thighs, and a tenderness deep in her body, but what she felt was more awareness than discomfort or pain. She was different.

It was a difference she liked. She stood at the top of the steps leading outside and waited for Cyrus, smiling as she smoothed his coat over her arm. The storm had dropped the temperature considerably so that it felt almost like autumn, and the air had a fresh-scrubbed smell. Gray clouds still lay heavily overhead, but they didn't look particularly threatening now, and it was obvious the storm was over.

It was a few minutes before she heard the sounds of the buggy, and she looked up to see Cyrus driving it around the corner of the house. He'd tied his horse to the back of the buggy. Neither animal was wet, so she assumed there was an old barn or some other shelter she hadn't seen. It didn't seem important.

She went down the steps to meet him, and held his coat up as he got out of the buggy. "You forgot this." She had to stand on tiptoe to hold it for him as he shrugged into it, and thought again how big he was.

"Thank you, sweet." He tipped her chin up and kissed her lightly, then helped her into the buggy.

"I blew out the lamp," she told him as she settled into the padded seat, wondering vaguely if he intended to make it a habit to kiss her no matter where they were. She had a peculiar idea that he would.

"Thank you for that too," he said, getting into the buggy beside her and picking up the reins.

Julia didn't speak again until they were on the road to Richmond, and when she did her words were hesitant. "Cyrus? Will I live with you? In your house?"

The question surprised him. He shifted the reins to one hand and slipped his arm around her, drawing her closer to his side. "Of course, love."

She glanced up at him. "Lissa too?"

"When she isn't at school and until she marries, certainly."

"I was . . . just wondering," she murmured.

Cyrus was puzzled for a moment, but then he realized what Julia must have been thinking, and he chuckled. "I'm sorry, my sweet. I've been unclear about future plans, haven't I?"

"I shouldn't have asked—"

"Julia, you have every right to ask. My only excuse for not making myself plain is that I haven't been thinking much beyond the utter delight of being with you."

The glance she sent him this time was startled, and he chuckled again.

"Sweetheart, as soon as you're free of Drummond, we're getting married."

"What?" That was so unexpected she could only stare up at him in total shock. Married? He wanted to marry her? But he wasn't a marrying man, everyone said he wasn't and besides, why would a man like Cyrus Fortune choose a woman like her?

In a chiding tone he said, "I know I'm considered to have few graces and a tendency to do things my own way, but I'm really not such a reprobate as you seem to believe. Ruining your excellent reputation by setting you up as my mistress would be bad enough; taking Lissa into my house as well would be inexcusable."

"I didn't think you—cared about reputations," she managed to say unsteadily.

"Not mine, no. But I know too well how important a woman's reputation is to her. And how cruel society can be when the most rigid rules are broken."

After a long moment she said very quietly, "I won't marry to protect my reputation."

Cyrus glanced at her, and immediately drew the horse to a stop. She looked so numb he couldn't bear it. He gathered her into his arms and merely held her for a moment, then pulled back just a bit and gazed down at her gravely. "Julia, I love you. I want to spend the rest of my life with you."

"You said—"

"I said what I did because I thought the reason would persuade you more than any other. I'm sorry, sweetheart—that was inexcusable." He cupped her face in his hands and held her eyes steadily with his own. "I want to marry you because I love you, not for any other reason."

His eyes weren't fair, she thought, they just weren't fair. "I don't know . . . I can't think," she whispered.

Cyrus kissed her gently, then kept an arm around her as he picked up the reins and urged the horse on again. "I won't force you," he said quietly. "I don't want you to feel you have no other choice. Whatever happens, I'll take care of you and Lissa; you can be sure of that. If marriage—to me or anyone—is repugnant to you after what you've been through, I'll understand. I'll do my best to change your mind, because I believe we belong together, but I'll try not to pressure you."

Her thoughts were awhirl. It had never crossed her

mind that he might want to marry her, and she didn't know how she felt about the idea. It would, of course, make her situation and Lissa's much more acceptable in the eyes of society if she eventually married the man under whose protection she was living. But she wasn't at all certain she wouldn't rather take her chances with society's condemnation than tie herself legally or morally to another man. Even Cyrus.

At least there would be time for her to think; she was grateful for that. Even if Adrian were completely agreeable to a divorce, the process would require months; since he was extremely unlikely to be agreeable, it would take longer. Perhaps by then she'd know what was best for her to do.

Julia felt Cyrus tense at that moment, and when she looked up at him, her thoughts scattered. He was staring straight ahead, his face almost masklike in its stillness, and his black eyes were filled with a radiant intelligence so intense it was almost shocking. She only just stopped herself from crying out, and was vaguely surprised her voice sounded so normal when she said, "What is it?"

"Something's wrong," he murmured.

"What?"

"I don't know. I can't see it." He blinked, then looked down at her, the intensity gone or hidden. But his expression was grim. "We'd better hurry." He slapped the reins against the horse's rump to urge it on.

She felt a cold touch of fear, but bewilderment as well. How did he know something was wrong? It was precisely like the moment he'd slipped the wedding band off her finger, something which should have been impossible. How could he do such a thing?

Cyrus was silent as he drove the buggy rapidly into Richmond. He had to slow down once he reached the city streets; the break in the weather had apparently stirred the populace, and everyone seemed to be taking advantage of cooler temperatures to run errands or simply get a little fresh air.

He swore softly as he threaded the buggy through brisk traffic, using both hands on the reins now to guide the horse. Worried, Julia sat very still beside him, her hands tightly clasped in her lap. She didn't think about what anyone might say after seeing her with Cyrus in an open buggy with his horse trotting behind; all she could think of was the worst possibility that had occurred to her. If Adrian had come home. And Lissa was there.

They reached the elegant neighborhood where both the Drummond house and Cyrus's were situated, and given the direction they'd come from, it was easier for Cyrus to pull the buggy over and stop across the street from the Drummond house. There wasn't so much traffic on this residential street; a couple of carriages tooled along briskly, quite a few people were strolling along the sidewalks, and far down the block a heavily laden ice wagon pulled by two huge, placid draft horses rumbled slowly toward them.

Cyrus got out of the buggy and handed the reins to Julia. "You wait here, sweetheart," he said. "I'll go and get Lissa."

"I should—"

"No." He covered one of her hands with his and squeezed gently. "Wait here, please."

"All right," she murmured, a little pale.

He turned and paused to wait for a carriage to pass. Glancing to one side, he saw Noel standing a few yards away on the sidewalk, and couldn't repress a faint flicker of amusement even though he was feeling unsettled and worried. His friend looked as if he'd been stuffed, mouth slightly ajar and bushy eyebrows climbing his forehead in surprise.

Noel took a step toward the buggy, then stopped, his head swiveling around as a door slammed violently across the street. Cyrus looked quickly as well, and his heart lurched when he saw Lissa running from the house. Her face was paper-white except for the brutally plain, reddened mark on her cheek; her hair was falling down and her white blouse was torn away from one shoulder.

Weeping hysterically, she darted across the street and, though tears must have made her half blind, unerringly found Cyrus and flung herself into his arms.

"He—he set the house on fire!" she sobbed, clinging to Cyrus with terrified strength. "And he has a gun! He said he'd kill Julia and me—"

Immediately, Cyrus swung her up and put her in the buggy beside Julia. As the younger sister collapsed against the elder, he said sharply, "Drive to my house, Julia, now."

The instinct to obey was so strong, she lifted the reins automatically, but then said, "No, not without you—"

"Julia—"

A sudden report from across the street made him swing around again, and he saw Drummond stumble from the house, waving a pistol—which he had accidentally or with mad deliberation fired into the air. His clothing was disheveled, his blond hair standing up wildly, and his eyes were utterly insane. A torrent of filthy words and hideous threats poured from his mouth, shouted rather than spoken, and as he staggered down the sidewalk toward the street, his demented gaze was fixed on Cyrus and the two women in the buggy. He was trying to get the pistol cocked, using both shaking hands in the attempt.

Forever afterward Cyrus remembered that scene as if Mathew Brady himself had made a photograph to freeze the moment in time. Passersby, motionless now, shocked, stared at an armed madman, at the sight of flames licking windows and the open doorway of the elegant house behind him.

Cyrus turned his head swiftly, his eyes locating the plodding ice wagon less than fifty yards away. He looked back at Drummond just as the man stumbled into the street and lifted the muzzle of the pistol with a hoarse, triumphant cry.

At the last moment he must have heard the thunder of runaway horses and a massive wagon bearing down on him. But by then it was too late.

Nine

♥

"No one can determine what caused the horses to bolt," Noel said softly. "I can't understand it. I know those animals; both nearly twenty years old and completely without vices, and they've been plodding up and down these streets for a decade without shying at anything."

Cyrus was standing by the fireplace in his study, a forearm resting on the mantel as he gazed down at the cold hearth. He was expressionless, his eyes unreadable. He didn't look up, or respond to his friend's low words.

Noel tried again, unable to forget the quick, curiously intense sidelong glance he had seen his friend throw the oncoming ice wagon—just before the placid horses had inexplicably bolted. "Did you hear what the doc said? Virtually every bone in Drummond's body was broken."

"Don't expect me to grieve for him," Cyrus said.

Sighing, Noel decided some questions couldn't be put into words simply because they weren't meant to be asked. "There won't be anything left of the Drummond house," he offered. "We're lucky the storm hit today, or the whole neighborhood would have gone up in flames."

"I know. At least Drummond's servants managed to get out, and no one else was hurt."

Perfectly aware that he should leave, since it was nearly midnight, Noel remained because he was determined to get at least a few answers. "How's Lissa?" he asked.

"The doctor says she'll be all right," Cyrus replied. "Shock and bruises, mostly. We put her to bed about an hour ago, and Julia's been sitting with her."

"How is Julia?"

Cyrus half turned to face his friend, sliding his hands into his pockets and leaning back against the mantel. A slight smile curved his mouth. "Did anybody ever tell you you're a damned nosy bastard, Noel?"

"You've told me frequently," his friend replied without offense. "But that was a perfectly proper question."

"I know. It's the ones I can see trembling on your lips I'm leery of."

A short bark of a laugh escaped Noel. "Get your answers ready. In the meantime, how *is* Julia?"

"Numb. In control. Withdrawn. Shall I go on?"

"She was leaving him, wasn't she?"

"Don't cross the line, Noel," Cyrus warned quietly.

Noel leaned forward in his chair, staring at Cyrus. "I think our friendship can bear it. I hope so, anyway. Besides, it's a fairly obvious conclusion, and one I'm not alone in reaching. Cy, people are already talking."

"Do you think I give a damn?"

"On your own account, no. But what about Julia? At least two families offered to take her and Lissa in, and you refused both of them. As if you had a right to. A lot of people heard that, and took note. So the eyes of the curious are gawking at a very recent widow and her young sister staying with a bachelor to whom they are not related—who has a reputation for fleeting affairs. By morning every inquisitive soul in the city is going to be chewing on that little tidbit. Drummond's obvious insanity might make some people hesitate to brand Julia with a scarlet A, but it's only a matter of time."

"I'm going to marry her," Cyrus said quietly.

Though those words from his friend would have utterly confounded Noel weeks before, he was curiously unsurprised to hear them now. He didn't even wonder if the motive was to protect Julia's reputation; he knew Cyrus too well to believe such nonsense. "Well, it'll eventually give the gossip a new direction," he said wryly.

"I mean immediately. Next week at the latest. If I can persuade Julia, that is."

That was a surprise. "For God's sake, Cy, her husband isn't even in the ground yet!"

Cyrus hesitated, studying his friend, then said, "Noel, Drummond didn't just *go* insane—he's been insane for a long time. Years, at least. He hid it well, except in private. He didn't hide it from her. No one who knew what Julia's gone through could ever condemn her for not mourning him."

"You mean . . . he abused her?"

Again Cyrus hesitated. He knew Julia would be appalled if the hell of her marriage became a topic for speculation in the neighborhood. But he also knew too well the social set to which they belonged. Some part of the story would have to be known if Julia was to escape censure for a second marriage hard on the heels of her husband's funeral.

"Cy?"

Obeying one of the impulses that seemed to determine so many of his actions these days, Cyrus said, "He was brutal. In ways I hope you can't even imagine. If she weren't an incredibly strong woman, she'd have gone mad herself. As it is, she's scarred both in body and mind, and terribly vulnerable right now."

Noel's expression was unusually still as he looked at his friend, and his voice was very quiet. "I see."

"I could take her away somewhere," Cyrus said broodingly. "Start fresh in another city, where no one has to know she was married before. But her life's already been disrupted so much. She needs a sense of security, and I believe I can give her that here. In time. But if the people she knows in Richmond treat her badly—"

"You're right in thinking that if the truth were known, there wouldn't be many who'd condemn her for marrying again right away. The question is, how do you let the truth out without making Julia feel worse than she does about it."

Another impulse prompted Cyrus to say, "Noel, would you ask Felice to call on Julia in a day or so?"

"Of course," Noel replied slowly, his eyes very intent on Cyrus. "But what's on your mind? And why Felice?"

"I'm not quite sure what's on my mind." He thought about it for a moment. "I believe Julia needs to know all marriages aren't like hers was, and she'll be sure of that only if another woman tells her. She needs to talk to another woman, someone she can feel comfortable confiding in. Felice would be perfect. She has a happy marriage, she wouldn't condemn Julia, and her support would go a long way in influencing the other women in the neighborhood to accept Julia's remarriage without censure."

Noel looked at him for a long moment, then said, "Cy, you are uncanny."

"What are you talking about?"

Leaning back in his chair, Noel shook his head

slightly. "You knew Felice was a widow when I married her?"

"Yes. I remember when she moved to Richmond ten years ago. What's your point?"

Softly, Noel said, "Her first husband . . . she'll carry the scars he gave her to her grave."

Cyrus felt a shock. "I had no idea," he murmured.

"I think you did. Somewhere inside, I think you knew Felice would be the ideal woman to talk to Julia, even though I've never told you what she suffered."

Cyrus didn't say anything immediately, just looked at Noel steadily. "I don't know. Perhaps," he said finally. Then he shrugged. "My peculiar whims and notions don't interest me at the moment. I'm worried about Julia. Will it upset Felice too much to talk to her?"

Noel got to his feet. "No, I don't think so. And she'll want to help, you know that." He studied his friend for a moment, then obeyed an impulse of his own to say, "Something else is worrying you, though. What is it?"

He hadn't meant to say anything, but Cyrus had a feeling he might need help in finding the answers he needed and there was no one he trusted more than Noel. "Drummond returned home hours before he should have. Lissa said he was already raving when he came in the door, that he *knew* Julia was leaving him—and coming to me. There was no way he could have known—unless someone told him. And I have no idea who it was."

Julia rested her head on the lip of the tub, feeling the warm water ease her tension. Warm water, Mrs. Stork had said in her motherly way, because she'd feel chilled later if she didn't now; shock did that to people.

Cyrus's housekeeper had been wonderful, helping Julia get Lissa into bed and even persuading the shivering girl to drink enough hot soup to "warm her from the inside." Julia had intended to remain by Lissa's bed, but once her sister had fallen asleep, Mrs. Stork had returned with a smiling young housemaid and had urged Julia to take care of herself now, because Sarah would stay by the bed in case Miss Lissa needed anything.

Julia had protested. It was late, there was no need for Sarah to be kept from her own bed. But Sarah had spoken up shyly to say she'd be pleased to stay, and Mrs. Stork had said there was a bath ready for Julia and a tray would be sent up later. Not accustomed to being watched over by anyone—Adrian's servants were efficient but remote—Julia had allowed herself to be persuaded.

She hadn't had the time to feel a sense of strangeness in being in this house, and matter-of-fact acceptance of the servants turned what should have been an awkward situation into a relatively normal one. From the moment Cyrus had brought them there, she and Lissa had been treated as if they belonged. Not by a single word or glance had anyone betrayed surprise, curiosity, or censure.

Julia didn't know what Cyrus had said to Mrs. Stork, but he must have told her something, because the waiting bath was in the master suite. After everything that had happened that day, Julia had felt nothing more than a twinge of embarrassment when she realized she'd been taken to his rooms. She had been provided with a nightgown—heaven knew where it had come from—and Mrs. Stork had asked her to leave her things out in the dressing room so they could be cleaned for the next day.

It had hit Julia only then. Everything in the world she

could have called her own was nothing but a pile of ashes now. She tried to feel something about that, but was aware of nothing except weariness.

Now, lying in the warm, softly scented bathwater, she tried again to feel something. Not grief, no, but some emotion. A sense of relief, of freedom. Worry about the future. She was a widow now. Today she had seen her husband violently killed, had seen his mangled body lying in the street. She had seen the house she had lived in for two years blazing. She had taken a lover.

A soft knock at the closed door of the bathroom made her turn her head and regard the barrier a little blankly, then she heard Cyrus's voice.

"Julia? May I come in?"

She was vaguely surprised he'd asked. That he had knocked. Intimacy with a man meant a loss of privacy, didn't it? "Of course," she responded. What else could she say? This was his house.

He came in and knelt on the mat by the tub, his black eyes searching her face intently. As if he had to touch her, his hand rose to gently stroke her cheek. "How do you feel, my sweet?"

"I don't feel anything." She forced herself to think. "The servants? The house?" She meant Adrian's, of course, and Cyrus understood.

"The servants are fine, they got out in time. They've been given rooms here until we can get everything sorted out. I'm afraid the house was gutted." His voice was quiet.

"I wonder why he burned it," she murmured almost to herself. "The house was his pride."

Cyrus was on the point of saying a madman could hardly be rational about anything, but something stopped him. Julia knew Drummond's sickness better

than anyone, and if she found the arson surprising . . . Cyrus had a feeling that was important,
but he didn't know why. And he didn't want to probe the
matter now with Julia. She was too controlled, too
withdrawn; he didn't like her pallor or the darkened
stillness of her eyes.

"Did you talk to the police?" she asked idly in the
same soft, remote voice.

"Yes." He had dealt with all the official questions and
had talked to the firemen at the Drummond house,
preferring to spare Julia as much as possible. He was
afraid, however, that the worst was yet to come. The
mayor of Richmond had apparently gone berserk, setting
his house afire and then rushing into the streets with a
gun, shouting obscenities until an ice wagon had run him
down; the newspapers were going to have a field day.

Cyrus leaned over and kissed her briefly, wishing he
could protect her from the curious world outside this
house. "Mrs. Stork sent up a tray for us," he said. "You
need to eat something, love."

Julia wasn't hungry, but she didn't argue with him.
"All right."

He smiled. "Want me to wash your back for you?"

"No." She knew the answer was too quick, too sharp,
and her eyes slid away from him nervously. "Thank you,
but it isn't necessary."

He was silent for a moment, then said, "Today at the
house you were careful not to turn your back to me until
your blouse was on. You don't want me to see, do you?"

She had to meet his gaze again, drawn by the understanding in his incredible voice. "It's ugly," she whispered.

Cyrus made a soft sound, as if he were in pain, and

said, "Sweetheart, nothing about you could ever be ugly to me. I have to see, you know that."

"Not now." She knew her eyes were pleading. "I can't—please, not now."

"All right." He stroked her cheek for a moment, then rose to his feet. "I'll wait for you in the bedroom."

Julia nodded, and remained in the tub for a few moments after he'd gone out and shut the door behind him. What she wanted more than anything was to close her eyes and sleep, to forget for a few hours.

She got out of the tub finally, pulling the plug to let the water drain, and dried her body with one of the warmed towels provided for her. The nightgown she pulled over her head was fashioned of cambric and trimmed in pale satin ribbons, a lovely, expensive garment. It didn't belong to one of the maids, she knew. The nightgown provided for Lissa had also been a fine one, and Julia couldn't help wondering . . .

She pushed the speculation out of her mind, too tired to try to decide if the nightgown and the acceptance of the servants was merely due to past experience of women staying here. There was a hairbrush and comb near the basin; Mrs. Stork had said they were for her use. Julia took her hair down and brushed it, but didn't attempt to braid it for the night.

She went out into the bedroom, finding that a small, linen-covered table had been set near the window with a light meal. She still wasn't hungry, but when Cyrus came to take her hand and lead her to the table she didn't protest. He had taken off his coat, tie, and vest and seemed relaxed, but she knew he was watching her closely. She wondered vaguely if he expected hysterics, and almost wished she could have them; she thought anything would be better than the numb lack of feeling that encased her.

He talked to her while they both ate, though afterward Julia was never able to remember what he said. All she recalled was the inexpressibly soothing sound of his voice, the peculiar magic of it seeming to surround her with a sense of peace and contentment. She ate to please him, tasting nothing.

When they were finished, he piled the dishes on the tray and set it outside in the hall. When he returned to her, he lifted her up from her chair, cradling her body easily in his powerful arms, and carried her to the big bed. He settled her there, drawing the covers up over her because the room was cool, then sat beside her on the bed and looked down at her gravely.

"I want very much to stay with you tonight, love," he said in a gentle tone. "Hold you. May I?"

Julia was surprised, first, that he asked. This was his house, his room, his bed, and he had every right to be there, after all. Then she became aware of a crack in her numb cocoon as warm gratitude rushed in. Whether he was sensitive to the moral awkwardness of her presence in his bed on her first night of widowhood or was merely concerned about her state of mind, at least he was kind enough to ask her preferences.

Without thought she reached out a hand to him. "Please."

He carried her hand briefly to his lips, then rose and began undressing.

She lay still and watched him. Some part of her mind considered the idea that this should have seemed wrong. Every proper feeling should have been outraged, she thought. Women didn't sleep in the arms of their lovers on the very night they were widowed, it just wasn't done. It wasn't decent. She would be expected to mourn Adrian for at least a year; everyone she knew would be extremely disapproving if she didn't. And they'd be utterly shocked she was even in Cyrus's house—no less his bed.

Her upbringing insisted she conform to certain standards of behavior and obey society's rules.

But being with Cyrus, even tonight, didn't seem wrong. Every instinct told her she belonged with him. If she'd been offered another choice, she wouldn't have wanted to exercise it. How could such a strong certainty be wrong? How could she pretend to mourn a husband who had treated her as Adrian had, or feel any need to show respect for his memory? How could she bring herself even to simulate grief for the end of a marriage that had been nothing but hell?

Julia knew she couldn't do it. She thought fleetingly of the probable consequences, but when Cyrus slipped into bed beside her she dismissed them from her mind. He was naked, which somehow didn't surprise her; she couldn't imagine him in a nightshirt, and felt her lips twitch of their own volition at the very idea.

He gathered her into his arms, and her body instinctively molded itself pliantly to the hardness of his. Her head was pillowed on his shoulder, one of her hands rested on his broad chest, and she felt mildly surprised she could be so comfortable. He had left the bedside lamp burning, and she blinked with the same detached surprise as she watched her fingers toying with his silky black chest hair.

"I love you, sweetheart," Cyrus murmured, pressing a gentle kiss to her forehead.

She didn't respond, except to sigh softly and relax completely in his arms. It had been a long time since she'd been able to give herself up totally to sleep; Adrian had found more than one rude or violent way of waking her, and she'd never been able to feel safe enough to sleep peacefully. But tonight she did. She slept so deeply and dreamlessly, she never moved all night.

It was nearly noon the next day when Julia woke, alone in the big bed. She lay drowsily for a while, dimly puzzled, then sat up slowly as she realized where she was. In Cyrus's house. In Cyrus's bed. The clothing she'd removed last night lay neatly over a chair near the bed, obviously clean and pressed. Only the soft ticking of a clock on the wall disturbed the silence.

Julia looked at the clock for a moment, then threw back the covers and slid from the bed. As she got dressed and put her hair up, she gradually became aware she wasn't numb anymore. The feelings were somewhat distant, hazy almost, but they were there. A lingering shock over the violent suddenness of Adrian's death; a sense of loss for her belongings gone in the fire; worry about Lissa; and worry about the future.

Choosing to deal with one matter at a time, she focused her attention on her sister. It wasn't until she left the bedroom that she realized she didn't know her way around the big house, but Lissa's voice made the matter academic.

"Oh, good, you're up. Cyrus said you were, but I couldn't figure out how he knew since he's just come back." Lissa was a little pale as she came down the hall toward her sister, and the left side of her face was faintly discolored from the bruise Adrian had given her, but she was smiling.

"Are you all right?" Julia asked.

Lissa nodded reassuringly. "I'm fine. I still shake when I remember—but I try not to think about it. You? Cyrus said you slept well."

Julia's first impulse was to rebuke Lissa for so casually using Cyrus's given name, but even as the thought occurred she chided herself wryly. *We're in his house, and I slept in his bed! It's a little late to worry about propriety.* Still, she glanced at her sister a bit uncomfortably as they began walking toward the stairs together. "I'm . . . much better. Lissa, I know what you must think about—about—"

"About you and Cyrus?" Lissa's smile widened as she linked her arm with her sister's. "I think it's wonderful."

Uncertain if she should feel amused or appalled by Lissa's acceptance of the situation, Julia said, "For heaven's sake, you weren't raised to think anything of the kind. I hope you know how improper the entire situation is."

"Why, because people will say so?" Lissa's voice was calm. "Julia, people said you had a perfect marriage, and they were certainly wrong about that. Besides, you're going to marry Cyrus so it's not as if you're living in sin."

Julia stopped at the head of the curving staircase, staring at her sister. "Did he tell you that?"

"Well, he said he'd asked you, and he meant to persuade you. I don't know why on earth you'd say no."

Somewhat weakly, Julia said, "I've been widowed less than twenty-four hours." To her own shock, it was the best reason she could think of.

Lissa smiled a little, but her eyes were grave. "Julia, I saw what Adrian was yesterday. I *saw* it. I can't even begin to imagine what you went through these last two years, but I can guess the idea of another marriage— especially so soon—scares you to death."

Julia knew that was true; tangled with her painful awareness of the scandalous situation was a frightened reluctance even to think about binding herself legally to another man. Haltingly, she said, "Cyrus has been very kind. And I know I should be grateful he wants to marry me, but—"

"Grateful?" Lissa looked bewildered. "You talk as if he's being noble in asking you! Why? Because you've—what's that prim phrase I heard old Mrs. Hunt use?—Oh, yes, just because you've anticipated the wedding night? Or is it because you were leaving Adrian anyway? Julia, for heaven's sake, Cyrus loves you, don't you know that?"

"You don't understand," Julia mumbled, too dismayed by Lissa's extremely frank comments to pay much attention to the last confident statement. She wasn't much surprised at Lissa's muted cheerfulness. Her sister had always been able to adjust quickly to even the most disturbing changes in her life. But this complete acceptance of Cyrus, and Lissa's cool disregard of all the proprieties, was definitely upsetting.

Oddly, Lissa laughed, and took her sister's arm again as they started down the stairs. "I think you're the one who doesn't understand, Julia. But Cyrus should be able to make things clear to you. I like him so much. "

Julia sent her a puzzled glance, but before she could say anything Lissa was going on.

"His servants are wonderful, aren't they? Sarah went to one of the shops last night to get those nightgowns for us—I think Cyrus knows the shopkeeper, because he opened up after hours just so Sarah could get the nightgowns—and she and another of the girls got a complete list from me this morning before they went out shopping for us. Cyrus didn't think you'd feel much like going out, so he asked me to tell them what colors you preferred so they could get what we needed for now—"

"Wait." They had reached the bottom of the stairs, and Julia kept a hand on the newel post as she stood looking at her sister. She felt a little dizzy. "He's buying clothes for us?"

Lissa looked as if she'd had a feeling this wasn't going to be easy, but her voice was matter-of-fact. "Our clothes went up in smoke, remember?"

"But he shouldn't. It isn't right."

"Mrs. Stanton thinks it is," Lissa said firmly.

Julia felt even more dizzy. "Felice Stanton? I barely know her. How can you be privy to what she thinks?"

"She called to see you this morning, and I talked to her." Lissa eyed her sister for a moment, then said, "Her husband is Cyrus's best friend. She said she was delighted he'd finally found a woman he could love, and that he'd make you a wonderful husband. Reformed rakes always do, she said. And she agreed with me that after Adrian was so cruel to you, you certainly deserve a wonderful man like Cyrus."

"Oh, my Lord," Julia murmured, almost wishing she was still numb. This turn of events was utterly unnerving.

Lissa looked a little guilty. "Well, perhaps I shouldn't have been quite so talkative, but she was nice. And she didn't think there was anything at all bad or improper in us being here. She said that sometimes rules had to be broken, because under some circumstances they were idiotic. After all, nobody could doubt you'd been living with a lunatic, not after what Adrian did yesterday. So why should you wear black and refuse to marry anyone else for at least a year? It doesn't make sense."

"Lissa, are you busy spiking my guns?" Cyrus asked calmly as he crossed the entrance hall toward them.

She turned to him with a questioning lift to her brows. "I'm not perfectly sure what that means," she confessed naïvely.

His gaze went to Julia's face, then returned to Lissa's. "It means a man likes to do his own proposing," he told her in a wry tone. Before she could do more than look guilty, he added, "The parlor's filled with packages; don't you think you should go sort through them while I take Julia to the luncheon waiting for her?"

"I suppose I'd better," Lissa murmured.

As Lissa walked to the parlor, Cyrus tipped Julia's chin up and kissed her, very slowly and thoroughly. When he finally raised his head, she felt breathless and dizzy.

"Good morning, love," he whispered.

Julia cast about among her scattered thoughts and chose one at random. "I have to flee the country," she said.

Undisturbed and apparently unsurprised by the statement, Cyrus took her arm and led her through the house to a small breakfast parlor near the rear. "Where would you like to flee to?" he asked politely. "I'm partial to San Francisco, but since that's U.S. territory, I suppose you'd rather go somewhere else. London is nice. Or Paris." He seated her at a cozy table, sat down on her right, and poured two cups of coffee from a silver pot.

Julia had the strangest impulse to laugh, and chided herself with silent severity. This was not a laughing matter. She felt absolutely appalled that Lissa had talked so freely to Felice Stanton—even if the older woman did seem kind and wasn't known as a gossip.

She took a sip of coffee, then looked at Cyrus with wondering eyes. "You talk as if nothing's happened."

"Nothing more terrible than shooting a rabid dog has happened," Cyrus said with utter calm. "The poor brute's out of his misery, and everyone around him is out of danger."

"I should feel that way, shouldn't I?"

"Why?" Cyrus took one of her hands and held it, his black eyes serious as they rested on her face. "Did you have one moment's peace or pleasure in your marriage?"

Julia didn't have to think; she shook her head slowly.

"Did Drummond ever show you even the barest hint of any sort of kindness, or do anything to make you sorry he's dead now?"

Again she shook her head.

"Then why should you feel anything except relief? Julia, if you plan to live your life as others think you should, you'll never be happy. Did it make your situation any easier to pretend your marriage was a successful one?"

"No," she murmured.

"Then don't pretend now. He was a brutal, demented bastard, and the only decent thing he ever did was to die."

She looked at Cyrus for a long moment and, slowly, a heavy weight lifted from her shoulders. What did the opinions of others matter? She valued Lissa's opinion and, she realized, she valued his. What anyone else thought didn't seem very important any longer.

"Would you really flee to Paris with me?" She smiled.

"Just say the word, and I'll book passage on the next ship, love." He was smiling as well, his velvety eyes warm.

Julia was tempted. At the very least, Adrian's death would be a nine-day wonder, with curiosity and speculation running rampant; removing herself, for a while at least, would be the most painless solution. But as she looked at Cyrus, she realized she didn't want to run and hide—because of him. If she ran, it would be as good as proclaiming she was ashamed of her relationship with him because there was something wrong with it, and she couldn't feel that way no matter her upbringing.

Drawing a deep breath, her fingers tightening in his without her knowledge, she said, "Perhaps we can see Paris someday. I'd like that. But for now . . ."

He lifted her hand and kissed it. "Good. Spring is the best time to travel anyway. Besides, we have a house going up outside the city, and you're going to be very busy in the next few weeks choosing paint, wallpaper, and rugs, among other things."

"I am? But—" She broke off, staring at him.

He looked at her gravely for a moment, then said quietly, "I know you haven't had time to think, sweetheart, and I know I said I wouldn't press you. But I've never felt more strongly about anything in my life. We belong together. Take a chance on me, please. Marry me."

"You don't know what you're asking," she whispered.

"Yes, I do. I know the idea of another marriage terrifies you. I know you've been hurt so much you can't imagine not being hurt again. I know you dare not trust me, even though you want to. And I know I'm asking you to have more courage than you think you possess."

He did understand. She felt she was lost somewhere in those intense, beautiful black eyes, caught and held by a gentle grip she didn't want to fight. Everything in her, every thought, instinct, and muted emotion felt the pull of him so strongly, it was actually painful to resist. A dull ache swelled inside her, growing moment by moment as she remembered the astonishing pleasure she'd found in his arms, his passion and gentleness, his care of her.

"I love you, Julia. Will you marry me?"

"Yes," she said breathily, and the dull ache inside her immediately faded, replaced by a growing warmth. She was still frightened, still acutely aware of the risk she was taking, but her deep and certain understanding that she already belonged to him was too powerful to fight or deny.

"Thank you," Cyrus said huskily, kissing her hand again. "You won't regret it, I swear."

A little bemused, she shook her head. "You have the most unfair eyes," she murmured.

He grinned suddenly, the first time she'd ever seen him do so, and his lean, handsome face revealed such delight, she couldn't help smiling back at him.

"Tate always said I was sired by a warlock; maybe he was right. I've known for weeks it would take some kind of magic to win you, love." He laughed softly, then released her hand and said, "If you don't eat, Mrs. Stork will scold both of us."

Mildly surprised, Julia looked at her steaming coffee and the covered dishes that were no doubt still warm. It had been another of those interludes that had seemed to stop time, she realized, as if everything around them had waited patiently for Cyrus and her to come to an understanding. She thought it was peculiar. Very peculiar.

She unfolded her napkin across her lap and sent him a slightly shy look. "I'm not really hungry."

"You have to eat to keep up your strength," he said solemnly, a gentle laugh in his eyes. "You're going to need it."

"Why?" she asked warily.

"Because," he said, sitting back and lifting his coffee cup in a toast, "I'm about to try to persuade you to marry me next week."

All during the remainder of the day Julia had the strangest feeling she was being gently but inexorably carried along by forces determined to shape her life. Cyrus was only the beginning, very reasonably arguing against her scruples until her own arguments seemed weak and uncertain. He never once scoffed at her principles or belittled them in any way, he merely maintained that since her marriage had been a travesty and her husband a brutal lunatic, she owed no respect or consideration to either.

It was difficult for her to disagree on those grounds, but she tried because she was frightened. Society's condemnation was only a small worry, and one she had already decided wasn't as important as she'd believed; marriage itself was what terrified her, and though she'd agreed to marry him, she badly needed time to get used to the idea. He knew that, she thought, but remained gently insistent she marry him as soon as possible. He didn't demand an immediate answer, but at various times all day he continued to try to persuade her.

She was kept too busy to pay much attention to the frequent rattle of the door knocker as the butler turned away newspapermen and other curious visitors throughout the day. Packages continued to arrive full of beautiful clothing for her and Lissa. No matter how strongly she protested to Cyrus that he shouldn't be buying clothing for them, he just laughed and kissed her.

He kissed her often. He touched her a great deal as well, touches that were casual and yet curiously intimate in their manner. He couldn't seem to be near her without taking her hand, brushing a strand of hair away from her face, or putting an arm around her—and quite clearly didn't care who happened to be present to witness his actions.

Julia was a little stiff at first, but it didn't last long. She couldn't help feeling warmed by his affection and tentatively reassured by it. She even stopped blushing whenever Lissa, Mr. or Mrs. Stork, or one of the other servants happened to observe a kiss or embrace.

She couldn't quite bring herself to feel the unshadowed enjoyment Lissa obviously found in trying on new clothes, but she didn't try to curb her sister's cheerfulness. She tried on a few things herself when Cyrus went out after their late lunch, choosing that particular moment only because Lissa insisted she should and because Julia wanted to spend a little time alone with her sister in her—and Cyrus's—bedroom so they could talk.

The master suite itself was a little changed since morning, a fact that surprised Julia and gave her food for thought. She didn't know the extent of Cyrus's participation in making the arrangements, but a second wardrobe had been brought into the bedroom for her clothing, and a dressing table complete with satin-cushioned boudoir chair now occupied a prominent place in the dressing room. There was also a set of silver-backed brushes obviously for her, as well as a selection of perfumes and bath salts. Fresh flowers in delicate crystal vases graced the table by the window and her dressing table.

Julia realized only then that Cyrus had been unobtrusively busy all day making her transition into his home as smooth and comfortable as possible for her. He had made certain she wasn't disturbed by the shocked and curious world outside the house, and had kept her attention occupied with her sister and the activities of sorting through boxes and packages while he had dealt with other practical matters. She thought he had talked to the police again, as well as Adrian's—and his—attorney, but she wasn't sure.

In any case, it was obvious he had assumed responsibility for her and Lissa's welfare as well as making certain both felt entirely comfortable and welcome in his home.

"Oh, Julia, look at this! Isn't it beautiful?" Lissa had opened one of the boxes on the bed, and held up a stunning emerald green evening gown.

"Lovely," Julia agreed, hanging in the wardrobe the golden gown she'd just taken off. She was careful not to turn her back to Lissa except when buttons had to be fastened, and even then took pains to show as little of herself as possible; the scars were faint, she knew, especially on her upper back, but she didn't want Lissa to notice them.

"Sarah and Cathy have wonderful taste," Lissa said, holding the gown up to herself as she stood before the dressing mirror in the corner and studied the effect. "And since Cathy's a redhead like us, she knows what colors just won't do."

"Nothing black," Julia said almost to herself, suddenly realizing this as she gazed at the colorful garments hanging in the wardrobe and tumbled on the bed.

Lissa turned from the mirror, her expression more serious than it had been all afternoon. "I told Cyrus I wouldn't wear black for Adrian, and he said he didn't want to see you do so either. So I told the girls not to buy anything black, not even a skirt."

Julia sat down on the edge of the bed and looked at her

sister gravely. "Something else for people to talk about," she murmured.

After a moment Lissa hung the emerald gown in the wardrobe and then returned to sit on the bed across from her sister. Her pretty young face was still sober. "Is that so important, Julia? I mean, I know it's supposed to be, but is it? All those people who look and talk don't know anything. They can't. They didn't live with Adrian. They didn't see the life bleeding out of you because of him. They didn't see you stay in bed for a whole day, so white and silent."

"Lissa—"

"You think I haven't noticed, since we've been in here, that you don't want me to see your back? I—" Tears glittered in Lissa's eyes, and her voice broke for a moment with an anguished sound. Then she was going on fiercely, "I hate myself for not realizing, for being fooled by him just like everyone else was! He hurt you so badly, and I didn't know. You should have told me, Julia—you must have been terrified, and hurt so often— you should have told me—"

Julia quickly went around the bed and sat down beside her weeping sister, putting her arms around Lissa gently. "I didn't want you to know, honey," she soothed. "There was nothing you could have done. It's all right."

"No, it isn't," Lissa said huskily, dashing a hand across her eyes as she tried to get control of herself. "I should have known, but I was blind and I didn't see what he was."

"No one saw," Julia murmured.

"Except you." Lissa looked at her, the wet green eyes filled with an implacable loathing. "I'm glad he's dead. I hope he suffered the way he made you suffer."

"Lissa—"

"I mean it, Julia. I won't even pretend to grieve for him. I won't wear black, I won't go to his funeral, and if anyone offers their sympathies to me, I'll tell them I hope he's burning in hell!"

Ten

♥

It occurred to Julia dimly as she looked into her sister's hate-filled eyes that she herself hadn't been able to release the wild anger and bitter loathing trapped inside her because she hadn't even allowed herself to feel those emotions. Adrian had made her so aware of shame and humiliation, had branded them so deeply into her soul, she hadn't been able to blame him for the pain he had inflicted on her.

It was the worst thing he had done to her, and she realized it only then.

She drew a slow, deep breath, and her voice was both surprised and softly angry when she said, "You're right, Lissa. I've done nothing wrong. It was he. He was an animal; that's still the truth even though he's dead. I hate him for what he did to me, and I won't lie about that. I won't pretend. Not for one more moment."

Lissa hugged her tightly. "And don't let it be a secret you're afraid to talk about. If nobody talks about such horrible things, how will decent people ever know that men like Adrian exist and have to be stopped?" She pulled back a little and stared at her sister intently.

Julia felt a twinge of mortification at the idea of her bedroom door being flung open to the public—or any small part of it—but fought the emotion as hard as she could. "I did nothing wrong," she whispered vehemently, struggling to convince herself. "I have nothing to be ashamed of."

"Absolutely nothing," Lissa agreed flatly. "Julia, if the people we know want to go on being blind to uncomfortable truths, let them. But don't help them. Don't make it easy for them to cling to their stupid, sacrosanct rules as if pain and suffering don't matter as long as they're kept behind closed doors."

Somewhat to her surprise, Julia heard a shaken laugh escape her. "I had no idea you could be so articulate."

Lissa looked startled, then rather proud. "Neither did I. But ever since we talked—gosh, was it only yesterday?—about how the laws are so hideously unfair to women, I've been thinking about it. Something has to be done!"

"Maybe you'll be the one to do it," Julia murmured, realizing she had underestimated her sister's intelligence. "But for now, why don't you finish trying on your things while I put the rest of mine away?"

"All right." Lissa got up, then paused and looked almost pleadingly down at her. "Cyrus loves you, Julia, and that's as real as anything you can touch. He's . . . he's a very special man, I think. He could make you so happy. Don't run from the life he could give you because you don't think you deserve it."

Julia felt a shock, and for an instant her thoughts whirled in confusion. Was that part of her reluctance to trust Cyrus? Not because she had any real suspicion he was somehow deceiving her in his kindness now, but because something deep inside her stubbornly insisted happiness wasn't meant for her? Had Adrian twisted her emotions so badly he had convinced her she deserved to be hurt and disappointed no matter what?

She got up from the bed slowly, looking at her unexpectedly wise sister with a little smile she could feel inside her, tentative but, for the first time, hopeful. "No, I won't do that," she promised.

Lissa smiled at her, then went quietly from the bedroom.

Julia spent a few minutes putting clothing, hats, and shoes away—the maids had been more than thorough in getting everything she might need—and thought about herself and her emotions more carefully than she had in a very long time.

She was on the point of putting her plain dark skirt and white blouse back on when she paused, still thinking. After a moment she left the skirt and blouse lying over a chair and went to the wardrobe. She fingered several garments, finally drawing out an afternoon dress of olive green. It was elegant in design and very simple, but it was a long way from what anyone would consider a mourning dress. Julia put it on.

It fastened up the front of the bodice, and as she dealt with the tiny hooks and eyes, she couldn't help remembering what Sarah had said when she and Cathy had returned to the house weighted down by even more boxes a couple of hours earlier. Mr. Cyrus, she'd giggled with a slight blush, had been quite adamant about corsets, and alarmingly frank in his detailed description of what he did not want them to buy.

Conscious of the relatively comfortable garment beneath her dress now, Julia had to smile. The corset in no way exaggerated her shape, nor did it constrict her waist painfully, make it impossible for her to breathe normally, or turn every movement into a torture. Julia was delighted with it.

The dress in place, she studied her reflection for a moment and nodded to herself. Like virtually everything else she had tried on, it fit perfectly. She thought both the color and simple, elegant design suited her, and she hoped she looked attractive. Not for fashion's sake, but for Cyrus.

She left the bedroom, planning to check on Lissa, but stopped in the hall as Stork approached her.

"Mrs. Stanton has called to see you, Miss Julia," he said in his quiet, unexpressive voice. "She's waiting in the blue parlor."

Julia realized suddenly that, although he'd been turning away other callers all day, the butler had twice admitted Mrs. Stanton. Because of the woman's insistence, she wondered, or because Cyrus had left those instructions? Whatever the reason, it seemed clear she had to speak to this visitor.

"Thank you, Stork," she murmured, changing her direction to move toward the stairs.

"Miss Julia?"

She paused and looked back at him. "Yes?" she asked, realizing something else: she had not been called Mrs. Drummond since entering this house. Cyrus's doing?

The elderly man hesitated, some fleeting emotion crossing his stern features, then said precisely, "It's not my place to speak, Miss Julia, but I've served this house more than forty years and I feel I know Mr. Cyrus as well as anyone does."

"You went west with him, didn't you?" Julia said, remembering what she'd heard.

"Yes, Miss." Stork hesitated again, then said, "The tales told about him, they're wrong."

Considering the circumstances, Julia hardly wasted more than a fleeting thought on the impropriety of discussing Cyrus with his butler. "You mean his women?" she asked bluntly.

Stork nodded, betraying no embarrassment. "People saw, but they didn't understand. He has a—a gift for helping others. When there's trouble in their lives, unhappiness because of some problem they are unable to solve alone. Mr. Cyrus always seems to know that, and tries to help them. They were mostly women, perhaps because women have fewer resources when something goes wrong for them."

Julia knew that only too well. "I see." She felt mildly puzzled. "Why are you telling me this, Stork?"

Again the butler hesitated, and when he spoke his voice came slowly. "I've never seen Mr. Cyrus the way he is with you, Miss. I've never seen him so happy. I just wanted you to know he isn't the rake some people say he is. He's a good man. And *he* would never hurt you." There was only the faintest emphasis on the pronoun.

Julia gazed at Stork's impassive face, and as she looked into quiet brown eyes, she thought, *He knows*. The Drummond servants were staying there for the moment; had they known more than she realized and talked about it? Probably. Servants always seemed to know more than their employers realized. The odd thing was, Julia didn't feel upset.

"Thank you, Stork," she said softly.

"The entire staff is happy to have you and your sister here, Miss Julia."

"Thank you," she repeated, smiling, then turned away and continued toward the stairs. Another gentle push toward Cyrus, she thought bemusedly. First Lissa and then Stork—as well as the other Fortune servants, apparently. As she went down to greet Felice Stanton, Julia had the idea she was about to encounter another ally. Not particularly because of what Lissa had said about Felice, but because Stork had admitted her to the house . . . several times.

She walked into the blue parlor, a small room at the side of the house, feeling wary and uncertain. Felice, a small woman in her early thirties with dark hair and eyes, was unusually lovely. She stood near the window, holding a newspaper in one gloved hand, and when she spoke—obviously referring to Adrian—her voice was dryly ironic.

"A week ago he walked on water; now half the reporters writing about his untimely demise have the insufferable gall to claim they knew he was a lunatic all along."

It was hardly the accepted conventional speech to a very recent widow, but the unexpected greeting, combined with Felice's rueful smile, not only put Julia at ease but made her immediately warm toward the older woman. "It sells newspapers, I suppose," she said.

Felice uttered a faintly disgusted sound and tossed the paper toward a chair. She came to shake hands with Julia, her grip warm and firm, and said frankly, "Custom says this is a dreadfully inappropriate time to call, but etiquette can go hang. I've felt uneasy about you for months, Julia, and if I'd only said something . . . Well, at least you would have had someone to talk to."

"Uneasy about me?" Julia gestured toward a comfortable settee, and as they both sat down she studied Felice with a startled suspicion in her mind.

"You'll recognize the signs from now on too," Felice said quietly. "You won't see it often, thank God, but you will see it. Beatings do more than leave scars on skin, no matter how well we think we can hide what we feel."

"You?"

Felice nodded. "My first husband. That's why I wanted to talk to you today, Julia. It took me a long time to heal, and if it hadn't been for Noel . . ." Her eyes grew a little misty, then she smiled. "It's amazing, isn't it? How one man can heal the wounds another man inflicted?"

"I—I'm not sure that's possible," Julia confessed in a low voice, but her eyes were pathetically hopeful. "Is it?"

Taking the younger woman's hand in her own and holding it strongly, Felice said, "I wasn't sure, either, ten years ago. Then I met Noel. And I met another woman who'd been through much the same thing. You aren't alone, Julia. *We* aren't alone. And it helps to talk about it, to someone who understands. May I tell you my story?"

Her throat was so tight Julia couldn't speak, but she nodded, and she listened. In time, she talked.

Cyrus asked his attorney to wait for him in his study, then addressed Stork as they stood together in the entrance hall. "Where's Miss Julia?"

"In the blue parlor, sir, with Mrs. Stanton." The butler's voice was unexpressive, and few would have heard anything informative beyond the facts he imparted. Cyrus heard more.

"They've been talking?"

"For more than an hour, sir. Miss Lissa is walking in the garden with one of her young friends who called to see her. One of the new—footmen—you hired is stationed by the gate."

"Has Lissa seen him yet?"

"I don't believe so, sir."

"All right." Cyrus stood thinking for a moment, a faint frown drawing his brows together. Absently, he said, "I've found other employment for the Drummond servants, so they'll be out of your way by tomorrow. And if a Mr. Stevens should call, I want to see him immediately."

"Yes, sir. Another Pinkerton man, sir?" Stork inquired in a low voice.

Cyrus nodded. "Yes, but remember what I said—keep that information to yourself, Stork. I don't want Julia or Lissa worried, and I see no reason why the staff should know."

"Very well, sir."

Cyrus crossed the entrance hall to his study and went in, closing the door behind him. His attorney, Gabriel Rushton, was seated in a comfortable chair by the desk placidly smoking a cigar. He was a silver-haired man in his fifties, very distinguished, with shrewd gray eyes and a deep, mellow voice.

That voice was a little dry now as he said, "This is highly irregular, Cy."

Settling into his chair behind the desk, Cyrus said, "Legally, perhaps."

Rushton looked pained. "The law is my business. Why I ever had the misfortune to accept Adrian Drummond as a client I'll never know, but I am obligated to discharge my duties as his attorney in accordance with the law—and that hardly includes divulging any of the man's private dealings to you."

"Gabe, you know why I want the information. I have

an enemy who's determined to hurt Julia, and I need to know who he is."

"Are you sure he's your enemy? From what you've told me, he hasn't struck directly at you. If it was Drummond he meant to injure, Julia should be safe now."

Cyrus shook his head, frowning. "He was using Drummond somehow, controlling him, or just goading him. The false message that lured Julia out to the house that day wasn't only meant to compromise her; it was also intended to focus Drummond's attention on me as his enemy. Julia would have suffered for it if the plan had worked, and Drummond's suspicion would have forced me to keep away from her. Don't you see?"

The attorney puffed on his cigar for a moment, then shrugged. "No, Cy, I don't see. All you have is supposition and a wild theory. Who's to say one of Drummond's enemies—who has nothing against you—might have simply meant to make mischief?"

"I say so."

"Based on?"

"Helen Bradshaw's murder."

Rushton straightened in his chair, the lazy air vanishing as his expression turned grim. "They've found her?"

"Early this morning." Cyrus's voice was flat. "I hired a Pinkerton man a week ago, partly to look for the girl. Neither of us expected to find her alive. He was with the police when they found her."

"Was she in the river?"

"No. I suppose the killer decided not to take that chance with the water so low. She was buried in a shallow grave in a vacant lot here in the city. There wasn't much left of her, but the police think she may have been strangled. It's impossible to know for certain when it happened; I believe she died the day she left that message for Julia."

Rushton smoked his cigar in silence for a few moments, his eyes fixed on the younger man's face. Finally, he said, "All right, I'll grant there must have been a connection between the false message and that poor girl's death; I don't believe in coincidence. Clearly, there's a diabolical hand involved in all this. But I still don't see how you've reached the conclusion *you* are the ultimate target when there's been no direct strike against you. What if it's Julia, for some reason neither of us can fathom, who's the target?"

Cyrus hesitated, then sighed roughly. "Gabe, I know you're a practical man with a logical mind, and what I'm about to say fits none of your criteria in determining facts or evidence, but bear with me, all right?"

"I've known you a long time, Cy," Rushton replied, his eyes unreadable now. "I won't discount or dismiss anything you tell me without a great deal of thought."

"Do you believe in fate?" Cyrus asked.

"Sometimes."

"I never did." Cyrus leaned back in his chair and shook his head wryly. "Or maybe . . . Hell, I don't know anymore. But what I do know is that someone wants to destroy me. I think . . . I *feel* . . . it's been going on a long time. Years. For some reason I don't understand, he's wary of me. Perhaps afraid of me. So much so he hasn't been able to attack me directly."

"So he used Drummond?"

Cyrus hesitated, struggling to bring his thoughts into focus; it was becoming easier, yet because he lacked pieces of the puzzle, the picture forming in his mind was still incomplete. "I think he saw Drummond as a tool, yes, but I believe his initial motive was to keep Julia out of my reach."

"What?" Rushton said softly, frowning. "Why?"

"I'm . . . more of a threat to him since I met Julia, since I fell in love with her."

"How could that be?"

Frustrated himself because he didn't have all the answers he needed, Cyrus was almost angry. "Because I can't fight him until I'm complete, and I won't be complete without her. And he knows that somehow, he knows. Oh, hell, I realize it sounds mad. Gabe, from the moment I first saw Julia, I've been changing inside. I don't mean just falling in love with her. It's as if I were half blind until I met her, and now I'm beginning to see things I never knew were there."

"What things?" Rushton asked quietly.

"Patterns. Patterns of fate. When I came back to Richmond, I was doing more than coming home. I was obeying an urge so strong it was a compulsion. I had to be here. The day I returned, I saw Julia walking with Drummond, and I was obsessed with her from that moment. I didn't understand what I felt at first, but I know now it was a sense of recognition. I knew we belonged together."

After a moment the lawyer said, "People say love at first sight's a myth, but I felt it the moment I saw my wife. I understand—and believe—that much. Go on."

Cyrus spoke slowly now, tentatively but with an underlying tone of absolute certainty. "She was meant to be a part of my life. We were destined to be together. And it was meant to happen this year. This summer. I know that as surely as I know my heart's beating. It's why I had to come home, why I had to be here." He hesitated, then said, "But the pattern's wrong."

"What do you mean?"

"I mean it wasn't meant to happen the way it did. Someone or something tried to change what had to be, and they were partly successful."

Rushton shook his head a little, frowning now. "Forgive me, Cy, but that sounds—"

"I know. But you said yourself you didn't believe in coincidence, and I know you have a healthy skepticism regarding convenient accidents. Correct?"

"Yes to both."

"Then I'll give you a series of coincidences and convenient accidents. They prove nothing—but if you look at them from my point of view, there is a pattern. And if you'll accept, for the sake of argument, that my enemy *knew* I needed Julia in order to be complete, and knew he would be in danger from me once I fell in love with her, the pattern becomes clearer."

"All right, I'm listening."

Cyrus nodded, and paused a moment to think, just as he'd been thinking for days now. "Four years ago, Julia was preparing to leave the schoolroom behind and come out into society—where I would certainly have met her. I was fixed here in Richmond, and had no plans to leave. Then Tate was murdered."

"Murdered?"

"The longer I think about it, the more convinced I am his death wasn't the accident it appeared to be. He'd been hunting for fifty years and wasn't the least feeble; he wouldn't have carried his gun in such a way that it would have gone off even if he'd fallen. And what happened to his dog? That animal never left his side, but it vanished when Tate was 'accidentally' shot."

Rushton was frowning, in thought rather than in disbelief. "The first convenient accident?"

"I believe so. And my fault, in a way."

"How could it have been?"

"A few weeks before Tate was killed, I was at the racetrack with a group of friends. I don't remember how the subject came up, but I said something idly about how I'd always wanted to go west, and probably would one day. Someone—I can't remember who—asked what was keeping me here. I said Tate. He was getting old, and I didn't want to be away from him in his last years."

"And someone heard?"

Cyrus nodded. "I can't even know if it was one of the group of men I was with; we were at the rail, not in a private box, and there were people all around. Anyone could have heard what I said."

Rushton was silent for a long moment, then said, "If someone did want you out of Richmond, I suppose killing Tate might have seemed a solution. But it's a fiendish idea, Cy."

"Wait." Cyrus smiled thinly. "There's more."

"Julia?"

"Yes. After Tate died, I left Richmond. It wasn't going to be permanent, everyone knew that. I just closed up this house, I didn't sell it. Obviously, I meant to return. My enemy knew that. Even more, he knew I'd be drawn back here—this summer."

"He knows a great deal," Rushton muttered.

"That," Cyrus said wryly, "is the worst of it. He's known more than I all along. I have a distinct feeling *he's* never been half blind."

"I can certainly understand why you'd want to find him—assuming, of course, all this is true." The qualification was more or less automatic. "So he knew you'd be back. Is this where Drummond comes into the picture?"

Cyrus nodded. "Yes. And again, I'm partly to blame

for what happened. My interest in married women was well known. It wasn't something my enemy was likely to forget. So when he chose a husband for Julia, he chose carefully."

Rushton frowned again. "Why not simply kill her? I mean, if he had no compunction about killing Tate, and if he's responsible for the Bradshaw girl's death, it's clear he doesn't balk at murder. Why shouldn't he have taken the easiest and most foolproof way to keep Julia from you permanently?"

"I don't know. Perhaps because it amused him to see her married to an animal. He's . . . arrogant beyond belief, I feel that. Intricate plans seem to please him, and I think he is or was convinced of his own infallibility. Perhaps he was confident he had put her beyond my reach and, moreover, had found a weapon for himself in Drummond."

Shifting a bit in his chair, Rushton murmured, "My God, Cy, if you're right about this monster—"

"Yes, I know. Frightening. You don't seem quite so disbelieving now, Gabe."

"The whole thing's insane," Rushton said flatly, but immediately added, "Go on. How did he arrange the marriage?"

"He killed again. I've found out from one of his friends that Julia's father didn't care much for Drummond, and wasn't happy to have the man courting his daughter. Rather than openly object to Drummond, he'd told them he didn't want her to marry until she turned twenty-one. She's twenty-one now."

"You mean your enemy was afraid she'd still be single when you came back to Richmond?"

"I believe so." Cyrus paused, frowning in thought. "Here's where I may be able to gather some hard evidence, given time. A little over two years ago, Richard Brand made a series of bad business investments; so far, I haven't been able to find out who was advising him. If I can, I may be a step closer to identifying my enemy— because it was he. It had to be. In any case, Brand was up to his ears in debt when he and his wife went sailing on the river and drowned. The police were never satisfied as to the reason their boat went down."

"Another convenient accident," Rushton said.

"Exactly. Julia found herself, at nineteen, grieving, impoverished, and alone in the world except for a young sister. Because of her father's insistence, she hadn't gone away to school and wasn't trained to do anything except run a house. She had nowhere to turn. That's when Drummond stepped in. He was well off, handsome, charming, and he'd been courting her for more than a year. He asked her to marry him. She said yes."

Rushton leaned forward to put his cigar out in a crystal ashtray on Cyrus's desk, sending the younger man a very direct look. "You told me he mistreated her."

"As I said, my enemy chose well for his purposes." Cyrus met the steady gaze just as directly. "Julia's marriage didn't stop me from pursuing her, but the pain and terror she had suffered at Drummond's hands made an affair virtually impossible. Or should have. Except that I fell in love with her, which made me very determined, and by some miracle, despite her fear and the torment Drummond had put her through, she was able to feel something for me in return. Not love, not yet, but something."

The attorney sat back, his gaze still intent on Cyrus's face. "So, your enemy took another step to keep Julia away from you. He somehow persuaded the Bradshaw girl to deliver a false message intended to place Julia in

a compromising position and alert Drummond to the
danger you posed to his marriage."

"Yes. But the plan failed. I think that's important. He
was beginning to lose his mastery over events. The plan
should have driven another wedge between Julia and
me. Instead, it alerted me to the fact that someone
intended her harm. For the first time, I became aware of
one of his actions."

"And he killed the Bradshaw girl because . . . ?"

"Because he blamed her for the plan's failure. And
because I knew who had left the message. I would have
questioned her, and that would have led me to him."

"What about yesterday? You said Drummond came
home before he should have, and knew Julia was leaving
him?"

Cyrus nodded. "I don't know if my enemy planned all
along to goad Drummond into trying to kill me, or if he
hoped the lunatic would kill Julia. I do believe he'd
realized he could no longer control Adrian, the man was
coming apart, and had been for weeks. I'd done my part
in pushing him, because I was trying to protect Julia and
discover who was behind him. Then, yesterday, I knew
I couldn't wait. I had to get Julia away from Adrian."

"I assume you're trying to trace Drummond's movements yesterday, find out who he talked to?"

"Yes, I have a Pinkerton man on that."

"All right," Rushton said slowly. "Now Julia's here,
under your roof, and you plan to marry her as soon as
possible. You believe your enemy's still too wary to
strike directly at you? That he'll try to hurt Julia?"

"I'm sure of it. For now, at least, he doesn't want to
come after me. If he can take Julia away from me
before . . ."

"Before what?" Rushton asked intently.

Cyrus half closed his eyes, struggling to grasp the elusive snippet of knowledge. "I don't know." He sounded frustrated. Was frustrated. "Julia being with me, even marrying me, isn't the worst threat to him. There's something else. And he's running out of time. The pattern is . . . reweaving itself. He can't control it any longer. I'm almost where I was meant to be now, despite everything he's tried to do to change that, because Julia's a part of my life, as she was intended to be."

"So you'll be able to fight him, unless he manages to—to alter the pattern by taking Julia away from you?"

"Yes. I can't tell you how I know, but I'm certain of it."

Gabriel Rushton was silent for a long time, his gaze turned inward now as he brooded. Finally, his eyes focused on Cyrus again, and his voice was matter-of-fact. "I sure as hell wouldn't want to argue any of this to a jury. But I believe it. All right, I'll tell you all I know about Drummond's business affairs, if you think it might help."

"I'm looking for connections," Cyrus told him. "Whoever he is, my enemy is close by, and whatever his evil is, I can't see it. He knew Drummond well, and he knows me. Anything you can tell me could help."

Julia was alone in the blue parlor, studying the newspaper Felice had left. She frowned. The paper carried a photograph taken a month or two before, after the election of the new city council. The nine members were in a stiffly posed group with Adrian in the center. Julia had seen it before, but hadn't studied it until now.

There was something disturbing about it, but she couldn't quite pinpoint the reason. She knew all the men in the photo at least by name; they were all part of the social group to which she belonged. Her eyes went from one face to another, finally resting on the man at Adrian's right.

His eyes . . . She felt a curious chill. Odd she'd never noticed that about his eyes before, and she had seen him countless times during the last years. A trick of the camera, perhaps?

She was trying to decide why it bothered her so much when her sister walked into the room.

"Stork says Cyrus is in his study with Mr. Rushton," Lissa said without preamble. "Isn't he Adrian's attorney?"

Looking up from the paper, Julia nodded. "And Cyrus's as well. I believe he represents most of the prominent men in Richmond. Why?"

"I was just wondering." Lissa hesitated, then sat down beside her sister on the settee. "Monica came to call, and we walked in the garden. You've been with Mrs. Stanton, haven't you?"

"Yes, she left only a few moments ago."

"She is nice, isn't she?" Lissa asked, eager to have her own opinion confirmed.

Julia smiled, conscious of the feelings her visitor had inspired in her. The sadness, anger, and relief of knowing she wasn't alone in what she'd suffered. The comfort of understanding and support. And the seeds of hope. "Yes, she's nice. She's very nice."

"I knew you'd think so." Lissa hesitated again, eyeing her sister, then said, "Monica told me what people are saying, Julia. Actually, it isn't too bad. They're shocked Adrian went berserk the way he did, of course, and they're surprised we're here. But it's rather strange. Monica says quite a few people have spoken up against Adrian. She—she *knew*, Julia. That he'd been hurting you. She says it was probably the servants who put the word out, and apparently they did it to defend you."

More surprised than appalled, Julia stared at her sister. The Drummond servants had always seemed distant to her; but perhaps they had feared Adrian as much as she had? Once he was dead, they might have freely condemned him. Or had they truly meant to support her? How many other people had she underestimated? she wondered dimly.

"Julia? Do you mind terribly? Monica told me people are saying Cyrus is in love with you, and there aren't many of them spreading ugly gossip about it."

Conjuring a faint smile, Julia said, "I can't say it's a pleasant feeling to have my private life on public display. But I'll survive it, Lissa."

"You are going to marry Cyrus, aren't you?"

"Of course she is," Cyrus said, coming into the room and smiling at them both. "Lissa, Mark Tryon's just called to see you. I've put him in my study."

Lissa's hand went to her bruised cheek, and she was obviously both pleased and anxious. "Oh, dear, and I look—"

"You look very pretty. Go and see the young man before he paces a hole in my rug."

She smiled at Cyrus as she rose, leaving the room with no further hesitation, and when she'd gone, Julia said, "You handle her very well."

Cyrus sat down beside her, his smile turning a bit sheepish. "I've always been partial to girls."

"So I've heard," she responded with only a touch of dryness.

His smile remained, but his eyes were very intent on her face. "I can't go back and change the way I've lived my life, sweetheart. I don't regret any of my choices—

except the one that took me away from Richmond four years ago."

Julia was a little surprised. "Why that one?"

Lightly, he said, "If I'd been here when you came out, you never would have married Drummond."

"You're very sure of yourself," she murmured, but she was smiling faintly.

He lifted a hand to stroke her cheek for a moment, then leaned over and kissed her. It was a slow, warm, intimate kiss, deepening into a hunger so intense it awoke her own burning desire. She was trembling when he lifted his head, and looked at him with dazed eyes. He was still touching her, his fingers gentle as they rested on her neck, and his thumb brushed her throbbing bottom lip in a rhythmic caress. She had unconsciously grasped his wrist, and now became aware of the steady beat of his pulse beneath her fingertips.

"I'm sure of what we have," he said huskily. "I'm sure we belong together." Then he smiled. "You are going to marry me next week, aren't you, love?"

"I think I am," she said, somewhat awed by her own ready response.

Since Stork coughed politely in the doorway just then to announce supper was ready, Julia said no more. But it was enough. Cyrus kissed her again, reining the desire this time, and his black eyes were alight when he rose to his feet and helped her up. She was grateful for the help; she felt more than a little shaken.

It wasn't until hours later, when she walked beside him up the stairs and into the lamplit bedroom they shared, that a sudden wave of panic swept over her. What was she doing? Marriage was enslavement, a prison sentence; no matter what anyone said, she knew it was true. She couldn't marry Cyrus, the risk was too great. She couldn't marry anyone, not again—

"Julia." He surrounded her face with his big hands, making her look at him. "Don't, sweetheart. Don't be afraid." His voice was low and achingly tender.

"I can't marry you," she whispered, foreboding clawing at her even though she struggled against it.

"Yes, you can," he said, his gaze very steady. "I love you, Julia. I swear to God I'll do everything I can to make you happy."

The panic was still inside her, but as she looked into his eyes she knew the emotion couldn't hold against his determination. Neither could she. And when he bent his head to cover her mouth with his own, the heat of desire he'd kindled in her hours before with another kiss flared so strongly it overwhelmed her.

Her body hadn't forgotten what he had taught it to feel. Her body remembered the incredible delight of belonging to him.

Last night she had been aware of exhaustion and a kind of numb peace, not even realizing she could never have slept in his arms if some part of her hadn't trusted him. Tonight what she felt was a yearning so intense, nothing else mattered. Her response to his passion was almost wild, so frantic she would have been embarrassed if she'd been given a moment to think about it.

Cyrus didn't give her a moment. His mouth on hers was hard with hunger, his fingers swift and sure as he unfastened her dress and pushed it off her shoulders. Her petticoat dropped in a pool of material around her feet, and she was only vaguely aware of her own actions when she fumbled with his tie and vest buttons. All of her—body and soul—was filled with him, his taste, the heady male scent of him, the hot intensity of his desire.

Looking back later, she didn't remember much of those moments except for the driven urgency inside her. Clothing was left in jumbled confusion on the floor, and when he carried her naked to the bed she wasn't thinking of anything but her need for him. His lean face was taut, eyes burning with the black fire that never failed to push her own passion even higher.

He didn't put out the lamp, and she was glad. The way he looked at her made her feel far more beautiful and desirable than she'd ever imagined she could feel. He was different this time; his need seemed greater, or perhaps because she wasn't nervous, frightened, or confused he merely felt able to express that need without holding himself back in any way. His hands trembled as they touched her body, and his own powerful form was hard and filled with fever.

The same fire was consuming Julia. She held his head, whimpering, when his mouth caressed her breasts, her body shaking as the incredible pleasure seared her senses. She couldn't breathe, couldn't be still, because the spiraling tension was becoming unbearable. When his hand slipped down over her stomach, her legs parted eagerly for him, and a ragged moan caught in her throat.

"So beautiful," he said thickly against her breasts, teasing her stiff nipples with his tongue as his fingers gently probed the soft, damp folds of her sex. "So warm and sweet . . . my sweet Julia . . . I love you so much . . ."

Already, the taut, building pleasure was a torment that seemed to be burning her alive. Her hips rose to his touch, and her fingernails bit into his shoulders as another moan tore free of her. Her body knew what it wanted, and the need was a fierce, primitive demand, a desperate necessity. She couldn't plead with him because the words wouldn't emerge from her tight throat. All she could do when he lifted his head to look down at her was plead with her eyes and pull mutely at his shoulders.

Cyrus covered her mouth with his, kissing her so deeply she felt bombarded by the intensity of his passion. Her thighs cradled him eagerly as he slipped between them, and through her half-closed eyes she stared into his black ones as her body accepted his slow penetration.

She made a little sound. Her total awareness focused on the burning invasion. It was almost painful, still a shock to her body, but great shudders of pure pleasure rippled through her as her tight passage stretched to admit him. She didn't realize she was kissing him frantically, gripping him with her arms and legs as well as her pulsing inner flesh, and when his weight settled fully onto her, she didn't hear the guttural moan of satisfaction that came from somewhere deep inside her.

Cyrus lifted his head to look down at her, an almost savage expression of pleasure on his hard face, his night-black eyes luminous, and his incredible voice was low and raspy when he said, "God, you feel so good, love." His arms slipped under her shoulders, he moved slightly, pressing deeper inside her, and a sound like a growl escaped him. He moved again, every rigid muscle quivering with the strain of holding himself to the slow, lingering thrusts.

Julia could feel him, feel the throbbing fullness her body held so tightly, and the tension was building, coiling in her until it was maddening. The prolonged retreat and return of his manhood was a blissful, searing pleasure she could hardly bear. Dimly, she thought there had to be a point when pleasure was simply too intense, and she thought she'd reached that tormenting moment, but he pushed her past it.

There was only sensation. The hot, slippery friction of him moving inside her. The way the powerful, quivering muscles of his back and shoulders and the sweat-dampened slickness of his skin felt beneath her fingers. The rasp of his hairy chest over her aching breasts, and the smooth hardness of his hips between her thighs. The sound of harsh breathing, hers and his. The musky, drugging scents of their heated bodies.

Julia bore the wild, exquisite lovemaking as long as she could, but she broke before he did. Her body surged beneath him, demanding an end to the magnificent torture, and a whimper of intolerable need was wrenched from her throat. An answering sound rumbled from Cyrus's chest and his thrusts immediately quickened. She matched his rhythm perfectly, taking him as surely as he took her and insisting on a woman's ultimate satisfaction.

When it finally came, the release was so devastating it flung her into a storm of sensation. She cried out, her body going taut and then convulsing as wave after wave of pleasure swept over her. The internal spasms of her climax held him deeply inside her, caressing him, and he groaned harshly as the soft inner contractions spurred his own shattering culmination. Shuddering violently in unbelievable ecstasy, he poured himself into her.

Eleven

♥

The storm of the day before had broken the heat wave, but it was still August and the humid, heavy warmth of the afternoon lingered in the quiet bedroom even though it was late. Julia was aware of that, aware their bodies were damp with sweat, but she was too utterly drained to think much about it. She murmured a protest when he withdrew from her, but couldn't manage to open her eyes until he lifted her off the bed and into his arms.

He kissed her, which distracted her from the question of where he was taking her, and the next thing she knew she was being lowered into wonderfully cool water. One of the maids had apparently readied the bathwater before they'd come upstairs, though she hadn't noticed the light on in the room. The tub was large, which was a good thing; he never could have joined her in a smaller one.

She looked at him bemusedly in the bright light of the bathroom, and said the first thing she could think of. "We're getting water on the floor." She was vaguely grateful her hair was still up.

Cyrus eyed the small waves lapping over the rim of the tub and shrugged. "I'll have to remember," he murmured. "A bigger tub for the new house."

"Is this decent?" she asked, grappling with a dim idea that it wasn't.

He leaned over to kiss her, his wet hands sliding up her arms to her shoulders. "Of course it is, love." Then his smile faded a little, and his eyes grew intent. "If you don't want me to join you like this—"

"No." She felt the heat of a blush rise in her cheeks, which was, she told herself, absurd. "No, I—I like it. I think." She had yet to feel at all shy or self-conscious with him, which surprised her. And she didn't feel humiliated the way she had whenever Adrian had looked at her naked.

"Good." He kissed her again, then reached for soap and a washcloth. "I want to take care of you, sweetheart. Will you let me?"

Julia could only nod a wordless acceptance, still bemused by him and by herself. It seemed there was much more to intimacy with a man than she'd known or even suspected, and this new experience was both strange and very pleasurable. He handled her body with a gentle, familiar touch, kissing her often in a teasing way that made her smile at him. He clearly enjoyed touching her, yet he was also matter-of-fact with the mechanics of bathing so she wasn't made to feel at all self-conscious.

She even returned the favor, a bit timid at first but encouraged by his pleased smile. She hadn't caressed him when he made love to her, mostly because her own emotions and sensations had overwhelmed her, and now, for the first time, she became aware of a need to touch him. She loved the way his hard body felt under her soapy hands, and when she realized he was becoming aroused, the knowledge sent a dart of pleasure through her.

"I can't seem to get enough of you, my sweet," Cyrus murmured, a familiar heat kindling in his black eyes. He drew her closer in the tub and kissed her, his hands stroking her body with none of the earlier matter-of-factness. And her body certainly understood the difference.

She was still touching him, slowly exploring both above and below the water's surface, her desire building so quickly that she was only mildly surprised when she realized—

"Here?"

"Here," he replied huskily.

He saw her naked back for the first time that night. It was after he'd pulled himself from the tub reluctantly and wrapped a towel around his lean middle, then held another open for her.

"Come on out, sweetheart."

She had forgotten her scars and did not worry about rising naked from the water or stepping out of the tub—only wondering if her trembling legs would hold her up. She'd never felt so blissfully spent, and stood a bit dazedly as he gently dried her. It wasn't until he began to turn her that she stiffened.

He went still and waited, looking gravely into her eyes. She wanted to refuse him, but couldn't somehow. After a long moment she slowly turned her back to him, unconsciously bowing her head. There was only a brief pause before he began moving the thick towel gently over her back, and he didn't say a word.

After the way it had hit him so hard to see only part of
her scars, Cyrus had braced himself to see all of them.
But there was no way, he acknowledged now, to be even
remotely prepared for the evidence of such cruelty. No
way to look at what had been done to her and not feel
intolerable rage and agony tearing him apart.

Adrian had chosen her back as his target, and that
terrifyingly fragile, delicate area from the nape of her
neck to her waist bore the atrocious brand of his insane
rage. The broader welts of a strap were only faint marks,
healed now; more awful were the thin white scars of
some kind of whip, crisscrossing her back, and the tiny
pale crescents that were the wounds of a ring or buckle.
There were so many.

Cyrus dried her gently, then wrapped the big towel
around her and drew her back against his body, holding
her. "My poor darling," he murmured. "What you've
suffered . . . I'm so sorry, love. No wonder you've
been so afraid."

A little shudder went through her, and Julia let her
head fall back against his shoulder as she relaxed in his
embrace. "I'm not afraid of you," she whispered, realizing it was true, realizing she trusted him. Some part of
her, she thought, had always trusted him. "I know you
won't hurt me."

His arms tightened around her, and he kissed her
shoulder. "Never," he promised in a low voice.

They stood silently for a time, the closeness creating
an aura of peace and contentment. When they did move,
it was slowly, and they were still silent. Cyrus took her
hair down and brushed it for her. He let the water out of
the tub and turned off the lights while she went into the
bedroom, and when he rejoined her she was waiting for
him, naked under the sheet.

He turned out the lamp on the nightstand and slid into bed beside her, drawing her into his arms. She cuddled close with a little sigh, so weary that giving in to the need for sleep was like tumbling into a well of warm darkness. Her only clear thought before that pleasant state claimed her was a wistful yearning. She wished she could love him.

Cyrus slept deeply as well, but only for a few hours. It was before dawn when he woke abruptly, something pulling at him. He got out of bed, careful not to wake Julia, and crossed the dark room to one of the windows. This room was at the front of the house, facing the street, and in the predawn hours all was dark and silent outside. The night was still, warm, humid.

It took him a few moments to realize his eyes were intently probing the darkness, and when he did, he had no idea what he was looking for. A threat, he thought. Danger. But he saw nothing except the normal shadows of night.

There were two Pinkerton men in his house playing the roles of footmen while they watched over Julia and Lissa; two more shared the task of keeping guard outside; yet another investigator was working to find the answers—and the evidence—Cyrus needed to identify his enemy. He should have felt some sense of security, of safety for those he loved, because he had taken every possible precaution. Instead, his strongest certainty was that whatever was meant to happen would.

There were things he could change. He knew it, had known it for a long time now. But his own future was set, marked in a pattern he could see only vaguely and had little hope of altering. The next few months would be critical, he felt it with everything inside him.

And he felt, for the first time, a kind of loneliness. He

had said to his old friend and attorney that he couldn't be complete without Julia; he wasn't complete, and he'd never been so aware of the empty place inside him. She had given him her body, and, astonishingly, she had given him her trust, but unless and until she gave him her love, he'd never be whole.

"Cyrus?" Her voice, soft and drowsy.

He turned away from the window and the nebulous danger he felt out there, and went back to her. She made a sound of contentment when he rejoined her and drew her into his arms, her delicate body utterly relaxed. She was already deeply asleep again, her head pillowed on his shoulder. He held her close, one hand stroking her back gently. He could feel the scars.

Adrian might be roasting in hell, but Cyrus knew there was another man just as guilty of sick cruelty, just as responsible for hurting Julia—and he was still walking around alive. He was worse than Adrian had been, not so much demented as evil. Cyrus could almost feel the darkness, almost smell the rotten odor of corruption. But what disturbed him most of all, what had begun to torment him, was the growing conviction that there was some deep connection, some bond, between him and his enemy.

He held Julia in his arms and stared into the darkness of night. He didn't sleep again for a long time.

Adrian Drummond was buried on Sunday with surprisingly little fanfare. The mayor of Richmond was laid to rest in the cemetery of his family's church with few well-wishers in attendance to bid him good-bye. Reporters far outnumbered the mourners, and though his fellow councilmen showed up, they had clearly agreed among themselves to betray no emotion and make no comments to the press. They were successful on both counts.

Neither the widow, her sister, nor Cyrus Fortune attended the funeral.

The evening edition of the city's newspapers contained numerous articles running the gamut from a rancorous interview with an ex-employee to a summary of Drummond's will—which had been read, in private, to those his attorney summoned to hear the details. The story concerning the will was a definite spur to gossip, especially since it accurately stated that Drummond's widow and sister-in-law inherited nothing. Drummond, it seemed, chose to leave his money to his political party.

That information wasn't news to Cyrus, and since Julia wanted nothing at all from her late husband, it suited her perfectly, but it gave the people of Richmond something else to talk about. Those outside the social circle the Drummonds had occupied talked the loudest; those who had known the couple, or thought they had, were more quiet and thoughtful.

On the following Friday afternoon Julia Drummond married Cyrus Fortune in a private ceremony in the neighborhood church. The bride was attended by her sister, the groom by his best friend, Noel Stanton, and the only guests were Felice Stanton and Mark Tryon.

The newspapers, uncharacteristically subdued, ran simple announcements followed by the information that the newlywed couple had chosen to postpone a honeymoon trip.

The people of Richmond shook their heads, but since rumors had been flying thick and fast from the day of Drummond's death, no one knew what to think. Most settled down to await developments, puzzled and curious—and unusually reluctant to judge.

"But Cyrus, I don't need a footman." Julia kept her voice low, partly because the stalwart young man in question was only a few feet away, waiting by the door to accompany her. She was venturing out alone for the first time since Adrian's death and less than a week since her quiet marriage. It had taken her this long to get up the nerve to show her face in public without the comfort of Cyrus's presence. They had walked in the park a few times, and he'd taken her to the new house more than once, but since they hadn't encountered anyone they knew during those outings Julia's courage hadn't been put to the test.

She thought it was time. Lissa was out with friends, Cyrus had an appointment at his office in the city, and she needed to do some shopping. He had arranged accounts for her and Lissa at a number of shops as well as providing extremely generous allowances for both of them.

He seemed reluctant to have her go out alone. He betrayed his feelings by a subtle, almost imperceptible tightening of his handsome features, but Julia knew him better now and she caught the fleeting expression.

"Humor me," he said lightly, smiling down at her. "Take Nelson along with you."

Julia drew on her gloves, a twinge of unease disturbing the peace she'd found these last days. "Why?" she asked finally. "Because of what happened to Helen? Is that why you've hired a footman to stay with Lissa and a footman to stay with me?"

Cyrus hesitated, then nodded. He bent his head to

kiss her, a gesture that no longer made her feel the slightest bit embarrassed no matter who was watching, and said, "It's partly that, yes."

"Partly? What else?"

He was stroking her cheek gently, as he so often did, and for a moment she thought he wouldn't answer. Then he sighed. "We'll talk about it later, all right, sweetheart?"

Julia felt uneasy about whatever it was, but her trust in Cyrus had been growing steadily and she was able to smile at him. "All right."

He kissed her again, lingeringly this time. "And don't stay out too long in this heat," he said.

"No, I won't."

Cyrus stood looking after her even when the closed door hid her from his sight. He hated letting her go out without him. The fear of losing her was with him constantly now, a coldness that never eased. He'd made no progress in identifying his enemy, and his odd instincts told him there wasn't much time left. But those same instincts also told him he would bring about the very thing he wanted desperately to avoid if he didn't allow Julia as much freedom as possible: he would lose her.

He had done what he could to keep her safe without locking her up with an armed guard to stand watch. All he could do now was trust in his precautions—and wait.

Julia was aware of her unobtrusive escort, though not particularly troubled by his presence, and the worry about what Cyrus hadn't told her was also on her mind, but most of her attention was focused on keeping her chin up and her expression calm. She wasn't wearing the social mask she had created during her first marriage;

that had been a lie and she was determined never to lie—to herself or anyone else—ever again.

When the first acquaintance she passed on the sidewalk tipped his hat with a murmured greeting and slight smile, she felt a bit more secure, and by the time she had visited two shops her confidence was much steadier. People she knew spoke to her, guardedly perhaps, but without condemnation, and no one asked awkward questions or looked at her as if there were any reason she should feel defensive or defiant.

When she returned home just over two hours later she was smiling, bemused but intensely relieved; her happiness with Cyrus had grown stronger with every passing day, and she'd wanted nothing to mar that.

"I'll take these upstairs, ma'am," Nelson murmured, indicating the several boxes he carried.

"Thank you, Nelson." She drew off her gloves as she watched him ascend the stairs, and turned in surprise as Cyrus came out of his study. "I thought you had an appointment," she said.

"I did, but it didn't last long." He put his hands on her small waist and pulled her to him, kissing her, then smiled down at her. "How about your meeting with public scrutiny?"

"It was . . . surprising." She absently smoothed his lapels. "Everyone was perfectly polite. Was that your doing?"

Cyrus lifted an eyebrow at her. "How on earth could it have been?"

Julia felt her smile growing as she gazed up at him. "I don't know, but I have a strange feeling it was another one of those things you wanted—and got. Like magic. Perhaps I did marry the offspring of a warlock after all."

He was smiling, but there was something unusually

hesitant in his black eyes. "Would it bother you if that turned out to be true?" he asked lightly.

Despite the tone, his question was serious. It was a strange question, yet she was curiously unsurprised by it. And her reply was made almost without thought, matter-of-factly. "No, of course not. How could it? Wherever your . . . magic came from, there's no doubt it's a—a positive force. If anyone knows that, I do." She reached up to touch his cheek, aware of an odd urge to comfort him. "How could anything about you disturb me?" she asked him softly.

Cyrus wished he could see love in her beautiful green eyes, hear love in her gentle voice. But he didn't. She felt trust, desire, and gratitude—perhaps even caring— but not love. And it was the one gift he could not get, no matter how often or winningly he asked for it.

He hugged her briefly, reminding himself they'd been together a very short time, and that she had a great deal to put completely behind her. "You realize I have no idea who or what my father was?" he asked, keeping his voice casual.

She nodded, still looking up at him. "Yes."

He wanted to avoid, if possible, telling her what he knew of his elusive enemy, at least until he had more information. He didn't want to disturb her peace, or worry her unnecessarily, but he did want her to know about the cane, about his fruitless search so far for some clue to his beginnings. So he said now, "Shortly after you and I met, I received a package. Why don't you come upstairs with me, and I'll show you what was apparently a gift from my father."

Julia was surprised, and intrigued. She was even more intrigued when she saw the cane. Though he remained casual about the subject, she knew he was disturbed

about it—how could he not be? She had no answers for
him, but during the following days she found herself
going often to his wardrobe and taking out the cane,
studying it intently. It seemed familiar to her, as if she'd
seen it, or one like it, before, but she couldn't remember
when or where.

During those next days she became so accustomed to
being accompanied by her footman whenever she left
the house on her own that she completely forgot Cyrus
had any reason other than Helen's murder for asking her
not to go out alone. There were so many other things for
her to think about.

Cyrus was busy, but he managed to spend time with
her during the days, and at night he made love to her
with a desire that seemed to grow more intense each
time. More than once he woke her in the morning
making love to her. It no longer either surprised or
shocked her that she could feel such incredible pleasure;
she was simply grateful and delighted she could.

It wasn't until the second week of her marriage that
Julia realized there had been one argument Cyrus hadn't
used in persuading her to marry him. In all truth, it
hadn't occurred to her he might have made her pregnant, until the familiar cramps woke her just after dawn
one morning. She slipped from their bed, careful not to
wake him, and gathered up her nightgown and dressing
gown; she always slept naked now just as he did, but
kept her sleepwear near the bed in case of need. She
went into the bathroom and softly closed the door.

Her cycle was extremely regular, and her body so
sensitive to its rhythms that the discomfort she felt now
heralded rather than accompanied her monthly flow; she
wouldn't begin to bleed for hours yet, and once she did
the cramps would diminish. As usual, she felt hot and

restless, and along with sharp twinges in her lower abdomen there was a dull ache in her back and deep in her pelvis.

She put on her nightgown and dressing gown, and splashed water on her face, then paused to gaze into the mirror above the basin as she realized that her body, in its normal cycle, was signaling the absence of new life. She wasn't pregnant. The wave of disappointment she felt surprised her in its intensity; she hadn't known until that moment how much she wanted to have a child. Cyrus's child.

Adrian had desperately wanted a son, and all she'd felt about it was her sense of duty as his wife; she had been aware of no urge to be a mother. Cyrus had said nothing about children, but she wanted them so fiercely it hurt now to know she wasn't pregnant already. She wanted to feel his child inside her.

"His child," she whispered, vaguely aware of the shock on her face but with no clear idea of what she was feeling. It was the strangest sensation, as if she were poised on the brink of some understanding just beyond her reach.

Then a soft knock on the door distracted her, and the peculiar feeling faded.

"Julia? Are you all right, sweetheart?"

She dried her face and went to open the door, smiling up at her concerned husband. "I'm fine. Sorry I woke you."

He shook his head slightly, dismissing the apology, and his eyes were intent on her face. "You're in pain."

She supposed the discomfort she felt might have been visible, but doubted it. He simply knew, just as he seemed to know so many things. Still smiling, she murmured, "One of the trials of being a woman." By now she knew Cyrus well enough not to expect him to react as Adrian had—and she had a better understanding of just how abnormal her first husband had been. Adrian's attitude toward the perfectly natural female cycle of her body had been open disgust.

Quick understanding flashed in Cyrus's black eyes, and the concern remained. He put his arms around her gently, one hand slipping down to massage the small of her back in a steady rhythm. "I'm sorry you're hurting, love. Can I help?"

The ache in her back diminished under his touch, and she was barely aware of the murmur of pleasure she made as she relaxed against him. He hadn't gotten dressed, and she rubbed her cheek against the thick, soft mat of hair covering his broad chest as her arms went around his waist. "That helps," she said.

"You should rest," he said after a few moments, still massaging her back gently.

Julia tilted her head back to look up at him, slightly amused but warmed as well. "I'm fine, really. In a few hours there won't even be an ache." She hesitated, then said, "I didn't think about it until just now, but do you want children, Cyrus?"

"A little girl with green eyes," he said promptly, smiling.

That surprised her. "I thought all men wanted sons."

"Not this man." He bent his head briefly to kiss her, then looked down at her gravely. "I'd love to have a child with you, sweet, girl or boy, but having you is what matters to me. I don't want you to feel it's your duty, or any of that nonsense. We don't have to have children if you'd rather not. There are ways to prevent it happening."

She could think of only one way, and the very idea of

no lovemaking absolutely appalled her. She didn't realize it showed so clearly in her expression, until he
grinned down at her.

"No, my love, I don't mean separate bedrooms—or
even beds, if it comes to that."

"I should hope not," she murmured, her face hot.

Cyrus chuckled and kissed her again. "I'm so glad you
agree with me on that point. No, I meant other ways. If
you'd rather not have children, we'll talk about those
ways."

Julia was staring intently at a point somewhere near
his chin. She was mildly curious to learn how to prevent
a pregnancy, but not interested enough to ask at the
moment. "I want a baby," she said almost inaudibly.
Your baby. Why couldn't she say that, she wondered,
say it was his child she wanted?

"Are you sure, Julia? You're still very young; we could
wait a few years, just to be sure it's what you want."

"I'm sure." Her eyes met his, steady and certain.

He smiled crookedly. "Then we'll relax and let it
happen, if and when it does."

"If?"

"Not all men are able to father children, love," he told
her seriously. "And some women are barren. We'll have
to wait and find out if we can have a baby together."

She wanted to tell Cyrus she'd be happy with him
even if they didn't have children, but somehow the
words wouldn't come. Instead, she managed a nod and
smile, and kept to herself the puzzling inability to tell
him how she felt.

From his secure vantage point, he watched the house,
the rage growing and twisting inside him. *Bastard*. The

bastard had deflected the blows aimed at him. He was virtually untouched, and he was guarding his new wife with all the care of a man who had more than a suspicion of a threat.

He knew. Not all of it, no, but enough. The "footmen" he'd hired were detectives, like the men who guarded the house at night, and they were very, very good at their jobs. Neither the woman nor her sister was ever alone.

The watcher stood at his window, his hands clenched into fists at his sides, unable to admit even to himself that he felt as much panic as rage. But the knowledge was there, burning like a brand in his mind. He was losing control, all the threads slipping from his fingers. He'd made a bad mistake in pushing Drummond when he had. The man had gone over the edge, and in so doing he had freed the woman.

And *him* . . . He was in love with her, a fact he didn't trouble to hide from anyone. Somehow, he'd won her trust. They were married now. Mated. A bond existed between them, a tie that gave the bastard added strength. He was almost . . . complete. Almost able to see the truth. When that happened, he would recognize his twin, and move immediately to destroy him.

The watcher wanted to howl, to rant and rave and tear something apart with his hands. His twin had been blind, but so had he, and he hadn't known it. He had discounted the importance of the woman except as a vessel for new life, never realizing it was her union with his twin that was the binding thread of fate. Like his own hate, love was the core of his twin's strength; now that he loved, he was stronger, and when she loved him he would be whole.

And invincible.

A muted sound erupted from the watcher's throat, low and primal. His lifeless eyes, empty even of the rage that was malignant inside him, stared through the window while the brilliant, dark brain behind them coldly considered.

He had to kill the woman. It was the only way, now, to destroy his twin.

August ended more pleasantly than it had begun, with frequent afternoon thunderstorms damping the heat of summer. Autumn arrived early, blowing cooling breezes through the drying leaves prematurely in September, and by the end of the month it was obvious summer was over.

For Julia, the passing days were almost dreamlike. With Lissa back at school, she and Cyrus had more time alone together, and her confidence as a woman, as well as his wife, grew more secure with every passing day. He talked to her, and listened when she talked, his interest in her thoughts and opinions unfailing. He began teaching her to understand business matters, saying it was her right as his wife to have a complete knowledge of his affairs—now *their* affairs—and he was both patient and thorough in teaching her.

He continued to encourage her blooming sensuality, making love to her with tenderness and passion. He taught her to laugh again, teasing her with obvious delight.

And he gave of himself so completely that the only shadow on Julia's happiness was the barrier she knew existed inside herself. It was deep within her, a wall around her heart, and no matter how often she tried to break it down, it stood firm. There were times, brief moments, when she thought she could reach through it, but she was never able to.

Some instinct, hardly understood, told her there were victories that couldn't be gained by force, and that she had to be patient, so she tried. Whenever her awareness of the barrier began troubling her, she found something to occupy her mind.

There was always something. She was spending a great deal of time now at the new house, which was nearly finished. Cyrus had given her a completely free hand with decorating, offering his opinions when she asked but showing behind a gleam of amusement the traditional male indifference to colors and furnishings. Felice, who had become Julia's first real friend, said that Noel had found sly ways of keeping her busy during the first months of their marriage, and it had proven to be a wise tactic. She had emerged from her guarded shell without even being aware of it.

"And so are you," Felice said with a smile, "in case you haven't noticed."

"I have." Julia looked up from a jumble of fabric and wallpaper swatches on the worktable set up in the foyer of the new house. They were alone for the moment, though the sounds of hammers and saws came from other parts of the house as the carpenters completed the final interior work. "Part of me wants to hold back," she confessed. "To wait and see. I'm not afraid Cyrus will hurt me, it's just that . . ."

Felice nodded. "I know. When you've been knocked down often enough, it's difficult to believe it won't happen again."

"But what am I waiting for?" Julia asked, bewildered. "I trust him."

After a thoughtful moment Felice asked, "Has Cyrus lost his temper with you?"

"No," Julia replied instantly. She hesitated, then added, "He was angry when he . . . when he saw my back, but he wasn't angry at me, and I knew it."

"Then that's what you're waiting for."

Julia felt a faint shock. "I don't want him to be angry with me," she protested.

"No, but you're afraid to trust him completely until he is angry and still doesn't hurt you."

It made sense once Julia thought about it. Since she'd been with him, Cyrus had never so much as raised his voice to her. In fact, his voice held a gentleness that seemed only to have deepened during the past weeks, a constant and consistent part of his personality. She trusted his gentleness, but since she had never felt his anger, how could she trust that?

Somewhat helplessly, she said, "What am I supposed to do, deliberately make him angry at me?"

Felice sat down on the third tread of the stairs, and sighed, a look of rueful amusement on her face. "You know, I'm really not sure you even could. From what Noel's told me, Cyrus has never had a temper, and the only time I've seen him in a bad mood was when he was upset because the two of you couldn't be together. You may never see him lose his temper with anyone—much less you."

"Then what can I do? Felice, I don't want to hold back, not with him."

The older woman shook her head. "I don't know. Unless . . . Well, if you could somehow convince yourself he simply isn't capable of becoming violent, even in the worst of situations, then that would probably do it."

Increasingly anxious, Julia thought during the next days about what Felice had said. Cyrus frequently told her he loved her, and she believed him; more and more she was painfully aware of the responses she wanted to make and couldn't. The barrier inside her stubbornly resisted the words that represented the ultimate act of faith and trust.

She told herself he wasn't capable of violence, not Cyrus, but no matter how insistently she tried to convince herself, there was still a tiny doubt, a wary hesitation in her mind. What if he were?

October brought chilly winds and rains, and no resolution for Julia. She was kept busy with the house and the few social functions she and Cyrus chose to attend, still surprised by the guarded acceptance she encountered. By the third week in October the house was virtually complete and the moving had begun. One by one, the rooms in the city house were emptied and closed, the furnishings hauled out to the new house. The valuables Cyrus had packed and stored before their marriage were also moved, as well as innumerable trunks and boxes filled with items that wouldn't be needed until they were settled in the new house.

Cyrus said they should have stayed in a hotel during that final week of the month when both houses were in total confusion, but since Julia enjoyed the bustle and needed to supervise all the activity anyway, he didn't insist. He did complain once, mildly, when he discovered every pair of shoes he owned except the ones on his feet had been packed and moved to the new house two days before they were due to take up residence there, but only laughed at Julia's guilty dismay.

Moving day was chilly but sunny, and with numerous hired wagons as well as extra workmen to do the loading and transporting, the last of the furniture was taken out to the new house by midafternoon. All the servants, as well as both Julia and Cyrus, were kept busy arranging and unpacking, and it wasn't until nearly five o'clock that Julia realized something had been left behind.

She was in the master bedroom, working with one of the maids to unpack the last of the trunks, and as she hung one of Cyrus's coats in his wardrobe she noticed what was missing.

"Cathy, did you pack that long, narrow wooden box I left on the windowsill in the old house?"

The young maid looked up, frowning a little. "No, Miss Julia, I don't remember seeing it."

The cane. It had been left in the old house. Julia hesitated, then went to the window and looked out. The bedroom was at the rear of the house, and she could see Cyrus down below talking to a well-dressed man who was apparently a business associate; she'd seen him coming and going a few times during the past week. She turned away from the window, thinking, and rapidly made up her mind.

"The buggy's still hitched, and tied out front; I'm going to drive back to town."

"I'll fetch Nelson," Cathy said, beginning to get up from her kneeling position beside an open trunk.

"No, it isn't necessary. He's helping Stork downstairs. I can make the trip in an hour or less, and be back by dark. Finish up in here, would you, please, Cathy?"

"Yes, Miss Julia."

Julia found her gloves and a coat, but didn't bother with a hat. She went down the curving staircase and crossed the foyer, hearing the sounds of busy people but encountering no one. The front of the house was deserted, all the wagons and extra men gone now, but the horse and buggy she usually drove was there.

A few minutes later she was on the road to Richmond, the horse moving at a brisk pace. She had a faintly guilty thought that Cyrus wouldn't like her going back to town alone like this, but she was less worried by that than by what could happen to his cane, left in an unlocked house. She had every hope of being able to get it and return before he even knew she was gone.

There was little traffic, and she made good time. She pulled the buggy over to the sidewalk in front of the house and used the tether block, then went inside. Empty now, there was an almost eerie feeling of vastness and silence in the house, and Julia wasted no time in heading for the master bedroom. She caught a whiff of kerosene as she went up the stairs, and paused for a moment before continuing on, a little unnerved. All her instincts told her to get out of the house, and she could feel goose bumps breaking out all over her body.

Definitely hurrying now, she went on to the bedroom, and felt a sharp pang of relief when she saw the box just where she'd left it on the windowsill. It was half hidden by the drapes, which was probably why no one had seen it. She went to the window and lifted the lid of the box, relieved again to see the dull gleam of gold and polished wood.

"Hello, Julia."

Twelve

♥

Cyrus broke off in the middle of a sentence, his eyes widening as he stared through John Stevens. He saw nothing, but he felt shock and fear, and he knew it was Julia's.

"Mr. Fortune?" The Pinkerton man's question was quick and sharp. "What is it?"

"My wife!" He heard his voice as if from a great distance, the sound of it hoarse and afraid. "She's—God, she's gone back to the house alone. And he's there."

Instantly, Stevens turned away, shouting for Nelson. Cyrus didn't wait to have confirmation; he ran for the stables and saddled his fastest horse, a terror unlike anything he'd ever felt before clawing inside him. He should have told her, should have warned her instead of believing she didn't have to know of the threat. But he hadn't. And now—now, when he'd finally gotten the evidence he needed to put a name and face to his enemy—Julia was miles away facing the soulless monster.

Alone.

It didn't occur to Cyrus until he was halfway to town

that he wasn't armed, but he made no attempt to slow his
horse's headlong gallop. Instead, he urged the animal
even faster, crouching low in the saddle as the wind
whistled past. He didn't need a gun. He didn't need the
Pinkerton men no doubt only minutes behind him. All
he needed was enough luck to reach the house in time.
That was all he asked.

Julia felt very cold as she looked at the man standing only
a few feet away from her in the empty bedroom. She
knew him. He had dined in her house when she'd lived
with Adrian, had talked to her at various social events,
had even danced with her. He was handsome and had
always been charming, smiling.

He was smiling now. A lighted kerosene lamp hung
from one hand, its bright glow holding the gathering
darkness outside the house at bay, and he was swinging
it gently back and forth as if to some music only he
heard.

"You look so surprised, Julia." His normally pleasant
voice was toneless and remote. "Didn't you know it was
I? Couldn't you feel it?"

The first shock of his presence had faded quickly, but
Julia felt trapped. "I don't know what you're talking
about," she whispered, a strange, primitive terror surging inside her. She wanted to run, to get as far away from
him as she could. But she couldn't move.

He cocked his head to one side and took a step nearer
to her. "Ah, I see. You really don't know. I've been
controlling your life for a long time, Julia. A very long
time. I married you to Adrian—after I got your parents
out of the way, of course. I made sure he treated
you . . . right. He talked to me, you know. Nobody

else, just me. He told me how much he loved hurting you, how it excited him."

A brief frown flitted across his handsome face and then vanished. "I wanted him to get you pregnant, but the stupid bastard couldn't. That was the only mistake I made when I chose him for you. I didn't know he really didn't like women. He hid that from me, until it was too late for me to get rid of him and choose someone else."

Julia's mind was working sluggishly. "You . . . killed my parents?"

"They were in the way," he explained almost politely. "People were always getting in the way when I arranged your life. Or making mistakes. That stupid cow—what was her name?—Helen, I think. She was a friend of Lissa's, so I used her. She thought I was going to marry her. I told her I had a wife in an asylum. That kind of tale always appeals to silly little bitches. She wasn't bad, really loved being tumbled in a stable. But she disappointed me. She made a mistake with the message I told her to give you. You got it too late, and that ruined my plan. So of course I had to kill her too."

Sickened, Julia stared at him.

His vacant smile widened. "I'm really surprised you didn't figure it out. *He* did. I suppose he was trying to protect you in that way as well, not telling you about me. I wish I could see his face when he finds out it was all for nothing."

One of her hands was still resting on the wooden box behind her; without really being aware of her action, she closed her fingers around the polished wood of the cane. *His eyes*, she thought, *they're so empty*. She'd never seen that before—except in the newspaper photo she'd all but forgotten about.

"What was all for nothing?" she asked, trying to think, to understand.

Adam Prescott chuckled softly, the sound like wind rustling through dry leaves. "He thought he could win. When he took you away from Adrian and put guards around you. He thought he could defeat me. Today is our birthday, did you know that? No, of course not. Neither does he. I've always known, though. Just the way I've known you had to be kept from him because he couldn't be allowed to make himself whole with your love." The final word was almost spat out, and he took another step closer.

"Whole?" Julia was bewildered, and yet some part of her understood.

In a suddenly reasonable tone, he said, "My gift isn't dependent on anything outside myself. That's my strength. But he has to have you. He has to be connected to you. All I have to do is cut that tie, and I'll win. It'll be easy to destroy him then. Once I kill you, he'll be alone, and his gift dies with you."

"Magic," she whispered.

"Fortune, actually. He even got the name, but it was mine by rights. I believe I'll claim it for my own. When he's gone. You do understand why I have to kill both of you?"

Julia shook her head slowly, her terrified gaze fixed on his dead eyes and blank smile as he took another step toward her; he was barely more than an arm's length away now. Every muscle in her body was tense and quivering, and her fingers gripped the cane so tightly they ached.

Adam made a little "tsk" sound, mildly impatient. "He'll fight me now that he's beginning to realize what we are; that's why I have to destroy him. And if I don't kill you first, he'll just keep getting stronger. I can't have that—" He broke off, stiffening, and tilted his head as though he were listening to some far-off sound.

For the first time Julia became aware of crackling sounds and a dim roar, and she caught the acrid smell of smoke. The house was on fire, she realized, the lower floor burning. She thought that was what he was listening to, but when he spoke she realized it was something else.

"He's coming," Adam murmured. He leaned over to set the lamp on the floor. "I have to finish it now, before—"

Julia didn't wait to hear the rest. She pulled the cane from its box and swung it with all her strength. The heavy gold handle struck him a solid blow on his shoulder, the force of contact numbing her hand, and he went over sideways with a startled cry of pain.

Still holding the cane, Julia ran. The hallway was thick with smoke, making her cough and making her eyes water, but she didn't slow her pace until she reached the top of the stairs. The roar of the fire was louder now, the smoke even thicker—and the stairs were burning. There was a secondary stairway at the rear of the house for the servants' use, but it was back the way she'd come, and not even a fear of burning could make her retrace her steps.

She hadn't knocked him out, just down; he'd be coming after her. Desperate, she darted into one of the salons on the second floor, hoping she could open a window and escape that way. But before she could cross the room, she heard the front door crash open, and heard Cyrus shout her name. That wonderful voice jerked her back around. She wanted to call out to him, to go out into the hall so she could see him, but something held her motionless and silent as she pressed herself against the wall beside the open salon door. The cane still gripped in one hand, she pressed the other over her mouth to muffle the sounds of her coughing, and strained to hear . . .

Cyrus went straight up the stairs, ignoring the flames all around him, and didn't stop until he reached the top. The smoke burned his eyes and throat, but he saw Adam Prescott standing motionless a few feet away, a gun in his hand.

"Where is she, you bastard?" Cyrus demanded, fighting the murderous urge to throw himself at the other man. He could feel Julia nearby, and he was almost sure she was unhurt, but the house was burning and soon none of them would be able to escape.

Adam laughed, a strange, high sound filled with the primal terror of an animal for fire. "A mistake, another mistake, I used too much kerosene." The words had a singsong rhythm, and his wide, empty smile was like a death's-head grimace. "She'll burn—we'll all burn now. But I win. Yes, I win. Say good-bye, brother." He lifted the gun.

"*No!*" Julia burst from the salon, closer to Adam than to Cyrus, the cane held high in her hands. Without hesitation she rushed across the landing and struck, bringing the heavy cane down on Adam's extended arm.

The gun fell and he stumbled back away from her. The smoke was so thick it was almost impossible to see, and he probably never realized how close he was to the fragile wooden banister until he fell against it. The decorative barrier splintered, and he dropped like a stone to the marble floor far below.

"Julia—" Cyrus reached her just in time to support her as she sagged. Her wide green eyes, tearing from the smoke, looked up at him for a moment out of her white face, and then a hoarse little sigh escaped her and she crumpled against him.

Her dreams were dreadful at first; she wanted to wake up. There was fire all around, the flames roaring with a maniac's laugh, and she held desperately to the cane because it was all that would keep her safe. Cyrus stood in front of her, but there were two of him, and she knew only one was real. Which one? It was terribly important that she guess correctly, because one was life and the other death.

She couldn't trust herself to choose. And if she didn't choose, if she held back and waited, then maybe she could be certain. But the flames were getting closer, and she suddenly realized what would happen if she waited. The chance for happiness gone. The chance for life gone. And, after all, wasn't that the point, to take the chance? To trust beyond knowledge, because that was where love came from?

She chose, and when his strong arms closed around her, she felt a kind of happiness she'd never known before. The flames faded away. There was softness, and cool peace. Her body seemed peculiarly aware of itself, as if all her senses had turned inward. In her dream, a little girl with dark hair and green eyes talked to her, seriously explaining what it would mean to be Fortune's love, and Fortune's wife.

Julia listened with gravity equaling the girl's. Magic, oh, yes. And love. So much love. She wasn't wary of the future anymore, or frightened of anything at all. The little girl smiled and went away—but not very far.

It was very quiet when she opened her eyes, and only

one lamp was on in the bedroom. She was in the new house, she realized. She was in bed, naked beneath the covers. She turned her head slowly and saw Cyrus sitting in a chair close beside the bed. He was holding her hand, and as she looked at him he leaned forward and kissed it, smiling at her.

"You're always taking care of me," she murmured, wondering vaguely why her throat wasn't raw from the smoke she'd breathed.

"You took care of me today," he reminded her in his black velvet voice. "I'm sorry I didn't tell you about him, sweetheart, warn you. If you'd known there was a reason to be wary, you never would have left here alone. I didn't know who the threat was until today, but that's no excuse."

Julia wasn't upset he hadn't told her; she thought she had needed the weeks of peace, or she wouldn't have been able to do what she had in defense of herself and Cyrus. "It's all right," she said. "But how did you get us out of there? The stairs were burning."

"They weren't when I carried you out."

The statement didn't surprise her, and she merely nodded. "He's dead, isn't he?"

"Yes, love."

"Who was he?" She hesitated, then added, "He talked a bit before I got away from him. He said he'd killed my parents. And Helen. And that he married me to Adrian to . . . to keep me away from you. Did he do all that?"

Cyrus nodded. "I believe he did. He's manipulated people and influenced events for years. As for who he was—well, I'm not sure. He called me brother. Maybe he was my brother."

Julia's fingers tightened in his. "He was no part of you. He was evil."

Looking down at her hand, holding it in both of his now, Cyrus spoke very quietly. "He was evil. But he was like me in some way, connected to me. I don't know how. Now that he's gone, I may never know." His gaze rose to her face, the liquid black eyes nakedly expressive. "It doesn't matter. As long as I have you. That you're safe is the only important thing. I was so afraid he'd take you away from me."

"I love you," she said.

Cyrus went utterly still.

Julia smiled. "I didn't know it until I thought he was going to kill you. I'd been afraid to let myself love you, to take the chance. But when I thought I was going to lose you . . ."

"Sweetheart . . ." He came over onto the bed, drawing her up against him. "God, I love you so much." He was holding her, his head bowed and face buried in the curve of her neck. "I searched for you all my life and never knew it until I found you."

She was holding him as well, happy and not worried about all the questions still unanswered. She had an odd belief that the answers would be provided eventually. Some of them, at least; the important ones.

"Come to bed with me?" she murmured.

He drew back just a little, and then kissed her tenderly. "You haven't eaten anything since lunch. Aren't you hungry, love?"

"For you." She stroked his lean cheek, smiling a peculiarly feminine, intimate smile. "I always seem to be hungry for you. I think it's part of your magic."

This time, his kiss was deeper and more intense. "Then you have magic too," he murmured against her mouth. "Because I can't get enough of you, my sweet."

Her green eyes gleamed at him in the dim room. "I'd

say we were perfectly matched. Make love to me, darling."

She didn't have to ask him again.

On a warm, pleasant afternoon of the following May, Cyrus leaned against the back of a park bench and watched his wife and Felice Stanton as they stood a few yards away talking to another woman. Julia was glowing, her lovely face alight with happiness and her vivid green eyes serene. Pregnancy agreed with her; she hadn't suffered even a single bout of morning sickness and, though well into her sixth month, retained the grace of movement that was peculiarly hers.

Cyrus never tired of looking at her. And he never ceased to feel a sense of wonder. During the last months, her love, given so freely and completely, had deepened the bond between them. Cyrus never felt lonely now, and the place inside him that had been empty was filled with her love and his own.

"Revolt won," Noel said.

Glancing aside at his friend, Cyrus said, "Did it?"

"Yes. By ten lengths. How'd you know?"

Mildly, Cyrus said, "A paddock tip, as I told you."

Noel made a rude noise. "The nag was a thirty-to-one long shot, and the jockey was so surprised he nearly fell off at the finish. I made a small fortune, thank you very much, but I'd like to know how *you* knew which horse would win the race."

"A lucky guess."

Sighing, Noel shook his head a little. He'd expected that sort of answer. "Well, take a lucky guess about tomorrow's races, would you?"

Looking at his wife again, Cyrus said absently, "I

shouldn't have done it yesterday. You don't need to make more money, Noel, and I shouldn't abuse knowledge for the sake of gain."

"Not even for a friend?" Noel's voice was dry, and he wasn't surprised when he received no answer. Wherever his friend's peculiar talents came from, they had grown stronger—and even more mysterious—during the past months. Cyrus had changed a great deal since returning to Richmond the summer past. There was a new calmness about him, a vivid wisdom in his black eyes, and Noel had come to the conclusion he was now literally incapable of raising his voice; it remained always soft and unruffled.

His humor was kinder and never sardonic, and not even the most cynical person in Richmond doubted that he absolutely adored his lovely wife.

Still, people occasionally commented on the strange events of the past year, and eyed Cyrus in puzzlement. Thinking of those events himself, Noel said, "The last time we spoke, your Pinkertons hadn't managed to dig up any more information about Prescott; is that still the case?"

"The case is closed," Cyrus replied, looking at Noel again. "They traced him to an orphanage in New York, but the place burned shortly after he left."

"Burned," Noel murmured. "He did like fire, didn't he?"

"Apparently. Two people died in that particular fire, including the priest who ran the place. If Prescott wanted to obliterate every trace of his beginnings, he did a good job. All the records were destroyed."

After a moment Noel nodded to the gold-headed cane under Cyrus's relaxed hand. "What about that?"

Cyrus lifted the cane and held it in both hands,

studying it thoughtfully. "This is still a mystery." Even more so than his friend knew, he thought.

The night of the fire, Julia had clung to the cane long after he'd carried her from the burning house. In fact, he'd had to gently pry her fingers off it, even though she'd been unconscious. When she'd first awakened, he had seen her eyes flicker to the nightstand where he'd placed the cane, but she hadn't said anything about it then. Only later did she tell him it had saved her as well as him from Prescott.

It had also been Julia who had first noticed the birthmark on Cyrus's arm—or, rather, its disappearance. The day of the fire it had marked his arm with a blood-red crescent; the day after, it was gone.

Cyrus had stopped asking himself questions about any of it. Like Julia, he felt sure there would be answers eventually. In any case, he was so happy with her and so delighted by a new appreciation of life and love, he was perfectly willing to be patient.

He wasn't particularly surprised, on that May afternoon, to find a visitor awaiting him and Julia when they returned home. But when they walked together into the parlor, he stopped and stood staring in wonder at the woman who rose to face them.

She couldn't have been much above fifty, and was stylishly dressed, elegant. Her hair was thick and richly black, her face still strikingly beautiful. None of those attributes, however, was responsible for Cyrus's shock.

Her eyes were black.

In a voice that was the feminine counterpart of his own lyrical tone, she said, "My name is Catherine Wingate. I—I believe you know who I am."

Cyrus nodded slowly. "You're my mother."

Perhaps oddly, Cyrus felt no bitterness and, in fact, no

discomfort at all with the stranger who had borne him. Instead, he felt very calm and, curiously, had few questions now. It was as if her appearance had opened a locked door in his mind.

Moments later he was on the settee beside Julia as they both looked at Catherine, and she was speaking softly. No further introductions had been necessary, and she told her story simply from the day a seventeen-year-old girl had found herself pregnant and unmarried.

"My family was wealthy, and didn't disown me, but insisted I not keep my child. There was no choice for me. So they sent me away, to relatives, where I wasn't known. I was told my child would be given to strangers. That was when a Gypsy caravan passed through town. I—I'm not sure why I went to the Old One, the Gypsy. It was as if I was drawn to her."

Catherine drew a deep breath and quietly related the Gypsy's predictions and warnings. Then she said, "I couldn't kill my child, I couldn't. If I had known then what harm he'd do, perhaps I might have found the strength, but how could I believe such a terrible thing of the child growing inside my body?"

Julia, one hand resting over her rounded belly and the other clasping her husband's hand, looked at the older woman with compassion and understanding. "You couldn't," she murmured. "Of course you couldn't." Catherine sent her a fleeting smile in return, so like Cyrus's, it caught at Julia's heart.

Catherine went on. "The Old One told me what to do, though she knew I was making a mistake. She told me precisely where my sons were to be taken after they were born, and dictated the written messages I was to leave with them. I managed to persuade my aunt to help me, though she naturally didn't believe a word the Gypsy had told me.

"When the two of you were born, my aunt pointed out triumphantly that my firstborn was the dark one—you." She looked at Cyrus, her gaze turned to the past. "He was fair, almost angelic. But his eyes were lifeless even then. Yours were filled with delight." She blinked, then shook her head a little. "I did what I had to do. And for thirty-two years I lived with the knowledge of what I'd done, even though my life was a normal one afterward. I married a good man; he died ten years ago, and we had no children together. I never attempted to see my sons, because of the Gypsy's warning."

Catherine unfolded a newspaper that had been tucked beside her in the chair, and held it out to Cyrus. "Then, last summer, I saw this."

He studied it. There was a photograph and article about him, done when he'd returned to Richmond. Also on the page was an article about the newly elected city council, with a photograph of the nine men.

Softly, Catherine said, "I knew Fortune had given you his name; the Gypsy said he would. I didn't know *his* name—but I knew his eyes."

Almost to himself, Cyrus murmured, "He was able to hide the emptiness from all of us for so long. But a camera sees what's real, without illusion."

"I knew, when I looked at the pictures, that the Gypsy had been right about it all," Catherine said. "And I realized the enormity of my mistake. I had tried to break the pattern, to alter destiny, and because of that your life was in danger."

"Is that when you sent me the cane?" Cyrus asked, glancing toward it where it leaned against the settee.

Catherine nodded. "From the article about you, I judged you weren't aware of the gift you'd been given. The cane was your father's, and I knew it would be a—a spur to your understanding. He had told me he wanted his son to have it."

"Who was my father?" Cyrus asked quietly.

She hesitated, then said, "I can tell you only what I know, and what I sensed. The Gypsy was right—he was no ordinary man. He said his name was Fate. There was a kind of power in him, a positive force I've never felt in anyone else. Except you."

Cyrus's eyes held hers steadily. "He knew he'd have a son, yet he didn't stay with you?"

A slight smile played at Catherine's lips, a smile that held vast understanding. "He couldn't stay with me, I knew that. But he gave the world a gift. You." She nodded slightly, and her voice was certain. "To fight for love. To guard and protect love. To be the guiding hand love sometimes needs. That would be your destiny, he said. Just as he was Fate, you would be Fortune. Love's Fortune."

Cyrus didn't look away from her, and his lean face was still calm, his eyes still tranquil. "So I'm to be a matchmaker?" he asked mildly.

"You don't need me to answer that." Catherine smiled again. "Once you fell in love with Julia, your course was set. Without her you would never have understood what love could be; now that you do, your instinct is to help others find what the two of you share."

"A tall order," Cyrus said, a sudden hint of amusement in his eyes. "And a lifetime's commitment."

"Isn't love worth that?" his mother asked.

Cyrus didn't have to reply aloud; his agreement was

plain in his smile. He turned his head and looked at Julia, his face softening in an expression of wonder and delight.

"Yes," he murmured. "It certainly is."

FANFARE

Enter the marvelous new world of **Fanfare!**
From sweeping historicals set around the globe to
contemporary novels set in glamorous spots,
Fanfare means great reading.
Be sure to look for new **Fanfare** titles each month!

On Sale in August:
GENUINE LIES
By **Nora Roberts**
author of PUBLIC SECRETS
*In Hollywood, a lady learns fast: the bad can be beautiful,
and the truth can kill.*

FORBIDDEN
By **Susan Johnson**
author of SWEET LOVE, SURVIVE
*Daisy and the Duc flirt, fight, and ultimately flare up in
one of the hottest and most enthralling novels
Susan Johnson has ever written.*

BAD BILLY CULVER
By **Judy Gill**
author of SHARING SUNRISE
*A fabulous tale of sexual awakening, scandal, lies and a
love that can't be denied.*

 **THE SYMBOL OF GREAT WOMEN'S
FICTION FROM BANTAM**
Ask for these books at your local bookstore.

AN 323 8/91